THE QUERY

By E.P. McKenna

D1361819

CHAPTER 1

Mr. James Schlesinger

926 Nash Ave.

North Bessemer, PA 16112

Dear Mr. Schlesinger,

Thank you for sending your manuscript to my agency with the opportunity to represent you. I'm sorry, but I don't think that will be happening anytime soon.

I might start off by suggesting you take a course in character development, and then follow it up with a lesson in basic imagination.

I hope I'm not coming off too strong, but whatever gave you the idea you could write to begin with?

I'm afraid you're not ready for New York, yet. You'll have to stay in your little hamlet of North Bessemer until you raise your game.

Please don't take this criticism personally, it's just a representation of your work. I'm sure you're a fine man with plenty of good qualities. It's just I need a certain level of panache in order for my agency to represent you. I'm sure you understand.

Regards,

Herbert Keeler
Herbert Keeler Literary Agency
Oyster Bay, NY 11801

Herbert Keeler folded his letter and inserted it into the envelope. A smile of superiority warmed over his face. His pious, pretentious mug.

He peeled off a stamp and dabbed it onto the envelope, the anticipation of its delivery driving him into delirium.

On this late July morning, leaning back in his chair in his home office, he surveyed the room around him. He'd done quite well for himself, working from his remodeled farmhouse in Oyster Bay, forty-five minutes outside of Manhattan. It had windows only in the front. That's what appealed to him. Lots of privacy. The only home nearby, the farm house across the street, set back deep from the road, all surrounded by tall-grass fields and woods. He sat close to the big city, but lived on the outskirts of the small town.

Hanging on the walls were the accolades of his most prized accomplishments, representations of authors whose books sold in the millions, and copies of their respected awards.

Along with representing all of those great authors came the money, the golden, bloody money.

And along with the money came the nice things in life, the amenities. Rolls Royce's. Rolex watches. Cherry wood book shelves meticulously alphabetized with his favorite authors. Heated floors. All the trimmings in his house, remote-controlled curtains, in-house speaker systems, internet-TV's, smart refrigerators, smart-thermostats, and he could turn on and off the lights in his house, all of these things from anywhere in the world, right from his hand-held cell phone.

Simply a must.

Having all of this gave him all the rights to look down upon every human being on the face of this earth. The twits. Not only because he was tall, chiseled, and had the most perfect teeth. But, what could they possibly have to measure up to him?

Nothing, obviously.

His stature within the industry was gargantuan. Those that he took on as clients were all but assured to become icons, but his rejection letters were legendary. Crass. Hurtful. And deceitful.

Today, though, he was nice. He didn't have the heart to be as hurtful as he would have liked. Maybe he was getting soft in his old age.

Just as he was about to kick his feet up on his desk and reflect upon his success, the doorbell rang.

His dog ran to the door.

Not in the mood for company, he ignored it. "They'll go away, Reese."

Herbert adopted Reese from the rescue program. Part lab and part pit bull, intimidating as hell, but boy, what a lover. She'd lick your epidermis right off your face. Herb's kindness to animals exceeded that to his fellow man.

Ding dong!

Reese went wild at the door.

Ding Dong! Ding Dong!

"All right, I'm coming. Sit Reese."

Reese barked, and barked with relentless abandon.

"I said, sit. Sit Reese! Sit! Now!"

Reese sat, dying to jump on the man.

Upon opening the door, Herb came face to face with a delivery man for an express letter. "Morning. You have to sign for this, Mr. Keeler."

"Boy, what lengths people will go to."

He grabbed the clipboard.

The delivery man wiped the sweat from his brow as he handed the pen to Herbert. "Supposed to get up to a hundred and one degrees today. Strong storm system to follow...possible hurricane."

"You don't say."

"Yes. Category one."

"Perfect for staying inside." He put his signature on the clipboard with the same flare the President might exude if he were signing a peace treaty.

"I suppose another writer wannabe. Thinks express mailing his query letter will get him represented. When will people learn? It's all about the writing."

Shaking his head he gave the clipboard back to the delivery man.

He shut the door behind him, sat down at his desk and was about to throw the package into the corner, when he noticed the return address.

There wasn't one.

Curiosity getting the best of him, he opened the package. It was a letter. Just what he thought.

A smug feeling of preeminence ran over him.

He opened the letter, put on his glasses and began to read. It was typed.

Herbert Keeler
Herbert Keeler Literary Agency
Oyster Bay, NY 11801

Dear Mr. Keeler,

Someone very dear to me received one of your rejection letters some time ago.

As you know, you have quite a reputation in the industry, with all the great writers you have represented. Years of award-winning writers. Millions of books sold. You're the most sought-after agent in the business.

For that I applaud you.

Bravo!

You miserable piece of shit!

You're in a position of power where you could give so many people encouragement to continue and get better in their pursuit of becoming a writer. You could share areas where improvements could be made. You could nurture those precious souls.

Instead you chose to insult. You chose to belittle. You hurt.

What is wrong with you?

Are you so small-minded you need to treat people this way to make yourself feel important?

No more.

The insults are over. The belittling is over. Your disgusting, condescending behavior is over.

And so are you.

Herb's breathing began to quicken. His head turned in every direction. His eyes shot to the windows. He glared at the home across from him, surveying the windows. Some had shades drawn. Who was this quack? Was this some kind of joke?

He continued to read.

I can tell by the way you're squirming in your chair where you are in this letter. Right now you're scarred.

Oops! Did I misspell scared? Are you going to give me a condescending critique on my spelling? I don't think so.

You're too busy feeling like the stalked animal that you are.

Slow down. Slow down. I can see that your breathing is really picking up.

Are you beginning to understand the pain and dejection that you caused all of these years?

I don't think so. I don't think you can even begin to understand how defeating it is to have worked so hard on something and then to have an agent rip it apart and crush your dreams. Only in your case it's been a thousand times worse. Maybe a million zillion.

You fuck!

You not only tore people's dreams apart, but you peppered them with verbal abuse and humiliated them.

Your days of this are over.

I have news for you. You are trapped in your own house. Like a caged rat.

You see, after the delivery man left, I placed an activator onto your door. The mere act of opening it will cause your entire house to blow high into the sky. Hey, did you like my prose? My rhyming ability? I'd like to hear what smart ass quip you have going through your brain right now.

Yes, I placed that explosive in your house last week while you were at the Thrillerfest Writers Conference in New York. I knew you wouldn't be home. It was perfect timing.

All I had to do was activate the tripping device after the delivery man left. And don't you worry, I took care of the back door, too.

Must be creepy for you to know that I'm so close to your house. I'm practically right outside your door.

I'd assume your first reaction is to call the police, huh? That's what I'd do.

Sorry, that's not going to happen. I scrambled your cell phone. Give it a try. Go ahead.

Herb put the letter down and grabbed his cell. He tried to call his friend at one of the major publishing houses. It rang busy.

"Shit!"

He tried the gym where he worked out. Busy, too.

He wiped the clamminess from his palms onto his shorts, but couldn't still his shaking hands as he went back to the letter.

I bet you wished you hadn't dropped your land line, huh? How did I know that? I did my homework. I prepare.

You're probably wondering, which query did you reject?

I didn't leave a return address on this letter. I paid cash, so there's no credit card to trace.

I can see your mind racing. Who is this? What book?

I have to admit. I'm kind of enjoying this. Watching you squirm. Watching your condescending ass on the receiving end for a change.

I know the biggest curiosity that must be running through your selfish brain—should I take the chance and try the door?

Give it a try. I'm video-taping this whole thing, and far enough away that I won't get sprayed with your house, or your spineless blood.

You can either trust me, or try it and end it all right now.

So, who am I and what book did you reject? Sorry, pal, you're going to have to go to your grave with that one.

Now you're thinking, where do we go from here?

You can't leave the house. You can't call anyone.

I bet you're wishing you weren't such a bastard to all of those writers.

I have to admit, this one way conversation is very satisfying. It's exactly what you've done over all of those years.

How do they say? Paybacks are a bitch, buddy.

Any fair-minded individual would agree you're getting what you deserve.

By the process of deduction, you're probably thinking of some ways out of this mess. I know what you're thinking, the windows.

Yes, you could do that, break them and crawl out.

But, a few things could happen.

First, you could get cut from the sharp edges as you crawl out the window. A little blood would be spilled, but then again, who cares? It's your blood.

Do you think I would be so careless and give you a way out?

No way, friend.

If you even come close to breaking the windows this whole thing will be over. How? Because I set sensors on the windows. All of them.

I'm in the farmhouse across the street and I'm standing far enough back from the window, so you can't see me.

I wouldn't want you to be able to break a window and yell out to someone for help. No. I want you to feel fear.

After all, this is for all the writers you scorched.

This effort is for all of them.

Your mind must be racing. Did this guy really wire my doors with explosives? He definitely scrambled my cell phone. Is he really behind a window across the street?

The only way to find out is to try the door. Go ahead. I dare you.

Come on Herbert, or should I call you Herby. Now that we're good friends and all.

Go ahead, show me how smart you are. Or perhaps, show me how dumb you are.

If you open the door, that shows how dumb you are. And that will end all of the fun we've been having. I bet you're dying to correct my improper use of the word And in the beginning of the sentence.

Fuck you!

Boy that felt good. No one cares what you think anymore.

Okay, now that we've come to the conclusion that you're smart enough to not open the door, it's time to go to stage two of this game.

CHAPTER 2

Yes, that's right. There's a reason for this madness.

Herb paused to look up. He ran to the window, held his hand over his eyebrows to block the glaring sun. He peered hard to see through the windows across the street.

Was there really a man behind one of those windows?

He just stared. The silence hung in the air like a heavy cloud. All of his current concerns in his life... gone. Deadlines to publishers, contracts to lawyers. Not even on his radar. He found himself totally in the present.

Without warning, the lamp at his desk exploded, splintering glass all around his office.

He hit the floor, covering his head.

"Jesus!"

What happened? Did a bomb go off? Was someone shooting at him? He looked for a hole in the window. Nothing. His heart pounded like an anvil jumping on his chest. His mouth gasped for gulps of air, more than it could take.

Cowering under his arm, he peeked up and saw the lamp smoldering. "What the...?"

He kept his head down. Would more shots be fired?

He took a moment to assess the situation. None of this made sense. What started off as a normal morning, was now more bizarre than he could ever imagine.

He shuffled back to the letter.

I'm not sure what has transpired at this point in time, but if I see you starting to get smart, I'm going to ignite one of the many explosives I have placed throughout your house.

The first will be your lamp. Your precious little lamp from Ireland that honors Patrick O'Connor, the literary giant.

How cute.

If that's already gone off, I hope I have your attention. Are you with me, Herby? Friend.

The first thing I want you to do is to sit down at your computer.

I know what you're thinking. You're probably ready to contact the police or a friend for help. Too bad!

Not going to happen.

Unbeknownst to you, you're sharing your computer with me, and I'm set up to override yours. So, there'll be no shenanigans. You're all mine.

Do I have your attention?

Your head is buzzing. You must be dying to know what I want. Pun intended.

First instruction, put the letter down and wake up your computer. I'll be sharing your computer with you.

He put the letter down.

But rather than go to his computer, he looked under the couch. He opened every drawer in his kitchen. Under the sink. He opened the dishwasher.

Where was the bomb?

He looked in the fireplace. Nothing. Over to his beloved bookcase. His fingers ran across his rows and rows of books. First through the Non-fiction section. Next through the Memoir area. His eyes skirted down to the History area. Over to Romance. And finally to the vast expanse of Fiction.

His heart thumped. He scanned behind the shower curtain. Opened the medicine cabinet. The bomb had to be here somewhere.

Into his bedroom. Under the bed. Nothing. Every drawer. Under his socks. He threw his clothes into the air. Into his closets, he tore back his hanging clothes. Nothing. What about his night stand? In the drawers. No go.

His eyes darted like frantic windshield wipers. Ah, what about the lights. He looked up at every outlet hanging from the ceiling. He stood on the bed, felt every part of every fixture. Fondled every lamp, feeling, fumbling his fingers, hoping to find something. Anything.

He looked under the new ottoman he found waiting for him when he returned home last night. It had a typed note on it from his mother stating it was a gift. It had foot pegs sticking out on all four sides and was long enough to lay down on. He'd have to call her later to thank her. He ran his fingers along all the edges, hoping to find the bomb.

Nothing.

And after he'd gone in every room and exhausted everything he could imagine, frustration consumed him.

He sat on the edge of the couch and slouched over, his body limp, holding his heavy head with his hands. He began to cry.

One day, on top of the world. Today, trapped in his own house. How could this all be happening? It had to be a nightmare.

He pinched himself. Yep, he was awake. This was as real as ever.

Where could the bomb be?

He went to his computer. He entered his password and waited. His breath, fast and short.

If only he could get a message out to someone. What about his friend, Joe? Yes. Joe! He forgot. Joe would be coming by later! Hope drifted in the air.

A box for communicating opened up, with a blinking cursor.

"Hi Herby."

Eager to respond, Herb typed away. "Where's the bomb?"

"LOL. You're funny. You think I'm going to tell you? That would spoil the fun."

"WHERE'S THE BOMB?"

"C'mon, Herb. I can appreciate the stress you're under. Even though *I* didn't send you a query letter, I have an appreciation for the craft of writing, and what a writer must go through. This is what it must feel like for a writer who's been rejected countless times. Only to see some movie star write about their fucked up life, and to see an agent and a publisher drool over the prospects of representing them because they have a *platform*. Well, platform this."

A few moments went by and then another message.

"You with me?"

He didn't do a thing.

"Hey Herby, show me some love!"

He just stared into the screen. A minute went by.

"C'mon, I know this must be jarring, but I'd like to think we're friends. Give me a, *hi*, or a *hello*?"

He simply glared into the screen.

"Hey pal, wake up!"

Nothing. Minutes went by.

"Do I need to snap you out of this stupor?"

He sat there frozen.

"Okay, have it your way."

A loud bang emanated from his bedroom. He ran to the room. A cloud of smoke billowed off his wall, right where his Monet used to be.

"No. Not my Monet!"

He approached the wall cautiously. Could there be more explosives?

He ran his fingers around the charred edges of the frame, burning his hands as the smoldering cinders seared into his skin. He coughed on the putrid smoke.

Only the remains of the frame were still intact. Barely.

A hole in his wall bared the old newspapers used for insulation in the old farmhouse.

"You ruined my Monet. An original."

He ran to the front window searching for any hint of the bastard who did this. His eyes strained, trying to penetrate every curtain and wall possible.

"Damn you!"

He sat back down at the computer. And just as he was about to type, a message came across the screen.

"Sorry."

Herbert began to type aggressively.

"I don't know who you are or what you want, but whatever it is, you're not getting it. Capisce?"

"Now, now. I have to admit, I did expect you to be a bit perturbed, but you weren't responding, Herb."

"Who are you?"

"Who am I? I'm the spirit of every writer you burned. I'm the nightmare in your dreams. You will always wonder if I'm near. I will consume your every thought. For the rest of your life. Which won't be long."

"What did I say to your loved one? Who is he? Who are you?"

"Wouldn't you like to know? You never seemed to care when *my* loved one sent their manuscript to you, did you? Just your cold, mean letters."

"Is that what this is about? You ever think maybe your loved one wasn't good enough?"

"That's not the point. You didn't just reject. You ridiculed. You demeaned. You took a person of hope and possibility and tore them down. How could you think that was okay? You're a bully."

"That's nothing compared to what I'm going to do when I get my hands on you."

"Haha."

Herb scowled at the screen.

"You're forgetting something. I have all the cards. This is not you looking down on me and saying I'm no good. This is me holding you in your house with no way out and no way to call for help. YOU'RE MINE!"

Herbert slammed his desk.

"I have to admit, it's kind of amusing to see your initial fear turn to anger. It's cute."

He shot his glare at the windows across the street. The bending trees drew his attention away from this nut, if only for a moment, telling him the storm was getting near.

"Ha. Maybe we can start over. Now I know you're with me, maybe you'll respond when I correspond. We're establishing rapport. Every relationship has to start somewhere."

"What do you want?"

"Hey, hey, hey. Not so fast. We'll get to that. I think we should get to know each other first."

He sucked in a huge breath and blew it out forcefully. He scanned the windows across the street straining for a glimpse of anyone hiding behind a curtain, daring them to exchange glances.

"Let me ask? What do you think this is about?"

He sat there, reluctant to get into this game of entertain-the-psycho.

"Come on, go ahead, you know sooner or later we're going to have to communicate. It might as well be now. Answer me. What do you think this is about?"

Herb pondered the question, took a breath and gave it some thought. What could this be about? He typed back. "What do you want from me?"

"What do I want? Good question. What crosses my mind right now is, how does a prick like you get to be a prick like you?"

Herb swallowed deeply, and typed feverishly. "What do you mean?"

"You belittled so many. Why?"

"That's a fair question. But, what does it have to do with you holding me captive in my house?"

"Patience. I can appreciate your situation. First, let me say this. I realize I have issues. After all, I'm holding a man hostage in his own house, and I'm toying with him. What kind of person does that?"

Silence hung in the air with no response from either computer.

After a minute, Herb's computer sprayed more messages coming from the sender.

"I want to know, what made you so bitter? Why are you so hurtful? Maybe by understanding you, I might understand myself. Was your mother mean to you? Were you beaten often by your father? Were you even raised by your mother or father? What could possibly..."

Herb fired back from his keyboard.

"What makes you think I'm going to engage with you?"

"Because at this point...you have no choice. If you play along, we both might be able to learn something about ourselves, and maybe, just maybe, I might let you live."

Herb just sat there. Should he fire off his real feelings and incite the madman on the other end of the computer? Or should he play along, stall him, trip him up, maybe even befriend him, and find a way out of this? Choice two seemed obvious.

"What do you want to know?"

"Were you raised by your mother and father?"

"Mother."

"What happened to your father?"

"Left us when I was twelve. Tried to get back in my life when I became successful. Want nothing to do with the leech."

"Now we're getting somewhere. And your mother?"

"Enough about me. What about you?"

"What about me?"

"What's your story?"

"This is about you."

"You have a mother and a father?"

"Of course."

"You have a good childhood?" Asked Herb.

"Parents had issues. As a result, I have issues."

"Tell me more." Herb felt control coming his way.

"My mother used men."

"Elaborate."

A pause ensued. Two minutes went by.

"This is not about me. You're father left you. Found out you were big stuff and wanted some of the sweets?"

"Yes."

"Your mother raised you?"

"Yes."

"She a good mother?"

Herb interrupted the volley, "Tell me more about *your* mother. She exploited men?"

"Yes." The irritation could be felt through the screen.

As an experienced negotiator with publishers, Herb knew, whoever asks the questions stays in control. "Was your father in the picture?"

"Yes."

"What was the problem?" Asked Herb.

"Enough with the questions."

Herb could feel his irritation scheme working. He had to ask more questions. "Were your mother and father in love?"

"My mother used him, and other men, too."

"I see. Your mother and father still alive?" asked Herb.

"No and yes."

"Is your father still in your..."

Herb's typing was interrupted. "Enough about me. Your father isn't in *your* life anymore?"

"No." Typed Herb.

"And your mother? You still see her?"

"Every week."

"What a good son? Then why are you such a nasty person? Your father abuse you?"

"Yes, physically and verbally." Herb typed.

"Now we're getting somewhere. Did you like it?"

"Like it? What kind of question is that?"

"Because if you didn't like being abused, why've you been doing it to so many others?"

Herb just sat there, staring into the screen. The question, a good one. A question he couldn't answer.

CHAPTER 3

Herb looked up toward the ceiling in a daze. His mind wandered. If only she were here now. To have her in his arms. The warmth. The safeness. And yes, the love.

Katie.

The way he met her. Unforgettable. Exchanging glances on the subway. No big deal. Everyone's done that. Long brown hair, athletic build, strong figure. And clothes to accentuate it all. Black skin-tight yoga pants, a clinging soft-pink tank top, and tennis shoes. And the most alluring eyes he'd ever seen. Large olive colored marbles looking up at him. He couldn't help but notice. After all, he was a man. With all of that, she had a purse slung over her shoulder.

No conversation on the subway. Just appreciative glances. They both disembarked at the same stop. Being a gentleman, he let her off first. Her urgent gait took her thirty feet ahead of him. Just as she was about to take her first step up towards street level someone attempted to grab her purse and bolt.

The most amazing thing he'd ever seen flashed right in front of him. The tug against her shoulder jerked her completely around. The same instant this occurred she tightened up her shoulder and spun with the momentum, preventing the purse from slipping off of her shoulder.

It stopped the would-be-thief in his tracks.

Their eyes met, and she yanked the purse back towards herself drawing him closer to her.

She stepped her right leg behind his feet and placed her right arm on top of his upper torso and pulled him back over her leg putting him down on the ground. All in one move. His head hit the ground hard. He lay there stunned. She kicked him once in the head and ran up to street level.

Herb ran up and caught up with her at the top of the stairs. He yelled out to her. "You okay?"

She leaned against a light pole, clearly shaken. He held his hands on her shoulders. "That's the most incredible thing I've ever seen. You okay?"

The gravity of what she'd done hadn't sunk in, yet. She stared at him expressionless, hunched over, gasping, struggling to catch her breath.

"Want me to call the police?"

She simply shook her head, no. She still couldn't speak. "Your shoulder hurt?" He asked.

She hadn't enough time to process everything. To assess if she were hurt or not. She rubbed her shoulder. Turned the side of her mouth up, and shrugged. "I'm okay."

They looked into each other's eyes. The excitement of the moment forming a bond. "You were great back there. How'd you learn a move like that?"

She looked humbled by the comment.

"I have a teenage son. Made sure he knew how to take care of himself. Learned a thing or two myself."

Herb laughed. "He didn't stand a chance. I'll call the police, if you want?"

She looked around as if she were looking for an officer. "No. I'm sure he's long gone by now."

"Yeah, but might be good to report him, so the cops know what he looks like."

She gave it a short thought, and said, "Yeah, you're right. I should file a report."

Herb pulled out his phone and called the police. Within minutes two police officers were standing in front of Herb and Katie questioning their story and getting the full version of what had transpired. When it was done they were sitting inside a diner retracing how the whole thing went down. All over a bowl of soup.

He'd been with plenty of women, but none that ever drove his interest like her. Her strength, both inner and outer, like none other. The courage to stand up to a street burglar, put him down, and then put a finishing touch on him with a kick showed something. This girl had an inner core. A constitution. He couldn't explain it. He just knew he was hooked. Possibly for life.

If only she were here, now.

CHAPTER 4

Herb stepped away from his computer. He needed a break from this madness. He had to get himself together.

He went to his liquor cabinet and poured himself a scotch. The warmth slid down his throat and into his belly. For a few seconds it took him away from the turmoil surrounding him.

Reese came up to him wagging her tail. Herb crouched down and hugged her. Her affection well timed, well needed. Herb rubbed her belly.

At that moment, Herb knew what he needed most.

His instinctual craving took over.

It brought him back to his core. Gave him the base to move on. Made him feel like a man.

A cigar.

His reputation for cigars went with his name. Every picture, every public appearance, every signing always had him smoking a cigar.

It became his trademark.

He cut the end off, lit the end with a wooden match, and rotated it in his mouth as he drew in the smooth tobacco flavor.

As he blew out a relaxing breath, he turned towards his chair. His search-for-inner-peace chair. His I-am the-man chair. And plopped himself down.

This is what he needed most. A chance to gather his thoughts.

He reached for the lever on the side and leaned back.

Another big draw, and he tilted his head back and blew high into the air, the smoke hanging like the fog, filling the room with his presence.

He glanced out the window and saw his pine trees bending further than he ever saw them bend. Maybe a category one hurricane really would visit.

He rolled the cigar in his fingers, feeling like a man in control. This, his first piece of normalcy since this whole thing started. Could this all be happening?

It couldn't be. It just didn't seem real.

He looked down at Reese, licking her paws to pass the time.

All seemed normal.

He drew in his cigar again. The self-assurance swelling inside him again.

He got up and walked into his bedroom. The charred Monet lying on his bed.

Damn. He hoped it was all a bad dream.

This was real. Some lunatic not only had him trapped in his own house, but was toying with him as well.

How the hell would he escape?

He pulled out a tab of paper from his desk, grabbed a pen, donned his glasses and sat down. Time to think up a strategy. Putting on his glasses he inhaled a breath of cigar.

Pfft! Pow!

The cigar ruptured into his face. The flash blinding him.

"Ah!"

His face burned. His glasses coked up with flash-marks, scarring them. The heat pulsed into his cheeks.

He spat out the cigar and jumped from his desk. Did someone throw something at him? Was he hit by a bullet? Where'd this heat come from?

Windows all looked intact.

Throwing his glasses onto the table, he ran to the bathroom and looked in the mirror to assess the damage.

His vision, okay. The glasses saved him from blindness. His eyebrows, singed. His cheeks lightly burned.

He splashed cool water onto his face.

The thought he could have been blinded infuriated him. The anger inside picked him up and carried him over to his computer.

There'd been no new entries since he stepped away.

Herb sat down and began typing furiously.

"You nut! Game on. Nice try with the cigar. Youre dead!"

He waited a few minutes. Nothing.

Had this nut-job gone away? What was he doing?

He looked down. Letters started dancing across his screen.

"I'm sorry to bring this to your attention, Herb, but you didn't put the apostrophe in the word 'you're'."

Herb clenched his knuckles, squeezing them tight.

"Apostrophe nothing. You think ignoring what I say is going to allow you to get away with this?"

"Herb, Herb, Herb, silly boy. I'm trying to give you a little input to serve you better. Please, make no mistake about this. You're not going anywhere. Not until we take care of a few matters."

"Matters? What matters?"

"First, did you fare well with the premium cigar I had set-up for you? Just a pinch of extra punch. I hope it wasn't too much? I know you like a good cigar. Isn't that one of your trademarks?"

"You almost blinded me! My face is burning. What's wrong with you? Why're you doing this to me?"

"I like that you're asking good questions. I will have them all answered by the time we get to the end of our little party. But, we're not going to answer them all at once. One thing at a time. I'm glad you're not blind. That wasn't my intention."

"What are your intentions?"

"The cigar was for retribution."

"Retribution for what?"

"The student."

"What student?"

"Oh for the love of god. Don't play stupid with me, you piss-ant. What student could I possibly be referring to? The one you drove to suicide. Everyone knows that."

"That's not fair to put that on me. That student had a lifelong case of depression."

"Yes, but maybe a few kind words from you could have made a difference. However, since kind words aren't your specialty, maybe if you hadn't been so sarcastic and so demeaning, he wouldn't have ended his life."

"He had mental issues already. Don't put that on me."

"Mental issues is one thing, but it stated in the papers your letter said, 'If you think you have a career in writing, I suggest writing the obituaries for a living where your writing is about as alive as the subject matters you'd be writing about.' You insensitive jerk!"

"I can't be responsible for the world's head-cases."

"The cigar was for the student. One score has been settled."

"One score? How many of these must we go through?"

"Herb, Herb, please settle down. Everything will come in due time. Like good writing, there has to be a flow. You, of all people must know that. Don't you?"

"What's next? What do you want me to do?"

"It sounds like you're ready to play. What's next? Let me tell you."

CHAPTER 5

"I think you should apologize to all the writers you lambasted over the years."

"Pardon me?"

"Yes. You're going to write a press release to all the writers throughout the country. And you'll start by putting an ad in the USA Today, full page."

"I'm going to do what?"

"You heard me. Pull up a new email and we'll get started."

Herb sat motionless. He didn't move for two minutes.

"In your new email you're going to type in the following: First type into the email address twest@usatoday.com."

Instead he typed in cblunt@aol.com.

Immediately he received in his communicator window the following: "You're forgetting I have control over your computer. Nice try. I give you points for effort. DON'T TRY THIS AGAIN! OR I WILL BLOW UP YOUR HOUSE. Type in what I told you. Moron."

Herb did as he was told.

"In the subject-line, type, Apology To All Writers."

Herb followed his orders.

"Now in the body, say the following:"

Herb interrupted him. "Since you have control over my computer, why don't you type this yourself?"

"Good question. The answer's simple. I want the satisfaction of *making you* do it. From your computer. Got a problem with that?"

"No."

"I didn't think so. Now, type this:

Dear Tammy,

I'd like to take out a full-page ad across the entire country on page two that says: This is Herbert Keeler at the Herbert Keeler Literary Agency. I'd like to formally apologize to all the writers I've criticized throughout my career. You deserved better than that from me and I'm truly sorry. I beg for your forgiveness.

Thank you for this opportunity.

Herbert Keeler
Herbert Keeler Literary Agency
Oyster Bay, NY 11801"

Herb typed in everything right to the letter.

"Very good. Now press SEND."

He paused. His eyes looked high to the ceiling, his senses dulled by the humility of it all. What could come of this?

The next series of letters walked across his screen.

"If you know what's good for you, you'll press, SEND."

Reluctantly, Herb pressed, SEND.

And then typed some more. "It's not free, you know?"

"Don't worry, you're paying for it."

"How will I pay for it?"

"Too many questions, Herb. You'll know in due time."

He slouched in his chair. Rubbing his face, he forgot it was burnt, the stinging accenting the crispness.

He nervously ran his fingers through his hair. Again and again.

His captor's request was honored. Would this be all? Could he leave his house? Could he have his life back?

CHAPTER 6

As if his computer had a life of its own, the words sauntered across his screen.

"Ready for the next assignment?"

"Assignment? Haven't you done enough?"

"Your debt to the world runs deep."

"What're you talking about?"

"You rejected someone very dear to me to such a degree, you drove her into depression."

"Who?"

"My mother."

"What was she writing? What's her name?"

"You mean what WAS her name?"

"Pardon me?"

"She's no longer with us."

"She's dead?"

"Yes, she's dead. Thanks to you."

"I'm sorry if your mother's passed away. But there's no way I'm responsible."

"Oh, you are. Believe me! Your rejection letter was one of the most demeaning things I've ever seen in writing, in my entire life. For that you will pay!"

"Please. What did she send? I remember a lot of projects." Herb wiped his hand across his forehead in nervousness.

"It was her memoir. The story of her life. I'll never forget the words that came from your letter."

There was a pause in the typing. As if catching a breath before spilling the beans.

Then it continued, "You told her to give up writing. You told her no one would find her life interesting. You told her no one cared if a little girl had been raped repeatedly, growing up with different men in her life. She reached out to you. Called you. Wanted to talk to you. You shut her down. Told her to just suck it up and move on. This was someone crying out for help. She broke, and began acting erratically, having sex with many men. She was never the same. And you, you didn't give a damn."

Several minutes went by. Herb sat there rubbing both hands through his hair. Over and over. Sweat crept out of his forehead. He jogged in place wiggling his arms and shaking his head, as if trying to displace a swarm of bees off his body.

His breathing accelerated, and he stooped over, hands on his knees, struggling to gain control.

He walked slowly over to the computer and sat back down. He held one hand on each side of the computer, and braced himself.

He typed. "I'm sorry. I'm truly sorry."

Back across the screen came an answer. "You'll be sorry, all right."

CHAPTER 7

Herb's thoughts drifted to his own mother. What he wouldn't give to see her now.

He remembered this past Mother's Day, beautiful sunshine spraying its presence all around them. Herb brought her a huge bouquet of pink daffodils into the retirement home. Walking past the main desk, the receptionist kidded him, "Oh, those for me?"

"You know it!" And he kept on walking.

When he turned down her hallway, her door was open. He knocked and walked right in. "Hey Mom!" He kept walking. On nice days like these, he knew where he'd find her. Out on the patio, soaking up rays of vitamin D.

"Happy Mother's Day." He bent down and gave her a hug. And handed her the flowers.

"Aw, those are so beautiful. Thanks." She stood up slowly and walked into the kitchen and reached up in her cabinet and pulled down a glass vase. She filled it with water and arranged the bouquet with deliberate placement inside the vase. "I think these will look good on my kitchen table. Brightens the whole place up." She flashed him her smile.

It made him feel good to see her smile.

She turned on the stove top and plopped a pot of water on to boil. "Two cups of tea coming up."

"Sounds good, Mom."

"How are you?" She said, her eyes piercing right through his. She was looking for something in particular.

And he knew exactly what *it* was. His love life. She asked every time they met.

"Doing fine. You know."

"Yes? Fine?"

"Yeah. Work's busy. People still reading books, and their reading books on their electronic gadgets, too."

"Oh, I don't give a damn about your work. What about girls? Are you dating anyone?"

"Yeah, I see a few different girls. Nothing serious."

She winced. "Why don't you ever bring any of these girls around to meet me?"

He paused, shrugged. "Someday."

"What are you waiting for?"

"When it's time."

"You're not getting any younger, you know."

"I know."

"Is it me?"

"No Mom. It's not you."

"Let me meet some of these girls. You're traveling all over with them. There's got to be one of them nice enough to introduce to your mother."

"We'll see."

"Is there something wrong with them? Are you dating weird girls?"

"That's it. I'm dating weird girls."

She swiped her hand through the air at him. "Oh, I don't even know why I bother. Can't get a straight answer out of you for nothing."

He chuckled. "Mom, there's more important things to think about than who I'm dating."

"Like what?"

"Like where to go for lunch."

She rubbed her belly. "I am getting hungry. But, don't think I'm going to let you off the hook. You need to settle down while you're still ripe for the pickens. Pretty soon you'll be too old to attract a good girl."

Herb laughed. "All right, Mom. I'll keep that in mind."

"Besides, grandkids don't grow on trees, you know."

The steam whistle from the tea pot started hissing. Just in time. "Tea's boiling," he said.

CHAPTER 8

The letters ran across the screen turning his attention back to the present.

"Time to make things right, my friend. You owe me. In fact, knowing you know what verbal abuse feels like, how could you ignore my Mom after what you went through? Huh?"

Herb looked at those words. And he looked at them again. And again.

Further instructions marched across the screen. "I want you to transfer most of that bank account to me."

That's what this was about. He was to be extorted for the misdeeds of his past. Part of him felt it as just. He waited. How much? How much did the extorter know he had?

"This is where it gets interesting, Herb. I know about your mansion on Lake Como in Italy. I know about your home on Nantucket Island. I know about your private memberships in Augusta and various other clubs throughout the world. I've seen your private yacht collection.

And Herb, I've traveled with you."

The typing stopped, as if to let that last statement sink in. And sink in it did.

They traveled together? Which meant he met this person. Their eyes had met.

And then it continued.

"Yes, does that freak you out? It should. That fancy travel club you belong to? I went on the trip that stopped at all the Ritz Carltons of Beijing, Kuala Lumpur, and Bali. Yes, we had dinners together, drank fine wines together, and fed the monks together. You had your eye-candy of a girlfriend. Nothing upstairs, but not bad on the eyes. Now, you're racking your pea-brain as to which one was me. Good. I want to give you something to chew on. If you remember, there were twenty two of us. The million dollar question is, which one was I?"

The writing stopped for a spell. Herb stared into the screen, stirring in his seat, comfort eluding his squirms.

Tapping his pencil on the desk at a pace only an expectant father would know, the anticipation drove him nauseous.

His blank stare up into the ceiling searched the outer reaches of his memory struggling to recall the faces on that trip. That long ago trip. He couldn't even remember which bimbo he had with him.

Was it the brunette who liked to get naughty in public places? Or was it the redhead who had a fixation for the oral? Hard to remember, they were all good. Just a jumbled blur of passion, flesh, and lustrous memories. Girls who were willing to do anything, and even had something from their own bag of tricks to offer.

An hour passed. No communication came across Herb's screen. What was this madman doing? Was this his way of torturing Herb? What would be next? How much money did he want? Blaming Herb for his mother's death—it all made sense. Maybe he was eating lunch.

Herb looked at his Rolex. Eleven forty-eight. Lunch time. His stomach twisted in thousands of tiny knots. How could he eat? Maybe he should force something down for nourishment. The madman surely had something to deliver soon.

Only God knew what that would be.

CHAPTER 9

Herb pulled the refrigerator open.

He jumped back.

Everything sat rearranged from the top shelf to the bottom. The butter and the cheese, the eggs, the relish, the mustard. All of them meticulously lined up. Rigid. Herb had them randomly thrown in before he left for the Thrillerfest. Now, everything had order. Organized. A purpose.

On the top shelf, a box. A note, stapled on top of the box.

With extreme caution, Herb pulled out the box. The note had scribbled on it in his mother's handwriting, "Hi Honey, I bought you your favorite cake. Enjoy! Mom."

The first thought through his head, *the psycho and his mother were both in his house while he was gone.* His second thought, *Mom never rearranged my refrigerator.*

Never.

He opened up the box. Perplexed by what he saw, one piece of cake. Did his mother eat the rest of it, leaving only one piece for him? She'd never done that before. Never. Always a whole cake. He loved her surprise gifts of his favorite cakes and pies.

He picked it up. Looked underneath it. Turned it over, and examined every part of the cake. He placed it on a plate and took a knife and cut it in half. He cut the halves in half.

Looking at the pieces closely, he found nothing. He proceeded to cut every piece in half again and again and continued until his entire plate spanned out to an artistry of cake crumbs. No sign of tampering stood out anywhere. Weird.

Herb grabbed the pickles, ham and mustard and made himself a sandwich. The sensation of taste tore his attention away from his current dilemma. Chewing, swallowing, and smelling, all the good things. All at no cost. Ah, the simple things in life.

He washed it down with a tall glass of milk. And sat there, waiting for what might come next.

If he only knew. It would be easier to deal with, but everything came out of nowhere.

His elbows supported his arms while he held his head in his hands, running them through his hair. His nervous habit.

He laid his head down in the crook of his arm, his face still sensitive from the burn, burying the outside world from his view. Exhaling a big sigh, he drifted off into a semi-sleep. A state of stressful weariness.

His mind searched through years of letters, wondering which one he pissed off to such vengefulness. Part of him wondered how many more were scorned to this degree.

His random thoughts rifled through a medley of visuals. Like a collage of movies, jumbled together in random sequence, he went from faces on vacations, to a litany of letters, all pulsing with a dark presence lurking behind them, threatening his existence.

He must remember the person on the trip.

He must.

CHAPTER 10

"WAKE UP, HERB! NO REST FOR THE WEARY."

The disguised robotic voice billowed out of the television at an alarming level. Herb awoke with a distressed breath. Short and fast. Panic breath.

"What the..."

The robotic voice continued. "GOOD MORNING!"

"Good morning?" How long have I been sleeping?"

"I LET YOU FIT IN A NAP. IT'S BEEN ALMOST A HALF AN HOUR."

Herb sat there, groggy, trying to get his bearings.

"I'M USING THE TECHNOLOGY YOUR TV OFFERS."

"How'd you know about that?" Anger oozing from his voice.

"I TOLD YOU, I PREPARED. YOUR TV OFFERS A GREAT WAY TO KEEP IN TOUCH. WE CAN HAVE LIVE CONVERSATIONS."

Herb wiped the sleep away from his eyes. "How could I nap at a time like this?"

"EASILY. YOU'RE UNDER A LOT OF STRESS. MOST FOLKS WOULDN'T UNDERSTAND HOW YOU COULD SLEEP AT A TIME LIKE THIS. BUT, I DO."

"Oh?"

"YES. I REMEMBER HEARING MY PARENTS ARGUING FOR HOURS, LATE IN THE NIGHT. THROWING THINGS. VIOLENT. I WAS TERRIFIED. STRESS BALLS IN MY STOMACH."

A curious expression brushed across Herb's face.

"WHEN IT FINALLY STOPPED, I DRIFTED INTO AN ANXIETY-STATE OF SLEEP. MY MIND RESTING FROM THE STRESS. THE SAME WAY A SOLDIER TAKES MINI NAPS ON THE FIELD OF BATTLE."

Herb didn't respond. His mind digested all he'd heard. His captor endured a turbulent childhood. The depths of that turbulence, unimaginable. Driven to the point of stepping over the line of the law. This gave him a window of understanding. "You've been through a lot."

"HMMM. YES. I HAVE. IT'S IMPACTED ME. AFTER ALL, I HAVE YOU TRAPPED IN YOUR HOUSE. AND YOU MIGHT GET BLOWN UP."

Herb paused.

"It's definitely impacted you."

"AND TO ADD INSULT TO IT ALL, I ATE MOST OF YOUR MOTHER'S CAKE."

Herb groaned.

"I WASN'T TRYING TO BE NICE," said the voice.

"That was her gift to me."

"YOU THINK I CARE?"

"You're heartless."

Loud laughter shot out of the TV speakers.

"OH BOY, THIS IS GOOD. YOU'RE CALLING *ME* HEARTLESS. COMING FROM YOU, I TAKE THAT AS A COMPLIMENT. THE MOST HEARTLESS PERSON I KNOW CALLING ME HEARTLESS.

HERB, YOU FUCKED OVER THE WRONG PERSON'S MOTHER. YOU HAVE NO IDEA WHAT I'M CAPABLE OF. BUT YOU'RE STARTING TO FIND OUT."

Herb sat there in thought. The noise from the TV ceased. A thought warmed over him. A sensation of possibility.

He got up and went to the refrigerator, opened up the door, and proceeded to pull every item of food out. He examined each one in great detail, looking for any deviation that may indicate an explosive.

Pickles. Milk. Ham. Every single item. The kitchen table was littered with cold food. No luck.

Next, the freezer. There had to be an explosive in there somewhere. Otherwise, why would he have reorganized the food? Confident he was on the right track, Herb removed every item out of the freezer. He melted every ice cube in the sink.

Nothing.

Herb dropped to his knees and looked underneath the refrigerator and ran his hand beneath it feeling for any little bump. Any little device.

Nothing.

What about behind the refrigerator? He pulled the large steel machine from the wall as his eyes scanned eagerly. Nothing attached to the refrigerator. Nothing to the wall. Nothing to the electric chord.

"Not a thing!"

"I'M SORRY. DID YOU SAY SOMETHING TO ME?" spoke the voice from the TV.

Ignoring the TV, Herb pulled the stove from the wall and looked for any sign of a foreign device. Methodically, his eyes scanned, back-of-the-stove, wall, chords connecting them both.

Nothing.

"Damn! Where is it? Where's the bomb? Tell me! Please!"

"NOT YET."

Herb slammed the refrigerator with his hand.

"What's with your irritating robotic voice? Is your voice too feminine? Are you ashamed of your own voice? Aren't you man enough?"

"YOU'RE ASKING GOOD QUESTIONS. THE PLAN DOESN'T CALL FOR YOU TO HEAR MY REAL VOICE. YET. IN DUE TIME, MY FRIEND. IN DUE TIME."

"When?"

CHAPTER 11

"WHEN I SAY SO."

"What're you waiting for?"

"THAT'S FOR ME TO KNOW AND YOU TO FIND OUT. DON'T YOU LOVE THE ANTICIPATION OF WAITING FOR A RESPONSE? THAT'S WHAT MY MOTHER SAID WAS ONE OF THE MOST FRUSTRATING THINGS IN SENDING OUT QUERY LETTERS. WAITING FOR THE RESPONSE. HOW DOES IT FEEL TO BE ON THE OTHER END?"

Herb slid his forearm across his brow, the sweat getting thicker and his skin still tender. He walked over to his thermostat and the temperature reading said eighty degrees. *Why wasn't the air conditioner working?* He always set it at seventy-one.

He notched it down, but some kind of override or temp-hold light kept blinking.

"What the...?"

He jammed the button with his finger again, and again. Five times. No response.

"HERB, I DIDN'T HEAR YOU. HOW DOES IT FEEL TO BE ON THE OTHER END OF WAITING?"

"Did you mess with my air conditioner?

"OH, WERE YOU PLANNING ON USING THAT TODAY?"

"Damn right. It's going to be a hundred and one today. Plus a hurricane."

"OOPS! MY BAD. I SOMEHOW OVERLOOKED THAT FACT WHEN I PROGRAMMED YOUR THERMOSTAT TO BE KEPT OFF, WITH ME AS THE OVERRIDING PARTY."

Herb slammed the wall.

Twice.

"Why're you doing all of this? Argh! Whyyyyy?"

"HERB. I'M TOYING WITH YOU."

Herb leaned against the wall with his hands, his head held low. He stomped the ground with his right leg.

His thirst kicking in, he went to the faucet and poured himself a cold glass of water. The cool drain of it flowed down his throat, the entire glass all in one breath. *Ah.*

For some reason he sensed the room getting warmer by the minute. *How?*

He went back to the thermostat and it said eighty-two. It had only been a few minutes. How could it go up two degrees?

He put his hand near the vents, feeling for cool air, or any flow of air. Nothing. Flat out nothing.

The gas fireplace? Not on. The pilot off for the summer.

"Okay, no air conditioning? Well, only one way to fight this."

Herb went to his closet next to the washing machine in the utility room and pulled out a small fan. Brought it out into the main sitting room near the TV and set it up. Turned it on high.

"Ha, two can play this game."

Loud laughter rang through the TV.

"What's so funny?"

"YOU'LL SEE. I WOULDN'T WANT TO BREAK THE SUSPENSE."

He plopped his feet up on the new ottoman and let the fan wash his body with air, warm air. He looked around the room, anticipating something else to happen. Nothing did. The fan did what it was supposed to. Blow air.

Rather than feel cooler, the rush of air felt warmer. *How?*

He got up and walked over to the thermostat.

Eighty-five.

"Now. What's going on?" Herb tried to think. "What're you doing?"

"MESSING WITH YOUR HEAD."

"How're you making it warmer?"

"IT'S YOUR HOUSE. THINK HARD. HOW DO YOU THINK I'M MAKING IT WARMER?"

Herb immediately went over to the large kitchen floor and dropped to his knees. He slapped the floor with his widespread fingers and felt the warmth radiating from the floor.

"You! You turned my floors on. You turned my heated floors on. How'd you know I had heated floors?"

"NOT ONE TO GIVE AWAY MY SECRETS, BUT IN YOUR CASE, YOU WON'T BE GOING ANYWHERE. I'LL SAY THIS. IT WAS EASY. AS I SAID, I DID MY HOMEWORK."

Herb let out a big sigh.

"HOWEVER, AS YOU KNOW, YOUR ELECTRONICS BOARD HAS EVERYTHING INTERCONNECTED, AND IT SHOWS ALL THE DIGITAL GADGETRY YOU USE FOR YOUR ENTIRE HOUSE RIGHT ON THE BOARD. I PROGRAMMED THE OVERRIDE, WITH ME AS THE MOTHER SHIP. TOUCHE! ENJOY THE HEAT MY BOY!"

Herb slapped the floor with both hands.

"This is supposed to be used in the winter so I can walk on a warm floor."

"TOO BAD! YOU'LL HAVE TO ROUGH IT JUST LIKE THE REST OF US COMMON-FOLK."

Herb pulled his t-shirt up over his head and tossed it on the back of the couch.

"I'm going to take this head on."

He reached for his glass and filled it up with another cold glass, only this time from his refrigerator water dispenser. He emptied half the glass, enjoying its nice cold feel.

He scanned the room, his thoughts a swirl of other possibilities that awaited him, this clever psychotic toying with his existence.

If he was going to get out of this, it would take cool and cunning.

A plan would need to be made.

CHAPTER 12

A plan would need to be made so he could see his girlfriend again. God, he couldn't believe he referred to her as his girlfriend. Never in his life would he think of anyone worthy enough to be girlfriend material. Yet, here he was, and she was the prime reason for giving his life a new purpose.

"ALL RIGHT. ENOUGH FUN. TIME TO GET DOWN TO BUSINESS. I NEED YOU TO GET ON YOUR COMPUTER AND WIRE OVER YOUR CASH BALANCE FROM YOUR BANK ACCOUNT, YOUR CHECKING ACCOUNT AND YOUR MONEY MARKET ACCOUNT. HERE'S THE NUMBER TO TRANSFER TO. 769 AED 437 G."

Herb yelled back to the TV. "You're high as a kite if you think I'm wiring my money."

No sooner had he released the last syllable on the word *money*, and a deafening explosion blasted from his garage. It shook the house.

Herb's eyes bulged from their sockets.

He leaped from his seat and ran to the garage where his Harley Davidson smoldered like a piece of scrap metal. The handle bars embedded into the wall. The gas tank, a display of warped jagged steel, resting next to the welcome mat near the door. The aroma of gasoline permeated the garage.

Smoke filled the air, and through the cloud he saw the frame of the bike resting on his golf clubs. The violence of it all contrasted with the quiet of the moment.

He strode back to the TV and shouted, "When will the destruction end? When?"

"I HOPE I'VE GOTTEN YOUR ATTENTION."

"That was my Harley Davidson Custom Vehicle. I've taken her across the country, and back."

"WIRE THE MONEY."

"We've been on road trips with friends. Attended biker events everywhere. She had custom chrome, Screaming Eagle engine. She was my baby."

"YOU ACT LIKE YOUR MOTORCYCLE WAS A PERSON. IF YOU WOULD HAVE THOUGHT OF PEOPLE THE SAME WAY YOU THINK OF YOUR OBJECTS, YOU WOULDN'T BE IN THIS PREDICAMENT."

Herb paused.

He looked up toward the ceiling, his thoughts in motion.

Some time elapsed. He paced the room.

Thinking. He rubbed his jaw. Ran his fingers through his hair. Drew in a breath, and sat back down.

"MAYBE IF YOU TREATED PEOPLE WITH RESPECT. IF YOU SHARED A SENSE OF DECENCY WITH THEM, YOUR LIFE WOULD BE RICHER."

Herb laughed.

"How could my life be richer? I've got everything I need. Money. Cars. Trips."

"HERB. HERB. HAVEN'T YOU LEARNED ANYTHING IN OUR SHORT TIME TOGETHER?"

"What do you mean?"

"YOU REALLY DON'T GET IT. DO YOU?"

"Um...."

"DO I HAVE TO SPELL IT OUT FOR YOU?"

Herb said nothing.

"HOW DUMB ARE YOU?"

Herb still said nothing.

"PEOPLE ARE MORE IMPORTANT THAN THINGS."

Herb sat there slumped in his chair. Like a scolded school boy. Minutes went by in silence.

"WAKE UP, HERB!"

"What more do you want from me?"

"WIRE ME THE MONEY."

"That's what this is about?"

"IT'S ABOUT A LOT OF THINGS. IT'S ABOUT EVENING UP THE SCORE. IT'S ABOUT MAKING YOU SEE THE WRONG OF YOUR WAYS. IT'S ABOUT MY MOTHER. AND, YES. IT'S ABOUT, THE MONEY."

"What makes you think you're any better than me?"

"NOW."

"If you think blowing up my things is going to make me crack, you're gravely mistaken."

"HMM, LET"S TRY THIS ON FOR SIZE. YOU WOULDN'T WANT ME TO PULL THE IGNITION SWITCH ON REESE'S COLLAR, WOULD YOU?"

Herb ran to Reese to examine her collar. He noticed it looked different. An extra attachment existed. He attempted to wrestle it off, but to no avail. He tried with all his might to muscle it off. Pull. Twist. Push.

No luck.

What drove him to panic? The very small electrical device on the collar underneath the chin he somehow didn't notice till now.

He jumped back in front of the TV.

"How'd you rig her collar? How? I beg you, please don't do anything to her. Please!"

"THAT WAS EASY. I WORKED AT YOUR DOG-WALKER SERVICE WHILE YOU WERE AT THRILLERFEST. I REQUESTED YOUR HOUSE WHILE YOU WERE GONE. IT WAS EASY TO GET YOUR ASSIGNMENT SINCE NO ONE WANTED TO RISK BUMPING INTO YOU. I WORKED THERE UNDER AN ALIAS. IT ALLOWED ME TO HAVE LOTS OF FUN WITH YOUR HOUSE. YOU WILL SEE. I THINK BY NOW YOU KNOW I'M NOT MESSIN AROUND. READY TO WIRE ME THE MONEY?"

"Yes. Yes. Please, I beg you. Don't do anything to Reese. Please. I'll wire you the money."

"EXCELLENT. FOLLOW THE INSTRUCTIONS ON THE SCREEN. IT ALREADY HAS THE ACCOUNT NUMBERS FILLED IN WHERE YOU WILL SEND IT TO. SIMPLY ENTER YOUR ACCOUNT NUMBER, NAME, AND THE AMOUNT, $450,000. I'M LEAVING THE REMAINING $2,000 FOR YOU. I DON'T KNOW WHY. I JUST LIKE ROUND NUMBERS. DO IT. QUICKLY."

Herb spoke not a word, entered his name, the account numbers, and the amount and hesitated for a second. He looked at Reese with her loving eyes staring right through him. Years of tenderness, soft hugs, unconditional love and a friend no one else on the planet could compare to. He went back to his computer and hit the "send' button.

He just depleted his bank account $450,000.

A few moments later the robotic voice thundered. "NICE WORK. WE'LL WORRY ABOUT YOUR RETIREMENT ACCOUNTS NEXT."

The word flew out of his mouth. "No!"

CHAPTER 13

The strong electronic voice surged out of the TV. "TIME TO GET DOWN TO BUSINESS. YOU SENT ME A LITTLE STIPEND. GRACIAS! NOW IT'S TIME TO SEND A LITTLE SOMETHING TO THE FAMILY OF THE STUDENT YOU LED TO SUICIDE."

Herb yelled back to the TV. "I didn't lead that student to suicide."

"SILENCE. PAY ATTENTION."

Herb looked at the screen and another money-wiring form appeared. It had names and account numbers filled in.

"It's not fair for you to put his suicide on me. I may have said some bad things, but I didn't contribute to his depression."

"WHAT YOU SAID TO THAT YOUNG MAN WAS WRONG. DEAD WRONG."

Herb thought for a minute. The voice had a point. "You're right. Looking back, I said a lot of wrongs things to a lot of people. I admit."

"GOOD. I'M GLAD YOU"RE BEGINNING TO SEE THE WRONG OF YOUR WAYS."

"Yes. But, please, don't put the suicide on me."

"YOU'RE BEGINNING TO IRRITATE ME. DO I NEED TO REMIND YOU? REESE'S COLLAR?"

"No. No. I get it. What do you want me to do next?"

"FILL IN YOUR PART AND HIT 'SEND'."

Herb read the screen and saw the account number being sent *from* was his retirement account. The amount, $1,000,000.

He barked into the TV, "How'd you get all these account numbers? Why one million?"

"IT WAS EASIER THAN YOU'D THINK. I SHOWED UP AT YOUR CUSTODIAN'S OFFICE WITH BOGUS IDENTIFICATION POSING AS THE IRS, STATED I WAS DOING AN AUDIT, AND PEOPLE PARTED WAYS FOR ME. I COULD HAVE PRACTICALLY WITHDRAWN THE MONEY MYSELF. SUCH MISLED RESPECT. WHY ONE MILLION? BECAUSE, I LIKE ROUND NUMBERS. NOW, FILL IN THE BLANKS."

Herb filled in the blanks, his hands shaking as he slowly entered the zeroes to make a million. He hesitated to hit the 'send' button.

"HERB, DO WE HAVE TO REVISIT THE PART WHERE I BLOW UP REESE?"

Herb looked at Reese, bit his lip, and hit 'send'.

"WELL DONE. WELL DONE."

Herb knelt down on the floor and scooped Reese into his arms, showering her with love. Reese licked him back showing her appreciation. It was like two lost souls, misfits to the rest of the world, but true friends to each other.

He grabbed her head between his hands, looked her straight in the eye and said, "I'll never let anything happen to you."

Herb's mind swirled. Picking up Reese at the shelter was the best thing he ever did. All the time he spent helping out with the animals led him to Reese. That's why he kept going back. To show his gratitude.

Reese licked his face. This animal showed him true loyalty. More than he could say for most humans. Herb would protect her with all his might.

For a couple of seconds, Herb forgot about the mess he was in. *And why pets were so great. They help you forget.*

Even for a couple of seconds.

CHAPTER 14

Pets help you forget.

But, Katie made him feel whole again. Whenever he had a bad day, she was there to get him back on track. Today she was in Chicago for a five day seminar with a thousand other pharmacists. And now he wouldn't be able to connect with her. She would wonder why he wasn't returning her calls.

He remembered their first date. He picked her up from her Manhattan apartment in his Rolls Royce. She looked stunning. High heels, black capris, and a white blouse that accentuated her alarming beauty.

When she saw the car she hesitated in her tracks. She slowly stepped into the front seat and looked over at him. "I hope you didn't rent this to impress me."

"Actually, I own it."

She let out a big sigh. "I'm impressed. But, I'm more impressed by the man than by what he drives. Just for the record."

He looked surprised. Most women were awestruck. This one proved different. He was slow to respond. He shrugged, "Just trying to share some of the things I've been fortunate to earn."

She threw a warm smile back at him. "Good recovery. I'll give you that."

A smug smirk ran across his face. "You hungry? I've got a favorite place I'd like to take you."

"Sure."

"Excellent. The ambiance is charming, and the cuisine, superb."

"Sounds good. Take me away."

They pulled up to the docks at North Cove Yacht Harbor at Battery Park. He ran around to open her door and led her by the hand. "Follow me."

She looked around. They were surrounded by yachts on all sides. She appeared skeptical, as he led her along the dock and helped her step up and onto his luxury cruiser. It felt more like a small hotel on the water. The one hundred ninety-six foot Italian built vessel sported a split-level sundeck with a Jacuzzi on the upper level.

He took her up to the steering wheel. "Maybe we can take 'er for a spin. You like the water?"

"Hmm...Yeah." She attempted to appear unimpressed.

"Nothing like being out there on a warm evening, the breeze gracing your cheeks."

"You sound like a poet trying to seduce his prey."

His eyebrows flipped higher. "I plead the fifth." He waited for a laugh.

She ignored all of it, his half attempt at a joke and a cheap try to win her over with his big boat. "So, is this the restaurant you were referring with the superb ambiance and the charming cuisine?"

"It was actually the other way around. Charming ambiance. Superb cuisine."

She flipped her eyebrow up at him. "You should never tell a girl she's wrong when you're trying to win her over."

Frustration started to swell inside. "I'll have to remember that." He sensed he better sway the conversation another direction and get the vibes going in his favor. "Shall we have a seat and look at the menu?"

It appeared she wanted the awkwardness to dissipate as well. "Sure."

He led her to a table on the back of the boat on the lower deck. Two chairs were positioned waiting for them. Linen tablecloth. A full set of silverware. Water glass. Wine glass.

A waitress approached them. "Good evening Mr. Wheeler. May I bring you and your guest a cocktail? A glass of wine?"

He said, "Hello Ingrid. This is my friend, Katie. Katie, this is Ingrid."

They exchanged pleasantries. He said, "Please bring us a bottle of the Chardonnay I ordered last week." He looked at Katie for her approval.

"Actually, I'm not a Chardonnay drinker. In fact, I'm not a drinker at all. If I could have an iced tea that would be fine."

"I'm sorry. How presumptive of me."

"That's okay."

"Have you always been a non-drinker?"

"Yes. I've never had a thing for it."

"Ingrid. Make that two teas please. Cancel my wine."

"Right away, sir."

Strong. Independent. Not afraid to stand her ground. Health minded. And beautiful beyond words. Hmm.

The dinner was ordered, devoured, desert followed. They sat there sipping their iced tea. "You ever been to Europe?" He asked.

"No. Never been out of the country."

"You'd love it. I know a place in Nice that serves the best beignets. Out of this world."

"Sounds nice." She nodded.

"There's so much to do there. You can drive to Cannes, where the film festival's held every spring, or you can ride to St. Tropez, this fashionable resort area. Or you can take in all that Monte Carlo has to offer."

She clasped her hands together, rubbed her thumb from her right hand into the palm of her left hand, folded them down upon her lap, looked up, and said, "Herb, you're nice. I've enjoyed talking to you this evening. And, it's obvious you're worldly beyond my realm of experience. But, I don't want you to think just because you treat me to a nice dinner on your yacht and lead me to the promise of traveling with you to Southern France that I'm going to go down below on your yacht and be your next notch of prey on your boat."

A look of disbelief took over his face. Even hurt.

"Katie. It's the last thing on my mind. I swear. I hope you know I'm sincere when I say that." He looked at her. For the first time ever in his life, a woman stood up to him. Called him on his attempts. Even more important, he was afraid of losing someone he truly wanted.

Fear raced through his heart. A fear he hadn't experienced before.

"Let's take a walk through the park." He said.

"Actually, it's a bit late. If you could take me back home, that would be great."

"I'm sorry. I feel like I've spoiled the evening just by having a yacht and by owning a Rolls. Please don't hold that against me."

"No, that's not it. It's getting late. I'm not a late night person."

"No problem. We can go now."

He opened the door for her and let her in. En route she answered his questions about being a pharmacist. He showed genuine interest in her work. And she was glad to elaborate about all the different types of customers that come in, and how she was trained to give flu shots. She even offered to give him one.

When the light turned green, Herb accelerated and a stray German shepherd ran out in front of him. He swerved to try and avoid hitting it, but to no avail. He clipped the dogs hind quarters. He stopped the car right there and clicked on his emergency flashers to stop anyone else from getting near. The dog lie there yelping. He could see his back leg was broken.

"It's going to be okay, boy. It's okay." He stroked the dogs back to help him feel safe. He looked up at Katie. "Can you please open the back door?"

After she opened the back door, he grunted and lifted the dog up and placed him in the back seat. "Would you mind riding in the back with him to make him feel safe?"

"Sure."

"Great. I'll take him to my vet. It's not far from here. They'll make him good as new."

On the way to the vet, he kept looking over his shoulder at the dog asking Katie how he was doing. "He's hurting. Are we almost there?"

"Yes. Just a few more blocks."

They pulled up to the front door at the vet's. Herb picked him up and took him in. "Can you park this for me?"

"Glad to."

The vet staff took the dog to the back and went to work. Herb and Katie waited out in the lobby. "I can take you home now." He said.

"What about the dog?"

"I'll come back and check on him. There's no collar on him so he's probably a stray. Once he's fixed up, I'll take him to the shelter I volunteer at."

"You volunteer at a shelter?"

"Yes. I've been doing it for years."

She sat up in her seat. "Interesting."

They talked for the next two hours while the dog had his leg worked on. Afterwards, they dropped him off at the shelter, and before they realized it, it was one o'clock in the morning. Herb pulled up in front of Katie's place. "Sorry I'm getting you home so late."

"That's okay. I had a nice time."

"I did too."

She gazed out through the windshield, gathering her thoughts. "I have to be honest. When you pulled up in your Rolls, I thought, boy, he tries too hard to impress. And then when you took me to your yacht for dinner. It sealed the deal for me. I wanted nothing further to do with you."

"And you still ate my dinner?"

She laughed. "It wouldn't have been appropriate to back out at that moment. Besides, I was hungry."

"You would've missed a good meal."

"More important. I would've missed the real you. Seeing you care for that dog let me see a side of you I didn't expect."

"I'm glad I hit the dog."

"Pardon me?"

"No. Not like that. So, you could see that side of me."

They both shared a weak laugh.

"You don't have to wow me with expensive things and fancy dinners. That's not me."

"I hope to have the chance to learn more about the real you." He said.

She tilted her head, flipped her hair to one side and said, "Next time, it's my date, my treat. Deal?"

"Deal."

CHAPTER 15

After day dreaming about his first date, Herb sat there waiting to see what would come next. A minute went by. Nothing. Then, five minutes. Nothing. Next thing he knew, it had been a half an hour since he'd heard anything.

The silence and the not-knowing drove him nuts.

Herb ran his hands through his hair a hundred times. He began pacing. He felt like poison was bubbling up in his stomach. Corrosive acid.

Stress.

He needed to grab control.

So, he did what he always did whenever life became overwhelming. He jumped on his treadmill in his office and started walking. Four miles an hour. A fifteen minute pace for the mile.

After twenty minutes he started to feel better. Despite the warm temperatures in his house, the acidic feeling in his stomach started to dissipate. He ramped up the speed to six miles an hour and started to jog. A ten minute mile pace.

After thirty total minutes on the treadmill he stopped, sat down on the edge and stretched his calf muscles. The physical exertion gave him a release he desperately needed.

His head churned with random thoughts. *How did he get caught up in this mess? Could he escape? If so, how? Would he ever find the man doing this? Would this be the final day of his life? What would the writing industry say about his life? Was he a good man? Did he help others? Was he good for the industry?*

Probably not.

Herb began to see his actions hurt others. *Why couldn't he have been different?*

His heavy head slumped into his hands. His hands rubbed his eyes, trying to soothe away the tension. He forgot the skin around them was singed. Tender.

His thoughts wandered, from one thing to the next. *This person had to come in here before, but how? May as well ask.*

"How'd you get in my house?"

"IT WAS EASY. WHEN I DID THE DOG-WALKING THING, I DID ALL KINDS OF FUN THINGS TO YOUR HOUSE. THERE'S MORE TO COME."

"More?" Herb scowled. He hated the condescending tone, and the last thing he wanted to be was a toy for some psycho.

"How'd you know so much about me and my house?"

"I STALKED YOU."

"You what?"

"THAT'S RIGHT. I STALKED YOU. I RENTED THE FARMHOUSE ACROSS THE STREET AND I STUDIED AND CHARTED YOUR EVERY MOVE. I EVEN FOLLOWED YOU WHEN YOU LEFT THE HOUSE."

Herb winced.

"When did you do that?"

"I DID IT SEVERAL TIMES. ONCE LAST WEEK WHILE YOU WERE GONE, WHERE I LAYED OUT THE FINAL PREPARATIONS. THE FIRST TIME A YEAR AGO, BEFORE YOU HAD REESE."

"Before I had Reese? Did you break into my house then?"

"YES. I DID."

"How'd you do that?"

"YOU EVER HEAR OF A THING CALLED GOOGLE?"

"I beg your pardon?"

"YES. I GOOGLED, 'HOW TO GET PAST HOME ALARM SYSTEMS'. WAS BLOWN AWAY BY WHAT POPPED UP. I SIMPLY FOLLOWED THE INSTRUCTIONS AND SENT RADIO WAVES IN TO BLOCK THE SIGNALS FROM THE SENSORS THAT CONTROL THE PANELS, AND IN ADDITION, WAS ABLE TO INTERCEPT UNENCRYPTED SIGNALS AND DISCOVER STORED PASSWORDS TO ARM AND DISARM THE ALARM. I USED A DEFINED RADIO WHICH COST ME SEVENTEEN HUNDRED DOLLARS. BOUGHT A USRP N210. IN CASE YOU WERE WONDERING."

Herb sat down on his couch and rubbed his chin. His mind went into assessment mode. He was dealing with a man of great mental capacity. Someone who would go above and beyond the norm to get what he wanted. Someone who sought out technology and was willing to take great risks to attain his goals. Risks that could involve prison, or great bodily harm. This would have to be a person highly motivated to do what they were doing.

He already knew what the motivations were.

Revenge. Revenge for his mother's depression.

If only he could find out who the mother was.

CHAPTER 16

Herb glared into the television.

"Where do you live?"

The robotic voice responded. "WHAT TOOK YOU SO LONG TO ASK?"

Herb huffed. "Where you from?"

"MICHIGAN."

"Michigan? What do you do in Michigan?"

"NOT SAYING."

"What're you waiting for?"

"WHEN I'M READY."

Herb rubbed the back of his neck, pondering what else he could ask. What other facts might the psycho be willing to reveal?

A loud noise emanated from the outside of his house. Like something blew into it. He looked out the window and could see gusts of wind carrying dust and light debris.

He brought his attention back to the matter at hand. "You said we traveled together. Tell me more about that trip. And since you're going to blow me up anyway, you might as well tell me your name."

A boisterous condescending laugh came out of the TV, robotic in every way.

"I HAVE TO GIVE YOU CREDIT. YOU MAKE A GOOD POINT. SINCE I'M GOING TO BLOW YOU UP, WHY NOT SPILL THE BEANS? WHY NOT TELL YOU MY NAME?"

Herb licked his lips. Anticipation grasping his awareness. Some information might arm him on how he could play against this mind. This disturbed, brilliant mind. "First name would be a good start."

The laughter continued. "YOU'RE PERSISTENT."

"Would you prefer I address you as mister, or doctor?"

"YOU DON'T NEED TO ADDRESS ME AT ALL. WE'LL KEEP THE NAME OUT OF THIS."

"But when I call you or ask for your attention, how should I address you?"

"THERE'S NO NEED TO ADDRESS ME."

Herb slumped back in his chair in defeat. Just as it looked like information would flow, his captor shut down.

"Please tell me more about your mother?" Herb asked.

"WHY?"

"To kill time. What'd she do for a living?"

"SHE RAISED ME."

"She work?"

"TOO MANY QUESTIONS."

"Where'd she grow up?"

No answer.

"Was she pretty?"

"GORGEOUS."

"You miss her?"

"MORE THAN YOU'LL EVER KNOW."

"How'd she pass?"

"TERRIBLY. VIOLENTLY."

"What happened?"

Silence ensued. Herb braced himself. He shouldered credit for her depression. How could he have contributed to her violent death? This couldn't be.

"Excuse me. Was it a car accident? Or, did someone do something to her?"

The sheepishness in his voice scratched the air.

"SOMEONE DID SOMETHING TO HER ALL RIGHT. MURDER."

Herb winced. A puzzled expression crossed his face.

"Excuse me, sir, but, how could I be responsible for that?"

A loud mechanical voice shot out of the TV.

"I TOLD YOU NOT TO ADDRESS ME."

"I'm sorry." He swallowed hard. "How could I be responsible for your mother's murder?"

"BECAUSE YOU DROVE HER TO DOING BAD THINGS."

"What kind of bad things?"

"THINGS WITH MEN. LOTS OF MEN. THINGS A HUSBAND WOULDN'T LIKE HIS WIFE TO DO."

Herb squinted in thought. The pieces started to come together.

"Your father killed your mother because she was fooling around?"

A loud silence swelled over from the TV. Herb crossed his arms consoling himself, knowing the person on the other end of the TV must have been doing the same.

"I'm sorry," said Herb. "I'm truly sorry."

"YOU'RE DAMN RIGHT YOU'RE SORRY. IT'S TIME."

"Time for what?"

"HANGMAN."

"What?" Herb's face scrunched up with puzzlement. He ran his fingers along his throat.

"HANGMAN. THE GAME."

"What about it."

"WE'RE GOING TO PLAY."

"I don't feel like playing a game."

"YOU DON'T HAVE A CHOICE."

"Yes I do."

"THE ANSWER WILL REVEAL IMPORTANT INFORMATION FOR YOUR EXPERIENCE. YOU NEED TO KNOW."

A serious composure washed over Herb.

"GRAB A SHEET OF PAPER AND PEN."

Herb took the pad in front of him and flipped it to a fresh page.

"Okay."

"YOU KNOW HOW TO PLAY?"

"Yes."

"GOOD. THIS VERSION HAS THREE WORDS."

"Three words?"

"YES."

"Why do I need to know?"

"YOU WILL SEE. GET STARTED. MAKE YOUR LITTLE GALLEY WITH THE NOOSE."

He did as told.

"OKAY. I'M GOING TO GIVE YOU ANOTHER HINT. THE FIRST WORD HAS FOUR LETTERS. THE SECOND WORD HAS TWO. AND THE THIRD WORD HAS THREE LETTERS."

Herb made corresponding dashes which he could write the letters on as he attained them.

"START."

He swung his tongue around his mouth in a clockwise manner. His curiosity at a peak. And the fear as to what this game would reveal just as elevated.

Herb started. "Okay. Here goes. A."

"STARTING WITH THE VOWELS. GOOD. YOU'VE GOT ONE. SECOND WORD. FIRST LETTER."

He wrote it in. And let out a sigh.

"E."

"GOOD AGAIN. TWO FOR TWO. THIRD WORD. SECOND LETTER."

He wrote it in.

He looked up towards the TV. "I."

"NEGATIVE. GIVE YOURSELF A BODY PART."

Herb drew a head.

"O."

"WHOA! YOU'VE GOT TWO ON THIS ONE. FIRST WORD, SECOND AND THIRD LETTERS."

He scribbled the letters in, his brows furrowed. His mind examining the letters in front of him, scanning like a computer searching for the possibilities.

"U."

"NO. ADD ANOTHER BODY PART TO YOUR STICKMAN."

He added on a neck. A short neck.

"Y."

"NO. Add another limb."

He drew an arm. And studied the array of letters in front of him. The second word only posed a few possibilities.

"N."

"YES. THIRD WORD, THIRD LETTER."

He was about to write the letter N on the end of the second word, but he caught himself. "Did you say *third* word?"

"YES. THIRD WORD. THIRD LETTER."

He marked it in the appropriate place. This left even fewer possibilities for the second word.

"S."

"WRONG AGAIN. ADD ANOTHER LIMB. YOU STARTING TO GET SOMEONE TO HANG?"

He said nothing. Added another arm. "Why does it matter if I even draw a stick figure or not?"

"JUST PLAY THE GAME."

"T."

"BINGO! SECOND WORD. SECOND LETTER. THIRD WORD. FIRST LETTER."

He printed the letters in and drew his head back from the page to look at the words. So far he had:

_ OO_ AT TEN.

He mumbled to himself. "Soon at ten. Look at ten. Book at ten. Cook at ten. Boot at ten. Cool at ten. Doom at ten?"

He looked up. "Is that it? Doom at ten?"

"WOW. I NEVER THOUGHT OF THAT. BUT, IT COULD WORK."

"What do you mean?"

"IT'S NOT THE SAME WORDS. BUT, IT MEANS THE SAME."

"Doom at ten. The bomb's going off at ten?"

"LET'S FOCUS ON THE GAME."

"Fuck the game! Is that it? The bomb's going off at ten?"

"YOU MUST GET THE WORDS RIGHT!"

"Jesus. The bomb's going off at ten!"

"FINISH THE GAME! IT'S CRITICAL!"

Herb swiped the pad and pen off his desk. "You're going to blow my house up at ten!" Panic filled his voice. The reality of it all kicking in.

"YOU MUST FINISH THE GAME!"

Herb's mind was a blur of emotion and overwhelm. His house would cease to exist at ten. And this crazy person wanted him to finish a game. "Just tell me the answer!"

"I'LL GIVE YOU A HINT. WHEN YOU SAID 'DOOM', ONE OF THE LETTERS WAS RIGHT."

He thought a second. Room at ten. Soon at ten. No similarities. Tool at ten. Wool at ten. No matches. If the D was in the front, he could have, Door at ten. Poor at ten.

What about M on the back letter. That's when it hit him.

"B. Boom at ten! You're blowing my fucking house up at ten?"

"EXCELLENT DEDUCTION. BUT. THERE'S ONE MORE THING."

CHAPTER 17

"One more thing?"

"YES. THE BOMB'S GOING OFF AT TEN O'CLOCK PM. TOMORROW."

Herb let out a big sigh and looked at his watch. 2:48 PM. He had a day plus seven hours. A look of urgency took over his face. He had to figure a way out of this.

Newly invigorated, he grabbed a pad of paper from his closet and sat down on his couch with a pen and began to write. At the top of the paper, he wrote: QUESTIONS TO ASK on one side of the paper, and STRATEGIES TO ESCAPE on the other.

Under QUESTIONS TO ASK, Herb wrote, 1) Where did you grow up?

Under STRATEGIES TO ESCAPE, he wrote 1) Tell him Reese needs to poop.

He looked up towards the ceiling, thinking. Tapping his pen on the desk. Another thought creeped into his head. *The tornado escape tunnel from the basement.*

He scribbled it as fast as he could under STRATEGIES TO ESCAPE.

"THE BOMB GOES OFF AT TEN." bellowed the electronic voice from the TV.

Slightly startled. "Yeah. I get it."

"SCARED?"

He paused before he answered. "No more than I was."

Herb went back to thinking. *Run and burst through the window. Get up and run. But, I'd probably get shot. Bad idea. This is brainstorming, dummy. There are no bad ideas. Write it down.* So he did. *Keep thinking. Then, it occurred to him. The voice never told Herb what to do. The captor waited for Herb to run into his next trap.*

Herb asked. "What do you want me to do next?"

A mischievous laugh echoed from the TV.

"What's so funny about that?"

"YOU JUST GO ABOUT YOUR BUSINESS BEING A RAT IN A CAGE AND LET THE EVENTS PLAY OUT ON THEIR OWN."

"Isn't there something you want to happen to me?"

"OH YEAH. BUT, I WOULDN'T WANT TO SPOIL THE FUN BY TELLING YOU WHAT TO DO. YOU'D BE ON TO ME RIGHT AWAY. THIS WAY, EVERYTHING'S A SURPRISE."

Herb wrote under *STRATEGIES TO ESCAPE*, "Out through the attic." More ideas started entering his brain. *"Try screaming."*

Like a river raging through a narrow canyon, his ideas flowed onto the paper. Both sides. Two ideas for ESCAPE. Three ideas for QUESTIONS.

He jotted questions about his family. Kids? Married? What he did for a living?

Maybe this would reveal something they had in common. If he could relate to him, maybe he could appeal to his emotional side to spare his life.

He wanted to ask him who inspired him. Regrets? How he came to know so much about sensors and explosives. Maybe he could appeal to his logical side.

If he were to die, what would be the worst way to die? He had to get in the head of this mastermind. Find a weakness. Find a pattern. A link. Something.

A posture of control perked up within. He continued to write. Furiously. Back and forth. One after the other. Before he knew it, he had a page and a half of QUESTIONS to ask. And half a page of ESCAPE ideas.

Maybe the questions would force the voice to reveal something about himself he could use to escape. Some type of leverage.

Feeling a small bit of control in the situation, it was time to try escape idea number one.

The hot room temperature and the stress embedded a strong thirst into Herb. The thirst for freedom, even stronger.

He grabbed a glass from the cabinet and poured himself a glass of water.

Okay, idea number one.

Here we go.

CHAPTER 18

"Excuse me. Reese needs to go to the bathroom."

A few seconds went by.

"WHAT?"

"You heard me. Reese needs to poop."

"LOOK AT THE CLOSET IN YOUR BEDROOM, I MADE PROVISIONS FOR REESE TO POOP THERE. AND PEE, TOO."

A look of puzzlement and frustration took over Herb's face.

He walked into the bedroom and walked into his large walk-in closet. Peeking out from behind his shoe bin laid a patch of newspaper. Underneath his clothes. Easy for him to miss last night when he came home.

"You can't expect her to go here. Poop and pee?"

"OF COURSE. THIS IS BY DESIGN. RIGHT BELOW YOUR CLOTHES. SHOULD EMIT A NICE ODOR INTO ALL YOUR CLOTHES."

A mischievous laugh followed.

Herb shook his head. "Why can't I go outside and let Reese go there? I'll come back in. I promise. If you'll disarm the sensor on the door first. Please."

"SORRY PAL. NOT GOING TO HAPPEN. I LIKE YOUR MANNERS THOUGH."

"But, Reese needs air. She needs to let out a couple of pees."

"IT DOESN'T SAY STUPID ON MY HEAD."

"I promise to come back in. If you could..."

"YOU MIGHT AS WELL QUIT YOUR WHINING. NO MEANS NO. THAT'S IT."

"What if you just let me out the door? We can go right there. If I try and run, you can just shoot me, right?"

"YOU'RE NOT GOING OUTSIDE."

"You're still right across the street, right?"

"YES. BUT THE DOOR STAYS SENSORED."

"Reese has never gone on paper before? I don't think this will work."

"I SAID I PREPARED. DIDN'T I?"

"What do you mean?"

"TAKE HER OVER THERE."

Herb snapped his command to Reese. "Here. Reese. Over here."

She came into the bedroom. Herb pointed to the newspaper. "Here. Reese."

She walked onto the paper and walked around it twice. Positioned herself. Squatted. And then the most amazing thing happened. She pooped on the newspaper. And followed it up with a pee.

Herb asked. "How'd you do this?"

"WHEN YOU WERE AT THRILLERFEST AND I WAS DOGSITTING FOR YOU, I TRAINED HER TO GO ON PAPER.

Herb looked pleasantly impressed. An accomplishment by Reese, for sure.

But the smell. Terrible. The poop, smoldering. The pee spreading out amidst the newspaper. The urine odor permeating his nostrils.

"The smell is terrible. I hope it doesn't seep into my clothes."

"HERB, YOU NEED TO LEARN. CLOTHES, ART, MATERIAL THINGS, THEY"RE NOT AS IMPORTANT AS PEOPLE. I'M TRYING TO TEACH YOU."

"By having my dog poop and pee in my closet and ruin my clothes?"

"EXACTLY. EXPENSIVE CLOTHES. SHOES. BELTS. FASHION BRANDS. THAT'S NOT WHAT'S IMPORTANT IN LIFE. IT'S THE PEOPLE. PEOPLE ARE WHAT MATTER. I'M GOING TO DRIVE IT INTO YOUR HEAD."

"But how does my dog peeing in my closet make me learn that?"

"BECAUSE RIGHT NOW YOU'RE TRAPPED IN YOUR HOUSE. IF YOU OPEN THE DOOR. KAPOW! WHAT'S MORE IMPORTANT TO YOU RIGHT NOW? FREEDOM TO GO WHERE AND WHEN YOU WANT? OR YOUR FUCKIN' CLOTHES?"

"You've got a point."

"WHAT'S THE POINT?"

"A person's freedom is more important than their clothes."

"EXACTLY. AND IF YOU LOOKED AT OTHERS WITH THAT SAME TYPE OF LENS YOU'D BE A HAPPIER PERSON. AND OTHERS WOULD BE THANKFUL TO YOU."

Herb scurried into his bathroom and grabbed a roll of toilet paper and ran back to his closet. He rolled up the newspaper and used the toilet paper to sop up the pee. As fast as he could. He walked it to his garage and tossed it into the garbage. One wet towel, some disinfectant cleaner, and a good wiping session, and his clothes were spared the terrible odors.

"Whew!"

He sat down on his bed. A posture of surrender slumped over him. The concept swarmed over his body. He ran his fingers through his hair, and leaned back resting his spine on the bed.

Turning his head, he stared at the spot where the newspaper had been sprawled out, on top of his oak-wood floor. The thought of it draining into his basement, appalling.

A view he never dreamed of.

His prized basement with pine-wood bar, thick carpet, and theater-style TV and seating. It hurt to think of urine dripping, drop by drop, as if torture were the plan of attack.

Something changed.

Herb's eyes grew wide. A ray of hope rippled in a mind of darkness.

Yes.

The basement.

CHAPTER 19

Herb jumped out of bed and lunged into a long stride towards the basement door.

The last time he was in the basement was two weeks ago. When his mother paid him a visit. The retirement home had several vans to be used for residents to take them on small errands and personal runs. Each resident could use the van up to two times a week. Herb's mom used one of these runs to visit him. It got her out of the building. Plus she could pester Herb about his love life. Besides, Mom loved the driver, John. One of the friendliest people ever.

The last time she came by, she brought her treat of the week. This time, rhubarb pie. They brought it into the basement, cut into the pie and accompanied it with a cup of hot ginger tea. And to add to the enjoyment, they watched the movie *Fried Green Tomatoes* on his theater-style TV.

Only this time when the movie ended, he had a question for his mother. "Mom, the abusive husband in the movie made me wonder, we all know Dad was abusive towards you. Was he always like that? Even in the beginning?"

She seemed taken aback by the question. Her posture shot up. "No." She shook her head sideways. "If I'd a seen that side of him early on, I never would've married him." She studied Herb. "Why do you ask?"

"I don't know. Things I wonder."

"What things?" Concern covered her face.

He withdrew in thought. Paused. His head down. "I wonder at what point his abuse started. What prompted it? Why and when did you finally decide to get out of there?"

"When I felt it wasn't safe for you to be around him anymore. I was devastated when I couldn't get a restraining order against him. I never felt comfortable allowing you to stay with him. That's why I tried to make those visits short. But failed many times."

He nodded. Didn't say a thing. Chewed on the inside of his mouth.

She asked her next question very slowly. Deliberately. "Did he hurt you during those visits?" Her stare, right into his eyes. Studying them for sincerity. Looking for any hint of deception.

He didn't answer.

Her hand went up to her mouth, "No. He did, didn't he?" Tears filled her eyes and flooded down the side of her cheeks.

"Herb." She gasped for air. "I'm sorry. Please. You've got to believe me. I never wanted to leave you there."

"Mom. I was fine. He didn't hurt me."

He stepped up and hugged her.

She buried her head in his chest. He wrapped his arms around her and she wailed.

"I'm okay, Mom. He didn't hurt me."

That was the last time he was in this basement.

He opened the door leading to the basement. Flicked on the light.

Down he went. Urgency in his step.

He walked passed the bar. Passed the theater screen, and opened a closet door. A huge closet door revealing plenty of storage space.

Inside, he flipped on another light. He brushed passed a stack of suitcases, some old tennis racquets, and a set of golf clubs.

He ducked his head down and followed along a long narrow tunnel. His escape tunnel for tornadoes. *These old farm houses thought of everything.* And if he ever got trapped in his basement due to fire, or if a tornado took the top half of his house away, he'd have an escape outlet.

Right here. Why hadn't he thought of it before? Herb felt lighter. Optimism. From every cell in his body.

The further he walked into it, the darker it got. He walked sixteen feet in, sloping gently up towards the ground, towards the door. The darkness too much for his eyes to adjust.

He reached out his hand to push back the latch on the door lock. A lump in his throat swelled with anticipation. He stepped up, reached both hands up and pushed the door.

Nothing.

No give. Not even a hint of giving in. The door held solid.

"What the hell?"

Herb stepped up again. This time, he buried his shoulder into the door. "Hmmf." He hit like a flea against a moving *truck*. Not an ounce of forgiveness.

How could this be?

Herb rubbed his shoulder, sore from crashing into the wall. His eyes adjusted.

"What's this?"

On the door, below the latch, a piece of paper. Some kind of flyer. Looked professionally done. Still too dark to read. He ripped it off the door.

Herb turned back toward the basement. As he stepped back within the light, he could read the flyer. It had a blue border on all four sides, and bright red lettering in the middle.

It stated: HI HERB. IT'S ME AGAIN. THOUGHT YOU COULD LEAVE FROM THE BASEMENT, DID YOU? NICE TRY SUCKER. THE NIGHTMARE CONTINUES.

Herb crumpled the paper up between his hands and threw it against the wall. "Ahhhhhhhhhh!"

"Argh! I'm going to find you."

He sat down on one of his bar stools and dropped his head onto his left arm, burying his face into the table.

Sobs reverberated off of the granite bar. Defeat pouring from every tear.

How could this be? Had this mastermind really thought of everything? Was there no way out? Was death the only outcome?

The worst part, some person reveled with satisfaction, as a result of all of this. The toying. The condescending banter. Hearing the frustration come from Herb's words. Sensing the fear. Detecting the delicious scent of desperation coming from his voice.

This could not be acceptable.

He dropped to his knees. He looked under the theater seats.

He stepped back to the bar.

Pulled out every bottle of premium liquor. Moved every bottle of craft beer in the refrigerator. Removed every bottle of wine from his collection, searching.

Searching for the bomb.

It had to be here. In the bottom of the house. He looked at every piece of carpet. Nothing looked re-pieced together. He looked at his Large Screen TV. Ran his fingers along every edge of the electronic device feeling for something out of the ordinary.

He pulled out the couch. Looked under every chair. Felt every lamp. Scanned every fixture with his fingers. Hoping for something. Something different. Some kind of hint.

The pictures on the walls. Pictures of him posing near the literary legends. John Irving. James Patterson. Nora Roberts. Sandra Brown. He removed them from the walls.

Carefully.

He looked at the backside. Expecting to feel an electronic device. A sensor tied to a bomb. How big would it need to be to blow up a house? Would it be on a timer? Could it be defused? How would that need to be done? Could he in fact do it? Did he have the courage?

After every article of furniture had been turned over, inspected, felt, and examined. After every picture, sculpture, memento, and souvenir had been scrutinized, he wilted to the floor.

Exhaustion enveloped him. Emotional drain.

Hope lost.

The only need alive...hunger.

Herb picked himself off the floor and made the long trek up the stairs. Each deliberate step, demanding every ounce of energy he had to make it to the next step.

Reaching the summit, he opened the refrigerator. The rush of cool air, a wave of heaven. He lifted his arms and basked in the coolness. He grabbed an apple, and bit into it. Its crispness, its texture soothing his soul. Putting a band-aide on a serious wound.

Just what he needed.

CHAPTER 20

Mozzarella. "Mmm."

Every bite gave him something to hold onto. He chewed and swallowed. The consistency satisfying.

He drew in short breaths. The last bite, euphoric. He held it in his mouth, swirled, chewed, and swallowed hard. Swallowed with appreciation.

Mozzarella never tasted so good. A thought crossed his mind. Did he need to be trapped in his house to appreciate how good cheese tasted?

He took in a gulp of air and wiped the sweat off his nose. The heat in the room, intense. He squinted at the thermometer. Ninety-nine degrees.

"What the..."

He jammed his finger at the setting, willing the thing to go down.

"Come on. Work you damn thing."

When that didn't work, he used his thumb. Push. Push. Push.

The override stayed in the "off" position.

He slammed the wall. Looking out the front window, he knew he couldn't go out. For two reasons. One. The sound of debris hitting his window from the hurricane sounded like a major league pitcher throwing handfuls of gravel a hundred miles an hour. And two, he remembered his predicament. Some asshole had him trapped in his home with a bomb.

"Damn."

He stomped his foot to the floor. Three times.

"Damn. Damn. Damn!"

Frustration ate at him from within. Like rust on an old bike.

Questions raced through his head.

How? How could this be happening? How could he have pissed someone off so bad? Why was he such a bad person? Did he deserve this? Would he ever get out? Would Reese be allowed to live? His dog didn't hurt anyone. She didn't deserve this. He would appeal to the mastermind for the dog. Would Herb be blown up? Or would another fate await him in his own house, ending his life?

Questions. Questions. Questions.

One after the other.

Was this a person of means? He seemed resourceful. He must have money. What profession did this person swim in? Was he a leader in his field? Was he a good person on the outside? Yet crazy enough to do this? Or, was it a poor person? Desperate for money, but bright enough to do this?

To be bold enough to do all of this, it would have to be a successful person, wouldn't it? Did he have a home in New York, too? Family?

Herb grabbed his paper and added these to his list. His list of questions.

Questions. Questions. Questions are what got Herb what he wanted. Questions helped him find out what publishers were looking for when they wanted a new author. A new story. Questions helped him line up the right author with the right publisher. Questions are what he used to find out how hard an author was willing to work to promote his book. Questions helped him determine whether or not he liked someone.

Basically, questions delivered his life.

That's it!

Questions delivered my life. Questions will save my life.

Herb reviewed his list of questions. Some were general. Conversational. Casual. And some were poignant. Specific. Highly personal.

He proceeded to give them numbers. An order for asking them. A priority.

Starting out with general, casual questions. To gain a flow. To make his captor feel comfortable. To get him to open up.

The same way you would if you just met someone. Where are you from? Where'd you grow up? Married? Kids? And then more focused questions. More personal. Career? Regrets?

Through this line of questioning, the hope, to find his captor's hot buttons. What makes him tick? What could be an area of common interest? A common bond that could make the captor empathize with him. To make him feel connected. To find one thing that could change his mind about all of this. And maybe, just maybe, he could get out of this thing alive.

At this point, he couldn't think of any other way out.

It was questions, or nothing.

Do or die.

CHAPTER 21

Herb grabbed a glass of water. Drank half of it. Picked up his list and sat down in front of the TV.

Grabbing his pen, he prepared to take notes. Copious notes. Notes that would deliver to him his formula for escape.

He cleared his throat. Shook his head clear. Exhaled a cleansing breath, and mumbled under his breath, "Okay, here we go."

He yelled at the TV. "Hey, you there?"

"OF COURSE I'M HERE. I'VE BEEN WATCHING YOU SINCE YOU CAME BACK UP THE STAIRS. WHAT WERE YOU DOING IN THE BASEMENT?"

He hesitated with his answer.

"Just relaxing with my entertainment center. Taking a break from all of this. From you."

"TAKING A BREAK, HUH?"

"Yes."

"HMM. WHAT ELSE WERE YOU DOING DOWN THERE?"

"Looking for the bomb."

"ANY LUCK?"

"You tell me."

"YOU DIDN'T FIND ANYTHING."

Herb's eyes grew wide. He noted on his pad, *Bomb not in the basement.*

"You're right. Nothing down there."

"WHAT ELSE DID YOU FIND DOWN THERE?"

"That you have a warped sense of humor."

"WHAT?"

"I explored the tornado escape and found your note. You went through a lot of trouble to print that up."

"LIKE I'VE SAID, I PREPARED. RIGHT DOWN TO THE LAST DETAIL."

Herb scribbled, furiously. *METICULOUS.* And underlined it, twice.

"You have a sense of humor. Although warped, it gives me hope. You just might have elements of a human being inside of you."

"I WOULDN'T GO THAT FAR."

"You don't think you're a nice person?"

"NO. I'M A NICE PERSON. I JUST DON'T WANT TO BE NICE TO YOU."

"This is all about me, isn't it?"

"YOU'RE GETTING SMARTER."

Herb looked down at his list, eyes scanning for question number one.

"Okay, I get it. I deserve this. I scorned your mother. My reaction to her query letter was harsh, and it led her to do destructive things to herself. I'm sorry. I really mean that. Please. I wish you could believe me."

Silence filled the room. But the presence of this person filled it even more.

"A SIMPLE APOLOGY IS NOT GOING TO RIGHT THE DAMAGE YOU'VE DONE."

"What must I do to satisfy your angst?"

"I'VE GONE THROUGH GREAT PAINS IN PLANNING THIS ALL OUT. IT MUST CARRY THROUGH."

"No. It doesn't. You don't have to carry this through. You don't have to have blood on your hands."

"I OWE THIS TO MY MOTHER. AND I OWE THIS TO ALL THE WRITERS IN THE WORLD. BUT, MAINLY, I OWE THIS TO MY MOTHER."

Herb looked down at his notes, looked up, and let her fly. "I understand. Maybe I deserve this. Maybe it's the way I grew up. Let me ask, where'd you grow up?"

"WHAT?"

"Where'd you grow up?"

"WHAT BUSINESS IS IT OF YOURS?"

"It's none of my business. I'm just trying to make conversation. Nothing else to do. No one else to talk to."

"THEN WHY ARE YOU LOOKING DOWN AT YOUR NOTE PAD?"

Herb looked out his window at the farmhouse across the street. Strange to think someone lurked behind one of those curtains, watching his every move. Maybe he would catch his captor slipping out the door for some air. Had to keep his own curtains open for a clear view.

"I wondered a few things about you, and I jotted them down before I forgot them."

"HAHAHA. YOU THINK YOU'RE DOING A BIOGRAPHY ON ME OR SOMETHING?"

"No. Just wondered some things."

"KEEP WONDERING."

"You won't tell me where you grew up?'

"NO."

"What've you got to lose?"

"NOTHING."

"Then, tell me where you grew up."

"NO."

"From here in the east?"

"NO."

"Out west?"

"NO. WHAT'S THIS? AN INTERVIEW?"

"Killing time. The south?"

"NO."

"That leaves the north. Or Midwest."

"YOU'RE BRILLIANT."

"Midwest. We're getting somewhere."

"Married?"

Silence emanated from the TV.

"I'll take that silence as a yes. How long?"

"YOU DON'T NEED TO KNOW. YOU'RE STARTING TO ANNOY THE HELL OUT OF ME." The anger in his voice rose with each syllable.

"Sorry. I'm bored. You seem like an interesting person. I'm curious. That's all. Kids? I can't imagine any parent treating someone like this."

"YOU ASK AS MANY QUESTIONS AS MY DAMN STUDENTS."

Herb's jaw opened with a gasp. Silence filled the air. This clearly slipped out.

"You're some kind of a teacher?"

No response. Herb followed up like a boxer advancing on his opponent. "Elementary? Kindergarten?" The intention to insult his captor with the lower levels of education, preying on his captor's ego.

"COLLEGE." Shot out of the speaker.

"Well, well, well, you're a professor. Which university?"

"YOU DON'T NEED TO KNOW."

Herb squinted his eyes. He riled his opponent. His ego, a fragile one. This gave him something to play with. Some ammunition to shoot with. "Hmm. If you're in the north or the Midwest, I'm going to assume a small community college. Five hundred students. Something quaint. A second-tear college. Something a little bigger than a high school. Perhaps part-time?"

Like a blast from a furnace in a steel mill, the words shot out from the TV, "BIG TEN. MICHIGAN STATE."

Herb's eyes grew large with excitement. His efforts making an impact. "All right. Michigan State. That wasn't so bad now? Was it? Getting to know each other a little."

Silence followed. No doubt, the person on the other side expressing disappointment in themselves for surrendering information.

"Nice to meet you. You have kids?"

"I'VE SAID MORE THAN I SHOULD."

"Boys? Girls?"

"NO INFO ON MY KIDS."

"So, you do have them? Good. You're a parent. High School? In college? Toddlers?"

"ENOUGH."

"All right. That's enough."

Herb scribbled on his tablet: *Assume captor WILL let me out of here. Don't even hint I'm going to get blown up. I've got to believe!*

He underlined that last sentence.

Three times.

"You're probably married since you have kids, and you're a professor at Michigan State. Where'd you meet your wife?"

"NONE OF YOUR BUSINESS."

A spell of silence hung between them. Like a wet, heavy fog.

"Okay. Fair enough. Having a family, a career, by all accounts, a full, busy life, and now, add to it...kidnapper, do you have any regrets?"

"NO."

"Hmm. Interesting. Not one little something? Something you wish you'd have done differently?"

"NO."

"Not something you wish you would have done? Or something you wish you hadn't done?"

"NO."

"Come on. Everyone has to have something. One little regret?"

"NO. EVERYTHING I'VE WANTED TO DO, I'VE DONE. ANYTHING I DIDN'T WANT TO DO, I DIDN'T."

Herb scribbled aggressively: *Extreme confidence. Narcissistic.*

Like a bullet, the words shot right out of Herb's mouth. As fast as they went into his brain, out from the mouth they came. "Does your wife know you have me trapped as your prisoner?"

"HAHAHAHAHAH." The laughter continued.

"What's so funny?"

Once the voice caught its breath. "THAT'S A GOOD ONE. YOU THINK I'D BE SO STUPID AS TO LET ANYONE KNOW HOW VINDICTIVE I AM?"

"Well, I didn't know..."

"COME ON. I MAY BE CROSSING THE LINE WITH ALL OF THIS. BUT I DO HAVE MY SENSES TO KNOW WHAT I'M DOING. I'M NOT GOING TO JEOPARDIZE MY MARRIAGE."

A perplexed look ran across Herb's face. He paused in thought, took a breath, and exhaled.

"You're interesting. I'd like to meet you. You're a professor, a family man, and yet highly motivated to carry out this bizarre revenge against me, despite putting you into the criminal element. What a contrasting psyche."

"I'LL TAKE THAT AS A COMPLIMENT."

"Will I get to meet you?"

"PERHAPS."

CHAPTER 22

Herb looked out his window. The debris kept blowing across his window, with the objects flying by getting bigger. The spray of dust pelted against the side of his house showing evidence the storm was getting stronger.

He sat up straight. His posture showed promise. With the chance he might meet the mastermind, maybe he could persuade his captor to release him. If he could win him over, get him to like him, then maybe, just maybe he might get out of this alive.

Questions. More questions.

That was the secret.

"We might have to evacuate if the hurricane picks up, you know?"

"IF IT DOES, I WILL BE THE ONLY ONE EVACUATING."

"You mean you'd leave me here to die in a hurricane?"

"YES."

"That doesn't seem right. Now that we're getting to know each other."

"SORRY. THAT'S JUST HOW IT IS."

Herb tried to appeal to his human side, but no luck there. Have to keep him talking. "How'd you ever learn about sensors and explosives?"

"I KNEW PEOPLE WHO WERE WILLING TO TEACH ME."

"Weren't they suspicious of why you wanted to know this?"

"I HAVE PERSUASIVE MEANS."

"What do you mean?"

"THAT's ALL YOU NEED TO KNOW."

"You asked someone to show you how to explode a painting, and you asked them how to trap someone in their house with sensors and a bomb?"

"YOU'RE FUNNY. I HAVE GOOD FRIENDS THAT KNOW THESE THINGS. THEY WERE WILLING TO SHOW THEM TO ME WHEN I ASKED. AND, ON TOP OF THAT, GOOGLE WAS A WORLD OF HELP."

"Interesting."

Herb sat there for a minute. His eyes scanning his sheet of questions.

His eyes blinked. He squinted, ran his hands through his hair, drew in a large breath, and asked another question.

"If you were to die, what would be the worst way to die?"

Laughter blurted out of the TV again. The robotic voice becoming a familiar sound to Herb.

"I THOUGHT I WAS THE DEMENTED MIND HERE. NOW, YOU'RE ASKING *ME* QUESTIONS ABOUT MY WORST WAY OF DYING? YOU'RE STARTING TO IMPRESS ME."

A subtle smile curled up on one side of Herb's face. A look of progress. Maybe he was getting somewhere. Getting the voice to like him would be critical in persuading him to walk out of the house alive.

"What would it be?"

"WHY?"

"I don't know. I think it tells a little bit about a person."

"LIKE WHAT?"

"It lets you know what their worst fears are, what drives them away from things."

"THAT'S A CROCK. THE WORST WAY I COULD IMAGINE DYING WOULD BE TO BE BURIED ALIVE, UNABLE TO MOVE MY ARMS OR LEGS, TRAPPED IN A SMALL CONTAINER. BUT THAT DOESN'T TELL YOU WHAT DRIVES ME ON A DAILY BASIS. IT MEANS NOTHING. ONLY THAT I'M INSANELY CLAUSTROPHOBIC. DAMN, JUST WHEN YOU STARTED TO IMPRESS ME, YOU COME UP WITH SOME B.S. WE'RE BACK TO SQUARE ONE."

"Well...what does drive you on a daily basis?"

"RIGHTING THE WRONGS TO THE PEOPLE I LOVE."

Herb asked, "Can't they fight their own battles?"

"NO. NOT WHEN THEY'VE BEEN KICKED AND BEATEN DOWN. NOT WHEN SOMEONE OF YOUR STATURE ABUSES IT TO DEMEAN OTHERS. NO. I'M HERE FOR THE UNDERDOG. THAT'S WHAT DRIVES ME."

Herb paused to think. He left the emotion coming out from the TV to resonate for a bit. And softly said, "You have heart. I commend you for that. Is there anything else that drives you?"

The voice paused for a minute, and then came out stronger. "AND CONTROL OVER PEONS LIKE YOU. YES. I LIKE CONTROL OVER PEOPLE. THERE, I'VE SAID IT. YOU HAPPY?"

"Yes. I am. I think we're getting somewhere. It's good you know what drives you."

"WHY?"

"Because, if we all know what drives us, and we want to change for the better, we need to know what our hot buttons are."

"AND YOU THINK KNOWING THIS IS GOING TO HELP YOU CHANGE ME SOMEHOW? HA."

"As your prisoner in my own home, it gives me a little insight into your mind. There's some comfort in knowing a little more about you."

"WELL, COMFORT YOURSELF AWAY. IT'S NOT GOING TO HELP YOU."

He could almost taste the vomit as he said the next set of words, "I just want to say thank you for sharing part of yourself with me."

He stood up and stretched his arms out. "You know, it'd feel more natural if I could call you by name. I'm not used to talking to someone without calling them by name."

"NOPE."

"Why not?"

"NO MEANS NO. PERIOD."

"Okay. Okay."

He looked back down at his list.

"Who inspired you?"

"COME AGAIN?"

"Who inspired you? Who played a big influence in you becoming what you are today?"

"LET ME ASK YOU. WHO INSPIRED YOU TO BE A WORLD CLASS LITERARY AGENT? WHO DEVELOPED YOUR TASTE FOR ART? CARS? MOTORCYCLES? TRAVEL?"

Minutes went by.

Herb rubbed his chin and looked up at the ceiling. It was apparent the question made him think.

"My mother."

"YOUR MOTHER? SHE STEERED YOU TOWARDS BECOMING A LITERARY AGENT?"

"Yes. Not by directly leading me to be an agent. She took me to the library as a young person. She took me often."

"I SEE."

"No you don't. You see, my father wasn't around often. Only in short bursts. I didn't have a dad to throw the ball around, or to play sports. My mother took me to the library. And we read together. And I fell in love with books because it made me feel close to her."

"YOU GOT INTO THE WRITING WORLD AND MADE YOURSELF A SUCCESS?"

"Yes."

"WHO HAD SUCH A MAJOR INFLUENCE ON YOU? WHO DO YOU THINK INFLUENCED YOUR CONDESCENDING MANNER? IT HAD TO COME FROM SOMEWHERE."

It was as if a black hole drained all of the energy out of the room into the TV screen, all on the wind of that last question.

Herb held his head down. Somber in breath. Gathering his thoughts. Wow. What a question. The answer, if there was an answer, could be written in the top psychology journals.

He shot his head up and fired back. "What about you? Who warped your mind where you're the type of person who traps people in their own home?"

No sooner had the words left his mouth, he wanted to pull them back in.

Silence filled the room. Like a heavy cloud of smoke in a poker hall. The weight of the answer waiting to explode from the TV.

What was he thinking? What was he doing? Was something about to happen?

Herb scanned the room, eyeing every fixture, every piece of furniture, every light-switch.

Was something about to explode, cave in, shoot out, fall apart, or bite him?

Herb stood up. He slowly walked around the room. His arms up, ready to protect his head. He widened his circle. He stopped, and looked at the farmhouse across the street. It was getting more difficult to see through the storm. The rain blew in at a side angle at a heavy pace.

"Hey, what's up? I know you're looking at me. I hope I didn't insult you on that last comment about being warped. I'm sorry. I was out of line. I just thought our relationship is at the level where we can be honest with each other. Where we can be real."

"YOU WANT TO BE REAL, DO YOU?"

"Yes. I hope that's okay."

"HOW REAL DO YOU WANT TO BE?"

"Well. If we can be honest with each other."

"THAT'S GOOD. MAYBE YOU CAN TELL ME, IF YOUR MOTHER INFLUENCED YOUR LITERARY CAREER, WHO LED YOU TO BECOME A CONTROLLING ASSHOLE?"

"That's just it. No one person can take credit for making me this way. I think the sheer dynamics of my life made me this way."

"EXPLAIN."

"Sure. No father figure. Different people in and out of my life. And..."

"WHAT DO YOU MEAN? DIFFERENT PEOPLE IN AND OUT OF YOUR LIFE?"

Herb coughed. "I think I shared too much already. The bottom line is this: When I became an adult, I needed to take control. I needed to control everything. Because up until that point, nothing was in control. No person can be blamed for making me condescending or controlling. By the mere need to survive, I became that way. Good enough?"

He rubbed his eyes with his rolled up index finger. A relaxed look of progress crossed his face. He felt better about himself.

The voice from the TV spoke. "I'D LIKE TO KNOW WHAT THINGS HAPPENED TO YOU IN YOUR LIFE TO MAKE YOU THAT WAY. I FEEL WE HAVE AN UNDERSTANDING. LIKE TWO TROUBLED SOULS."

"Me too. You said we traveled together in Asia. I have questions about that trip."

CHAPTER 23

Questions were his tool. His way of manipulating the world. But, someone else used questions as well.

Katie.

"This cuisine up to your culinary standards?" That was her question to him. On their second date. She called *him*. Asked *him* out. Her choice. Little burger joint. No franchise place. Hamburgers, cokes and fries. Mmm...good.

He showed up in jeans and a light blue golf shirt.

After they gathered their food and found a seat on a park bench, she asked him, "This cuisine up to your culinary standards?"

He took a big bite, threw a couple of fries into his mouth, and sipped his coke. Katie sat with anticipation. Like a restauranteur waiting for the food critics response. He chewed a bit, and then gave her a huge grin. "The burgers, sumptuous. The fries, delectable. The cokes, syrupticious. But, the company, divine."

She gave him a raised eye brow. "Wow. That's more than I expected. And syrupticious? I'm not sure that's even a word."

"It's not. I took the liberty of making it up."

"Nice. And the company divine?"

"Supremely good."

She raised her eyebrows again at him. "Wow."

They chuckled and finished their meal, enjoying all the savory juices coming from the gastronomic basics. Afterwards they took a stroll through Central Park, taking in all the fresh air. Holding hands.

"When I first met you, you mentioned you had a teenage son. Is he in high school?"

"Yes. Cooper. He's in his senior year."

"And he lives with you?"

"Yes. Great kid."

"College?"

"Harvard or Stanford."

Herb raised an eyebrow. "Of course. What's he want to be?"

"No clue. I tell him not to worry. He'll figure it out."

"Good advice. Sounds like a bright kid. Hope to meet him someday."

"Maybe. I try not to introduce him to anyone 'til I feel there's a chance of being around for more than a couple of dates."

"You don't beat around the bush do you?"

"Prefer to be honest. You know where I'm coming from. I expect the same from you."

A serious expression came over his face. "I like that."

"It's important. I want to know the people I'm bringing around him are safe. Stable people. You don't find that in a couple of dates."

"You're right. You're a model for single parents."

"Just looking out for his best interest. I love him."

"He's lucky to have you for a mom."

They stopped by the local ice cream parlor and grabbed a couple of cones. Herb ordered the chocolate, Katie the vanilla. He found an empty bench and they sat and licked away at the goods. After a couple of licks, she asked if he would like a taste of hers. He said yes. Leaning his head in towards her cone, she pulled away and put her lips up to his and they kissed. A long slow delicious kiss. Vanilla flavored.

When they separated, they looked into each other's eyes. He said, "I like your vanilla."

She said, "I like your chocolate."

"I like that you feel comfortable making the first move."

"I think I have good judgement. Don't prove me wrong."

They laughed some more. Talked for hours strolling through the park. And when it was near the end of the evening, he walked her home. They kissed the best good night kiss he could remember in years. Yet, he knew it was too early to meet her son.

The thing that surprised himself the most? After two dates, and he hadn't tried to bed her. He was afraid to. He liked this girl and didn't want to screw it up.

What was happening to him?

CHAPTER 24

That was a question he couldn't think about now. He had other questions on his mind. Only not for himself. For his captor.

So, he proceeded to ask. "Who was your travel partner?"

Laughter jumped out of the TV. "NOT GOING THERE."

"Why not?"

"IT'D BE TOO EASY TO FIGURE OUT WHO I AM."

"Really? What's the harm?"

"NOT GIVING THAT."

"Oh, c'mon. That wouldn't hurt."

"NOPE."

"So what if I know who you are?"

"YOU CAN QUIT ASKING. NOW."

"Okay. Okay. You can't blame a guy for trying."

Silence responded back to him. He looked up at the ceiling, and bit the right side of his lip.

"What do you remember most about that trip?"

The response came immediately.

"HALONG BAY."

"Ah, yes. Halong Bay in Vietnam. One of my highlights, too. Why do you remember that so fondly?"

"BECAUSE AS WE CRUISED THROUGH THE PINNACLE ROCK FORMATIONS JUTTING OUT OF THE SOUTH CHINA SEA, THE BAY LOOKED LIKE SOMETHING FROM A SPACE MOVIE, BUT ALL SO REAL, AND RIGHT HERE ON EARTH."

"You're right, it did look like a space movie, but I liked it because the families who lived on the small boats came up to our ship and tried to sell us prawns. I felt sorry for those families. They lived so simply."

"YOU'RE KIDDING."

"What do you mean? About what?"

"HERB, YOU'RE BEGINNING TO LEAD ME TO BELIEVE YOU MIGHT HAVE A HEART AFTER ALL."

"I'm serious. I wish I could've bought all those families clothes. Or a house. It was hard to fathom them living on those small boats."

"THAT'S WHY THEY REFER TO THEM AS BOAT PEOPLE."

"What else do you remember about that trip?"

"WAKING BEFORE DAWN TO FEED THE MONKS IN LAOS."

Herb's eyes gazed down to his hands. "Yes, I remember that fondly, too."

"WHAT DO YOU REMEMBER?"

"There was a young lady on the trip, a stunning beauty I might add, who had a soft spot in her heart for feeding the monks. I believe her husband was an auto executive. She went back to get more food to share. I found her inspirational."

"INSPIRATIONAL BECAUSE SHE FED THEM MORE FOOD? OR BECAUSE SHE WAS STUNNING?"

Herb paused in thought before he answered. "Both. I found myself going back to get more food for them because of her. In fact, I found my thoughts swirling around her for the duration of the trip."

"HMM. WHAT WERE YOUR THOUGHTS?"

His face flushed red. A slight smile curved up on one side of his face, and his right eye brow arched. With a cock-sure tone he said, "She was nice."

"YOUR VOICE CHANGED. YOU WANTED HER?"

"Yes. I wanted her."

"DIDN'T I SEE YOU AND HER HAGGLING OVER A SILK TAPESTRY OR SOMETHING?"

"Yes. Although we weren't haggling. She encouraged me to buy it, and she helped negotiate a good deal. Not that I needed the help. But, it gave me a reason to talk to her without her husband or my girlfriend thinking I was trying to hit on her."

"WERE YOU TRYING TO HIT ON HER?"

"I don't know. I was just going with the flow. Staying with the moment. Seeing where things would go."

"WHERE'D THEY GO?"

"Well, I bought the tapestry. It's right over there, on the wall."

"I DON'T CARE ABOUT THE TAPESTRY. WHERE'D THINGS GO BETWEEN YOU AND HER?"

"Nowhere. My girlfriend's intuition picked up my vibes and she didn't appreciate that. And her husband must have sensed things, too, because after that day, not too much conversation followed. Although, our eyes met often. And I mean, often."

"HMMM. YOU'RE A DOG."

"I wouldn't say that. I just have carnal urges like any other man."

"THAT BEAUTIFUL SILK TAPESTRY. IT MUST REMIND YOU OF HER, HUH?"

Herb looked at it with admiration. "It does. It reminds me of her and keeps her alive in my memory."

"IT MUST STIMULATE YOUR CARNAL URGES, TOO, HUH?"

"You're getting personal, and sick, too. But, yeah, it does."

"LOOK AT IT, HERB. BURN IT IN YOUR MEMORY."

The tone took on a sense of warning in it. It took a moment, but Herb's intuition shot through his veins. He bolted from his chair toward the tapestry, shouting, "No. Nooooo!"

Like a trail of gunpowder, the entire tapestry lit up and sizzled, burning right before his eyes. He attempted to grab it by its edges, only to be scorched from the intense heat emitting from the frame.

"Damn you."

Herb grabbed a dish towel and dabbed it on the tapestry to smother the flame out. Smoke filled the room, and the wall on which it hung displayed charred paint.

He choked a bit. Then grabbed the tapestry and stared down at it. He stroked the edges, as if he were consoling a loved one who'd had her heart broken, trying to soothe away the pain.

He brushed away the charred edges, and blew off the black dust. Pulling it away from himself, he assessed its status, as if saying goodbye to a long lost love.

In essence, that's exactly what he did.

CHAPTER 25

"I SEE YOU'RE A PLAYER. AREN'T YOU?"

He scowled at the TV. Biting his lip, he rubbed his neck. "You didn't have to ruin the tapestry."

"SORRY. PLEASE ANSWER MY QUESTION."

"Am I a player?"

"YOU KNOW WHAT I MEAN. YOU'RE NOT LOYAL TO ANYONE. YOU CHASE THE NEXT SKIRT IN FRONT OF YOU, DON'T YOU?"

"Maybe I never found the right person to grab my attention."

"AND YET, YOU HUNG A TAPESTRY IN YOUR HOUSE BECAUSE IT REMINDED YOU OF SOMEONE YOU'D ONLY KNOWN FOR TWELVE DAYS ON A TRIP. WHAT GIVES?"

"There was some kind of connection. Something special. It's like we were meant to be."

"I THOUGHT YOU SAID SHE WAS MARRIED?"

"I did, but you can't deny that feeling in your heart? That something you can't put a word on."

"MAYBE SHE WAS PLAYING YOU. EVER THINK OF THAT?"

"Why would she do that?"

"I DON'T KNOW. SOME WOMEN LIKE TO LEAD MEN ON. LIKE TO SEE THEM GET THEIR PANTS ALL IN A BUNCH. LIKE TO WATCH THEM TRADE THEIR SOUL FOR LOVE. LIKE TO WATCH THEM CRUMBLE FOR LUST. THEY LIKE TO LEAD THEM TO BELIEVE THEY MIGHT BE ABLE TO HAVE SOMETHING THEY NEVER COULD HAVE BEFORE. IT'S ALL A GAME FOR THEM."

"Hmm. You sound like you might know something about that."

"JUST SAYING. YOU PLACED THAT WOMAN IN A SPECIAL PLACE IN YOUR HEART, AND YOU NEVER REALLY HAD ANYTHING WITH HER. ARE YOU THAT PATHETIC?"

"Hey, I felt it. You wouldn't know anything about it. Only she and I would."

"HERB, SHE WAS MARRIED. DO YOU REALIZE HOW YOU SOUND?"

He paused. Thinking.

"I know it sounds ridiculous. But, when we looked at each other, a yearning arose between us."

Laughter launched out from the TV.

"YEARNING? OH BOY. YOU'RE LIKE A MIDDLE SCHOOL BOY THAT DOESN'T KNOW HOW TO HONOR SOCIETAL RULES. YOU DO WHATEVER THE HELL YOU WANT. YOU SAY WHATEVER YOU WANT. YOU HAVE NO REGARD FOR RULES, OR OTHER PEOPLE'S FEELINGS. THAT, MY BOY, IS WHY YOU'RE IN THIS PREDICAMENT."

Herb sat there, slouched. He slumped in his chair looking every bit of the person who'd just gotten scolded for inappropriate behavior.

"YOU'RE A PLAYER, AREN'T YOU?"

"I guess I am."

"YOU GUESS? DO YOU HAVE A STEADY GIRLFRIEND NOW?"

"Yes."

"HERB?"

"What?"

"ARE YOU FORGETTING SOMETHING?"

"What?"

"I TOLD YOU I PREPARED FOR ALL OF THIS, DIDN'T I?"

"And your point?"

"IN THE FEW WEEKS I STALKED YOU, I COUNTED THREE DIFFERENT WOMEN YOU ASSOCIATED WITH. FOR ALL I KNOW, YOU PROBABLY HAVE MORE."

"You saw them? You followed me for that long?"

"ARE YOU SURPRISED BY NOW? HOW MANY TIMES DO I HAVE TO TELL YOU? I PREPARED."

"I see."

"WHILE I MIGHT SAY THEY WERE GOOD ON THE EYES, THEY ALSO SEEMED TO POSSESS ELEMENTS OF CHARACTER. WHY DON'T YOU GRAB A HOLD OF ONE OF THESE JEWELS, AND MAKE A LIFE WITH THEM?"

He sat there in a daze, gazing at the seared tapestry, rubbing his fingers along the charred edges. In all the years of his philandering, he couldn't answer that question.

Not even to himself.

CHAPTER 26

Herb took in a big breath and placed the tapestry down, right next to his list of questions. The list reawakened his sense of purpose. *Stay focused. Got to get out of here. Questions.*

He read the list and followed down to the next question. Looking up, he fired away. "You're an accomplished professor in your field, but what would you say are your biggest accomplishments in your life?"

Silence followed.

He looked around the room, then glanced out the window at the farmhouse across the street. Nothing seemed to be happening. Could his captor be engaging his next move? Or maybe taking a bathroom break?

"Hello? You there?"

Maybe he hit a nerve with that question. He asked again. "What are your biggest accomplishments?"

"I'M THINKING." The robotic voice sounded irritated.

Herb waited, and tried to be patient. He got up and paced slowly. His body language said he sensed progress with this question. Or maybe the smug smile gave it away.

He sat back down and tapped his fingers on his knee. Maybe this question would reveal something.

"I HAVE MANY."

"Do you? By all means, please share."

"FOR STARTERS, MY PROFESSORSHIP IS SOMETHING I'M PROUD OF."

"That's good. What field are you in?"

"NOT SAYING."

"Okay. What other accomplishments?"

"MY SPOUSE. I'VE MARRIED WELL."

"How long have you been married?"

"NOT SAYING"

"What's her name?"

"NOT SAYING."

"Sorry. What else."

"MY TWO KIDS."

"I wouldn't call that an accomplishment."

"HEY. WHOSE LIST IS THIS? I'M PROUD OF THEM. AND THAT'S THAT."

"Okay. You're right. It's your list. What else?"

"I HAVE YOU IN THE PALM OF MY HANDS. THIS IS A BIG ACCOMPLISHMENT. I'VE BEEN PLANNING THIS FOR YEARS. AND IT'S ALL COMING TOGETHER."

"I'm really happy for you." The sarcastic tone weighing on every syllable. "What would you say is your greatest accomplishment?"

There was a slight pause for thought, and then the voice came right out, matter of factly.

"YOU. CAPTURING YOU IN YOUR HOUSE AND TOYING WITH YOU IS MY GREATEST ACCOMPLISHMENT."

"I beg your pardon?"

"YES. YOU'RE MY BIGGEST ACCOMPLISHMENT."

"Why?"

"MANY REASONS. FIRST, THE ATTENTION TO DETAIL I'VE HAD TO GIVE HAS BEEN UNPRECIDENTED. THE LONG ARDUOUS PROCESS OF STALKING YOU, STUDYING YOUR ROUTINE, COMING INTO YOUR HOUSE, RIGGING EVERYTHING UP, NOT GETTING CAUGHT, AND OF COURSE ALL THE RESEARCH IN SEEKING THESE THINGS OUT AND PUTTING THEM INTO PLAY HAS BEEN A GARGANTUAN TASK."

Herb twirled the pen in his mouth as he bit down on it. "Your motivation to do all this and to push you through must have been very strong."

"THAT MY FRIEND IS AN UNDERSTATEMENT. HOW WOULD YOU FEEL IF SOMEONE DID TO YOUR MOTHER WHAT YOU DID TO MINE?"

He shook his head. "I understand. I do. Please know this when I say it. I'm truly sorry. I don't know how I can ever show you."

"WE'LL JUST HAVE TO WAIT AND SEE HOW THIS ALL PLAYS OUT."

He looked over at Reese sitting next to him on the floor.

"Can I ask you a question? Something that really worries me?"

"WHAT WOULD THAT BE?"

"Are you going to let Reese get out of this alive?"

CHAPTER 27

"AM I GOING TO LET REESE GET OUT OF THIS ALIVE?"

"Yes. I beg of you. She didn't have anything to do with my actions."

"YES. YOU HAVE A VALID POINT. BUT, SHE'S LEVERAGE. SHE MEANS SOMETHING TO YOU. MY MOTHER MEANT SOMETHING TO ME, BUT THAT DIDN'T STOP YOU FROM TORTURING HER, DID IT?"

Herb didn't answer.

"WILL I LET REESE OUT? TIME WILL TELL. I HAVE ALL THE CONTROL. I HAVE AN IDEA OF HOW THINGS WILL END, BUT LIKE A GOOD BOOK, IT'S BETTER TO NOT KNOW HOW IT ALL WILL END. DON'T YOU AGREE?"

Herb sighed and shook his head.

"I understand your angst. This poor little dog doesn't deserve to be caught in this cage of revenge. She doesn't deserve to pay for the mistakes I made."

"I HAVE TO SAY, IT'S NICE TO HEAR YOU ADMIT YOU MADE MISTAKES. I TAKE GREAT PLEASURE IN HEARING THAT."

"I mean it. Please spare her whatever other plans you have for me. Please."

"WE WILL SEE."

"What type of plans do you have for me?"

Laughter rolled out of the TV. Sinister laughter. Devious, sick laughter.

"HERB, WE DON'T TELL THE END OF THE STORY RIGHT IN THE MIDDLE. YOU'VE SEEN A GOOD INTRODUCTION. YOU GET THE HOOK. AND NOW WE'RE WINDING OUR WAY THROUGH THE MIDDLE, SWIRVING THROUGH SUBPLOTS, FACING OBSTACLES ALONG THE WAY. "

There was a pause for effect.

"THE CHARACTER DEVELOPMENT JUST KEEPS GETTING BETTER EVERY MINUTE. I USED TO HATE YOU A LOT. NOW, I STILL HATE YOU, BUT A HAIR OF A FRACTION LESS. THAT'S A GOOD THING FOR YOU. YOU'RE KEEPING ME INTERESTED. I'M NOT BORED OUT OF MY FRICKIN MIND BY YOU. I THINK I'M GOING TO KEEP YOU AROUND A LITTLE LONGER."

He swallowed the large lump that had grown in his throat. His head tilted back, facing the ceiling, with both hands, he rubbed the swollen tension that ached around the back of his neck.

"If there's anything I can do to change your mind about all this, please, please tell me. I'm sincerely sorry. I'll do anything to live. I've done everything you've asked of me thus far. Please. If there's something else you'd like me to do, I'll do it. I want to show you my regret for doing what I did. I want to live. Please?

More silence trickled out of the speakers.

Maybe he would let Herb live. Maybe he was thinking. Or was he ready to unleash his next surprise?

The silence tortured him. The waiting, mind-bending.

He pounded his palms into his head. Over and over, again. "God, when is this all going to end? When? When? When?"

"QUIT YOUR SNIVELING, WOULD YOU? YOU'RE SUCH A WHINING TWIT. WHILE IT GIVES ME DELICIOUS PLEASURE TO DRIVE YOU NUTS, I DESPISE WEAKNESS IN CHARACTER, WHICH YOU TRULY POSSESS."

He glared at the TV, a look of judgement. *Who owned this voice? Who was he to judge his character?*

The son-of-a-bitch.

He looked down at his list, then tossed it aside. The emotional toll drained him. A glance at his watch told him ten o'clock. Twenty-four hours till the bomb goes off. And late in the evening. Good enough reason to go to bed.

He dragged himself to the bedroom holding Reese, plopped himself on the edge of the bed, glared at his Monet, and shook his head in disbelief. Herb snuggled his arm around Reese nuzzling his cheeks alongside her soft furry face. Reese licked him. The love desired and needed, more than ever.

He stroked Reese's head with his thumb. "Reese, I've done bad things. And now I'm paying for them. I've affected many people. I don't understand why I did them. I really don't."

Reese looked up at him with awe and wonderment. As if he understood all of Herb's woes.

"If I could take them all back, I would. If I could do it over, I'd be nice. I could've helped some of those people."

Reese licked Herb's ear. Showering him with approval. The love lulling him into peace.

Herb fantasized. Maybe he'd go to sleep and when he'd wake up find this whole thing was a bad dream. All a nightmare. No Reese with an exploding collar. No house rigged to blow up if he tried to walk out. No smoldering Monet and motorcycle. Maybe it would all be in tact when he'd wake up. Just maybe.

In one motion he brought his feet up and rolled over in bed. In a matter of minutes his breathing paced to a steady cadence.

PART 2

NOT ACCORDING TO PLAN

Like a marine sergeant yelling at the top of his lungs, the intrusive robotic voice called out to Herb, "WAKE UP! YOU MADE THE HEADLINES!"

Herb rubbed the sleep from his eyes and peaked at his watch. Ten minutes after seven. AM. What could he be talking about?

"GET IN HERE! QUICK!"

Herb walked into the living room and saw *Good Morning America* on. The robotic voice said, "SIT DOWN. I'LL ROLL IT BACK SO YOU CAN SEE THE BEGINNING. WE'RE A BIG STORY TODAY. IT'S A GREAT DAY TO BE ME. EVEN THOUGH THEY'RE TALKING ABOUT...YOU! HAHAHAHA!"

Herb sat down, directly in front of the TV.

The hard news of terrorism and financial meltdowns had already been delivered. The wholesome anchorwoman had that look that conveyed she had something interesting to share and you better tune in. "Good morning America, I'm Alison West. Trending now in our pop news, this morning we feature the literary industry's top agent placing a full page ad in the *USA Today* newspaper apologizing to all the past writers he ridiculed."

The screen transitioned to her head shot with a photo of Herb behind her on the screen.

"In an odd turn of events, legendary literary agent Herb Keeler placed a full page ad in the *USA Today* apologizing to prospective writers for his abusive rejection letters. We've tried to reach out to his agency for comment, but there's been no response."

She shook her head and winced before she read her next line. "The rumor mill in the literary world is there have been several suicides linked to his notoriously offensive remarks. We have reporters trying to reach him for comment, but have been unable to reach anyone at this time. Again, the ad was just released this morning and the entire publishing world is shocked."

"This is an interesting story because literary agents send rejection letters every day. In talking with agents, most soften the rejection with kind encouragement. We have our ABC affiliate in New York WXYZ with reporter Melanie Kathryn who has one of Herb Keeler's clients with her. Melanie?"

"Thank you, Alison. I have thriller writer Elizabeth Heiter here. Author of five books about FBI Profilers. Elizabeth, you're represented by Herb Keeler. What can you tell us about him representing you as your literary agent?"

She stood tall and confident, her long brown hair draping over her shoulder. "He's supreme. The consummate professional. When he took me on as a client, he called me, said he wanted to represent me, and he would make me a best seller. I signed. And he's done everything he said he would. At this point in time we are approaching over two and a half million books sold. I owe it all to Herb."

"Do you find him rude, or hurtful as other folks claim?"

"Not at all. I find him kind. He offers me suggestions. He gives me direction when I need it. He's been in the business a long time. He has the connections. I take his advice very seriously and I follow it. It's led me to where I am. I can't imagine him talking to people the way we're hearing. I've never seen it."

"Okay. Thank you, Elizabeth. As you can see there are two sides to every story. Back to you, Alison."

"Thank you, Melanie. The question everybody is asking, if these allegations of hurtful letters are true, and it appears they are, otherwise, why would he apologize in the newspapers? What led him to announcing this apology? Why the sudden soft heart. It's a good thing. It's a question we want to find out. There'll be more to this story and we'll keep you posted as this story develops. Other news, a weather system, currently a category one hurricane is heading up the east coast honing in on the New York coastline..."

Herb's attention drifted off. He glared at the farm house across the street, straining his eyes to see through the heavy rain and wind. Some lunatic behind one of those windows orchestrated this whole thing. The whole bloody thing.

The robotic voice spoke from the TV. "HOW'S THIS FEEL, HERB?"

"What do you mean?"

"IT'S ON NATIONAL TV. EVERYONE KNOWS YOU'RE MEAN AND HEARTLESS. THEY KNOW YOU'RE A SCUMBAG. HOW DOES THAT FEEL?"

Herb stared out the window. He rubbed the back of his neck and rotated his head around.

"It feels good."

"PARDON ME?"

"Yes. Actually, it feels great."

"HOW COULD YOU SAY THAT?"

"Because, they'll call me."

"YES. BUT YOUR PHONE IS SCRAMBLED. HAHAHA."

"That's right. Laugh all you want. And when they realize they can't reach me by phone, they'll show up at my door."

More laughter rang from the TV. A superior tone in the laugh. A condescending tone. "THAT'S NO REASON TO FEEL GREAT."

"That's not the reason I feel great."

"WHAT IS?"

"My friend is about to turn into my driveway."

CHAPTER 29

Herb waved out the window. His friend stepped out of the car and waved back. Seeing another person for the first time since this all started was paramount to receiving a life raft in the middle of the ocean after being left to tread-water for two days.

His friend ran up to the door through the rain. The doorbell rang and Reese went ballistic.

His friend, Joe Mathews, Senior Editor at Breakaway Publishing, one of the top publishing houses in the industry. He stood at the front door, his eyes met Herb's. A look of puzzlement consumed his face. His arms stretched out from his waist, "Let me in."

Herb yelled back. "I can't. I'm trapped in here. My house is rigged. I might blow up."

Joe's brow winced. "I can't hear you?"

"I can't open my door. You've got to get me help. Hurry! Run!"

No sooner than the last syllable left his lips a slender hooded figure darted onto the porch with a pistol in hand. Joe turned and contemplated the events before him. His friend wouldn't open the door. The form motioned Joe to move towards the street. The shock of it all overwhelmed him. He froze while the wind and the rain pelted him in the face.

In frustration, the hooded person fired a shot into the air. It motioned for Joe to move towards the street again. Confused, Joe asked, "You want me to walk to the street?"

Primal grunts and a nod of the head confirmed his notion. It waived the gun three times for Joe to move towards the street. To make sure he meant business the figure fired again into the ground.

Joe walked. And he walked with a special purpose. His life. He looked behind at the person, twisting as he walked, hoping his captor wouldn't shoot him. He walked forward, and looked behind again, looking for reassurance the direction he walked satisfied his captor.

As he approached the street, he turned behind and looked for confirmation from his captor. "This the way you want me to go?"

The gunman motioned towards the farmhouse.

Joe walked forward, deliberate and with determination. His heart thumping out of his chest.

He looked both ways. The street clear. *Damn, if only a car could be approaching now.* An old man going for a drive. A Coca Cola truck on a delivery. Something. Anything. No such luck. Bad timing.

The gunman pushed the pistol into his back hurrying Joe towards the front door.

Herb watched from his window.

His friend helplessly led into the farmhouse.

Questions swam through his dizzying mind. Were others involved in this nightmare? If so, how many? If not, who was this hooded figure? What plans did they have for Joe? Would they kill him? If not, would they feed him? How could I think about food at a time like this? How could they be so ruthless to others?

Joe didn't do anything to the captor's mother. This whole thing got more bizarre by the minute. Herb cried out, "Please don't hurt my friend. He didn't do anything to you."

As these questions consumed him, he watched the last glimpse of his friend as his captor pushed him into the farmhouse. Joe gave one last glance at Herb over his shoulder, his eyes telegraphing to him, "why?"

CHAPTER 30

Herb paced the floor. Back and forth. Staring blankly into the oak planks. His mind searching for answers. More questions surfacing then answers.

He looked at his watch. 7:39 A.M.

Who? How many? Will this end? Will he come out alive?

Reese sensed the turmoil circulating in the room. She came up to him and beckoned for a hug. He bent down and she met his hand with a lick. A lick of love.

"For the love of God my dear girl, I forgot to fill your water dish. And your food, too."

He scurried over and filled the bowl with food and rinsed and filled the dish full of water, careful not to spill a drop.

"With everything going on I forgot to take care of you." She looked up at him, clinging to his every word. Turning her head, listening for verbal commands.

"I also put a friend in danger. How could I have done this?"

He filled his coffee pot with water and poured it into the maker. A few scoops of his French Roast into the filter and the aromas filled the air within minutes.

By now, Reese had heard enough and focused her attention on her bowl of goodies. Every bite a crunch of canine delight. He watched her devour her meal, every sense completely in the present.

"Thank you, Reese. That's what I need, too. I need to take care of myself. I need a good meal."

He toasted a raisin whole grain bagel. When it popped up, he smothered a gob of peanut butter on it. He poured himself a cup of coffee and then dipped his bagel into his cup. Coffee dripped from his bagel as he inserted the coffee-soaked grain into his mouth. The rich creaminess lulling him out of his current misery and into the sensorial present. Mmm.

After several bites and numerous sips of caffeine, the nutrition the peanut butter provided seeped into his veins. His consciousness awakened.

He sighed a breath of relief. A feeling of calm enveloped him. He was in control. Ready to figure out how to get out of this. Funny how the basics of nutrition can make you ready to take on the day.

His mind took him back to when he first met Joe. Herb wanted to be a romance novelist. He'd sent two manuscripts to hundreds of agents. Most were ignored. He received rejection letters from a few.

Early one summer, while waiting tables at the Sagamore Yacht Club, he met Joe Mathews. They developed a friendship. Joe made Herb realize he wasn't cut out to be a writer, but liked his social skills and introduced him into the world of being an agent. After three years of learning his craft at a big agency, he struck out on his own. And their friendship deepened along with his success.

Sitting in his kitchen, an unfamiliar murmur came from his living room. His brow furrowed. "What's that?"

It sounded like an electric motor humming. From his living room?

What could possibly be making that sound? There were no motors of any kind he could think of. No gadgets. No maneuverable parts. No toys that moved. Yes, of course he had all the technology working for him. But, he'd never heard this noise from any of his devices.

He cautiously ran to the living room. And stopped in his tracks.

His jaw dropped open.

"What?" His eyes couldn't believe it.

Electronic drapes ran across his window closing him off from the rest of the world. The mood in the room became somber and dark.

He laughed. "If you think a little drape is going to stop me from connecting with the outside world, you've underestimated me."

The curtain closed completely. He attempted to grasp the curtain and pull it apart. His hand slipped off the steel-belted material. No grasp to be had. Impossible.

He tried again. This time with two hands. Digging in violently with full force, his fingers attempted to pry into the curtain-material. To no avail. He punched the curtain. "Come on." He attempted to dig his hands into the crease where the curtain ended, but it locked itself up at the seam.

"Come on. You break into my house. You hot wire it to mess with me. And now you install some fancy ass curtains to block me out? Huh? What's wrong with you?"

He struck the curtain. Beating it. Punching it. Over and over. His frustration transferred directly through to the curtain. The curtain unforgiving.

The expression on his face went humorous, like a light bulb went off in his head. A subtle laugh eeked out of his voice.

He ran to the kitchen, straight to his knife drawer. His eyes scanned the entire drawer and went directly to the largest and strongest knife. The one he used for cutting watermelon and pumpkins. He grasped it like it was the key to his salvation. And at that moment it *was* the key to his salvation. It represented his chance to avoid being blocked out from the outside world. It was *his* savior.

With the knife in hand he dashed back to the curtain and began slicing movements attempting to carve it up. Like a slasher in a movie, his arm-swings contained full-force and relentless repetitiveness. Again and again. He swung until his lungs could breathe no more.

He stood there, gasping for air. The result of his efforts? Nothing. The curtain appeared to laugh at him. All that work, all that effort, and this is all you have to show for it? Ha!

He slouched forward. He went over and turned on the light. "Reese, how come I didn't notice this before?" With closer examination he could see. He ran his fingers along his old drapes. "Ah, I get it." It became clear to him. The new curtains were installed behind the old ones.

"It doesn't matter now. I'm completely cut off from the rest of the world."

CHAPTER 31

With defeat permeating through his body, Herb slouched into the couch. Things couldn't get worse. A madman had him trapped in his house. The long-term outlook held for him...death. A violent, explosive death.

At 10pm.

And to top it all off, now he'd jeopardized a friend's life. And if that wasn't enough, the whole world saw another side of him. A terrible disgusting side of him.

People would despise him. If he were to escape from this misery, a new misery could await him. A world where no one would like him. An existence with no accolades. No clients. No riches. No travels. No women. The world would shun him.

The publishing industry that embraced him as their leader would ignore his cries for a second chance. They'd turn him away at social galas. They'd reject his offers to speak for free at publishing shows, venues that commanded $10,000 before. Friends wouldn't return phone messages he'd left.

His existence–a living hell.

The world would become much smaller. His world. His sentence.

But, maybe he deserved it, he thought.

Maybe if he did live through this, the actual living would be the penance for his past.

The price he must pay for belittling so many. And as the memories of his past discretions played out through his head, he sensed nature handling the gavel to balance the wrongs he'd delivered to so many. The wrongs he ground into the multitude of souls.

If that were true, then his future looked dark.

It must.

And if all of this wasn't enough, the lights flickered off and on. A power failure from the storm?

Herb braced himself and just looked around. Herb turned the TV back on to keep communication alive.

"LOOKS LIKE I SLIPPED UP." The mechanical voice slid out of the TV, smooth and direct.

Herb rubbed his hands across his face waking himself to a higher state of alertness. "Pardon me?" said Herb.

"YES. LOOKS LIKE I SLIPPED UP. I SHOULD'VE HAD THE CURTAINS DRAWN BEFORE YOU WOKE UP. BEFORE YOUR FRIEND SHOWED UP. MY MISTAKE. WON'T HAPPEN AGAIN."

"My friend. What have you done to him? Please don't hurt him. He doesn't have anything to do with my past behavior."

"DON'T WORRY. I WON'T. HOWEVER, HE DOES GIVE ME A TREMENDOUS AMOUNT OF LEVERAGE WITH YOU."

"Leverage?"

"YES. LEVERAGE. WHEN I ASK YOU TO DO SOMETHING, I EXPECT YOU TO DO IT WITH NO RESISTANCE. UNDERSTOOD?"

"Yes. I understand. You have my full cooperation. Please don't hurt him."

"YOU WILL BE GETTING LOTS OF VISITORS NOW THAT YOUR USA TODAY AD IS OUT. NEWS REPORTERS WILL BE FLOCKING TO YOUR HOUSE. THAT'S WHY YOUR CURTAINS ARE COMPOSED OF SOUND PROOF AND BULLET PROOF MATERIAL. YOU KNOW, SUEDE, VELVET AND STEEL-BELTED MATERIAL. A LOVELY COMBINATION. WHEN THEY COME KNOCKING ON YOUR DOOR, THEY WON'T BE ABLE TO HEAR YOU YELLING."

"How do you know?"

"I TESTED IT. I COULDN'T HEAR REESE BARKING WHEN I RANG THE DOOR BELL."

"How did you know how to get all this stuff?"

"LIKE I SAID BEFORE, I DID MY RESEARCH, MY BOY. I DID MY RESEARCH."

CHAPTER 32

The incessant pounding drove Herb mad.

All day long.

He didn't know which was worse, the recurrent rounds of knocks on the door or the ringing of his doorbell. If he was forced to choose he would have preferred to listen to the knocks on the door because each person offered a different cadence and a variation in volume that offered a slight alteration for his audio experience.

None of it would have been a bother if he weren't obliged to ignore it, with the threat of harm to Reese and Joe hanging in the air.

With each ring and pound that radiated through his wall, Herb gained a sense of touch knowing a human being stood on the other side of his door. It was a contrast of relief and frustration. Relief to know people were trying to reach him. Pursuing him. He felt wanted. Close to someone. Frustrated he couldn't let them in. He couldn't talk to them. He couldn't say, *I'm alive and okay, and I truly am sorry for the wrongs I dished to so many people.*

He made his bed, and he was definitely sleeping in it.

A CNN reporter and his crew pounded furiously on his door. The desire to talk to Herb rang strong.

Reese barked hard. Her job to protect taken seriously, evident by the hair standing up on her back.

The calm, slow voice spoke deeply and softly from the TV. "I'M GLAD TO SEE YOU'RE NOT ATTEMPTING TO KNOCK BACK OR YELL OUT TO THE FOLKS ON THE OTHER SIDE OF THE DOOR. NOT THAT THEY WOULD HEAR YOU ANYWAY. I'D HATE TO DETINATE THE EXPLOSIVES AT THIS STAGE OF THE GAME. AND OF COURSE THERE'S REESE, AND YOUR FRIEND. YOU'RE WISE."

Herb stood there speechless, glaring at the TV. He clenched his fist. Three times. He bit his lip and shook his head.

The TV turned on. CNN still the station of choice. The screen displayed the script on the upper left hand corner "LIVE".

Herb couldn't believe his eyes. The reporter standing outside his front door. Sporting a brown raincoat.

It struck him as odd that here in his own living room, he watched a national reporter reporting the news. CNN news for Christ sake. Only more than news. It was someone at *his* house. Someone he couldn't talk to. He couldn't reach out to them and beg for help. He couldn't say he was in grave danger. The whole thing seemed unreal. How could it be?

And yet, it was. Very real. And he couldn't do a damn thing. His worst nightmare times a million.

The reporter went on.

"Here in Oyster Bay, New York, I'm standing outside of literary agent Herb Keeler's house and office, in the middle of a category one hurricane."

The wind and the water pelted him in the face as he screamed into his microphone.

"He shocked the publishing industry when he ran a full page ad this morning apologizing to all the people he rejected in a less than professional manner. We're here hoping to allow him to comment, but at this time he's nowhere to be found. Herb, if you're out there, please give us a call, we'd love to hear your side of this story and to learn what prompted you to apologize in such a public manner. Reporting from Oyster Bay, New York, Wald Zoller."

Herb walked over to the door. He raised his clenched fist, cocked back, ready to pound on the door.

Reese, sensing activity at the door, ran over to him ready to greet the visitor. Her bark, happy and excited.

Herb's mind swirled. This was his chance for help. Maybe his only chance. He could pound the door and let someone know he was there.

Would his captor blow up the love of his life? His dog? Would he take further steps to harm his friend Joe? And would he ultimately blow his house up? And the CNN crew, too? Would it all end now?

Sooner or later, he would have to take that risk, or he may never get out. Maybe he would have to call his captor's bluff. Should he do it? Or should he wait things out a little further. Maybe try and win his captor over and eventually befriend him. Persuading him to let him out by showing he was truly sorry.

"It's now or never," blurted out of his mouth.

He pulled his fist back further and swung it hard towards the door.

Right before the point of contact, he stopped himself. "My God." He held his head in his hands. "I can't."

The exhilaration of what he was about to do overwhelmed him.

"What...am I doing?"

He drew in a large breath. He winced, broke down, and cried. His knees buckled and he sank to the floor, his fist dragging down along the door until he crumbled to his knees.

"Not yet."

His emotion took over his state. His head pressed hard against the door, tears poured down along his cheeks.

He'd almost took control of the situation. But he didn't know what would follow. Would it all have turned out to be a bluff? Or would he have forced his captor's hand to do the unthinkable?

From what he'd seen so far, this madman had the mindset, the motivation and the lack of conscience to carry out his threats.

Reese, sensing Herb needed love, licked his face, attacking him with aggressive kisses.

Overcome with emotion, he hugged her. "Reese, I can't believe I almost did it."

He hugged her and rocked her back and forth swimming in the love from his embrace.

He stared out with a blank stare, comforted by the temporary detachment from the moment.

Only to be brought back to earth by what he saw next on the TV.

CHAPTER 33

CNN again.

This time a film clip played. A reporter stood outside the Oyster Bay Animal Rescue Shelter. The camera zeroed in on a puppy being held by a gentleman. The puppy, a blend of chocolate brown with white stripes running up its chest. Beautiful dog. Appeared to be a blend of Bulldog and Pitbull, loving up the guy holding it.

Herb remembered that morning well. He was going into his second year of monthly visits. After breakfast on Saturday mornings, the first Saturday of every month to be exact, he would bring his second cup of coffee and intend on spending an hour at the shelter. But, he almost always ended up spending the whole day there. Feeding the animals, refreshing their water dishes, and what he liked most, holding them and giving them long walks around the neighborhood.

It just so happened on that particular day the local news people were there doing a segment on volunteerism. Being the guy there on that day, they interviewed Herb.

The slender news lady in the red dress asked him, "Herb, why do you volunteer here at the shelter?"

"I like dogs. I like all animals, but I especially like dogs."

"Do you have a dog of your own," She asked.

"I do. Reese. She's at home. I got her here from the shelter. Beautiful. Smart as heck. Love her to death."

"Would you recommend folks to come to the shelter and adopt a dog?"

"Without question. These dogs have an unusual sense, when they're taken home, they seem to know they're being given a special chance to have love in their life. I can't explain it. I know it sounds crazy, but if you ask every dog-owner who got their dog from a rescue shelter, they'll say the same thing."

"Really? That's interesting. What does volunteering do for you?"

"It's my chance to help these animals in some small way. There's an attraction with them I can't explain. Call it love if you will."

"I love it. May I ask what you do for a living when you're not volunteering here at the shelter?"

"Yes. I'm a literary agent. I represent writers and help them get their work published."

The young reporter's eyes sparkled with enthusiasm and he remembered the sensation he felt looking into them. It wasn't a week later he'd bedded her after a homemade meal and a couple bottles of fine wine at his place. The romance lasted a couple of months and he dropped her after her intentions became serious. His feelings were not the same. Not with her.

But, the news piece went out over the air and Herb's reputation began as a big volunteer.

The next segment showed him standing in front of the Bronx Zoo presenting a four-foot-long check for ten thousand dollars to the zoo director wearing a huge smile.

The announcer stating, "Here you have it, Herb Keeler apparently verbally abusive to potential writers, but a softy when it comes to animals."

The next video displayed him holding a falcon on his arm at the Theodore Roosevelt Nature Sanctuary. "The announcer saying, "Here's another example of Herb Keeler funding fifteen thousand dollars to the research of the falcons."

The Director at the sanctuary shared with the reporter, "Herb's been an integral part of our funding, but the time he's spent helping out here at the center has been invaluable. And his compassion for the program, exemplary."

The anchor continued on, "How could such an animal lover be such a detestable person to so many prospective writers? It says here he also made large donations to the Queens Zoo as well. It appears he has a heart, but maybe not for the human species. We haven't heard the last of this story. What a complicated individual this Herb Keeler is. We hope to find out more."

The video broke to newspaper clippings displaying headlines where he donated money to other shelters and anything related to animals.

The deep mechanical voice thundered out of the TV, "IF ONLY YOU TREATED PEOPLE AS WELL AS YOU TREATED ANIMALS. YOU MIGHT NOT BE IN THIS PREDICAMENT. I'LL HAVE YOU KNOW, I SUPPORT SHELTERS FOR BATTERED WOMEN."

Herb looked surprised. "You do?"

"YES. AND I DONATE MONEY AND I VOLUNTEER ONCE A WEEK IN THE EVENING SHIFT. SOMEONE'S GOT TO HELP THESE WOMEN."

He glanced up at the TV with a blank stare. "That's the first piece of relevant information you've shared with me. Why?"

"WHY WHAT?"

"Why you telling me this and why finally now?"

"YOU ASK TOO MANY QUESTIONS. BE GLAD I'M SHARING ANYTHING WITH YOU."

He pondered the question. How could he use this information to get out of this situation? His captor volunteered at a shelter for battered women. He *did* have a heart. Somewhere in that demented mind was a soft part he might try to appeal to.

"Why do you support a battered women shelter?"

"REALLY? YOU THAT POOR OF A LISTENER? YOU FORGET ALREADY HOW MY MOTHER WAS ABUSED? YOU'RE DAMN RIGHT I HAVE A SOFT SPOT FOR ABUSED WOMEN. AND, BEING A PERSON OF ACTION, I'M DOING SOMETHING ABOUT IT RIGHT NOW."

"What do you mean?"

"YOU. I'M DEALING WITH YOU AND THE PERSONAL ABUSE YOU DISHED OUT TO MY MOTHER. I'M MAKING YOU PAY FOR IT. COME ON. YOU'RE SMARTER THAN THIS. YOU SHOULD BE ABLE TO PUT THIS ALL TOGETHER. MUST BE GETTING A TIRED BRAIN."

"Hmm...You're right.

"YOU'RE DAMN RIGHT I'M RIGHT."

Herb sat up straight. His face winced. The voice was right. His brain tired. His whole body tired. And mention of his captor's mother led him to thoughts of his own mother.

CHAPTER 34

He remembered the emotional pain of almost losing his mother.

He remembered that day well. It started at a luncheon pitch, where he told a publisher he could improve the economy of the entire state of Michigan simply by publishing his client's book. Up till now, this was his most powerful push, ever. A pretty strong statement for a collection of seventy-thousand words bound by a hard cover. A page-turning thriller titled, *The Grand Secret*.

In the middle of lunch he received a call from Plainview Hospital telling him his mother was in cardiac arrest. Herb kindly excused himself and bolted out the door.

Upon arriving in the ER he saw her there, a team of doctors and nurses buzzing around her like a swarm of hornets, frantically working to keep her alive. The tone in their voices told him things were serious. He couldn't remember the details of their conversations, but the rapid manner in which they spoke and the volume of their voices he could never forget. When the beeping machine transitioned to one long high pitch sound, shouting kicked in. "Hurry!" Muddled shouts. Swift movement all around.

"Get the paddles! Clear!"

Thump!

More chatter. Direct orders. "That wasn't enough. Hurry!"

"Again! Clear!"

Thump!

"Damnit! Nothing."

The things that remained in his memory: a swirl of activity, more shouting. Direct orders being given. Do this! Do that! Check on this! Check that! None of it clear in his mind. A foggy mist of fear clenching his stomach. His world as he knew it about to be changed forever.

It may have been at that point where Herb reached out to God. Or was it the devil. Not a religious guy, but at that moment he would have reached out to anyone.

He held his head in his hands hunched over his lap. He blabbered through his tears. "Please God. Spare her for me. If not for me, for her. Please."

"Let's try this again! Clear!"

Thump!

And after what seemed like hours, the words spoken. "She's stable." Herb lifted his head. The heaviness in the room lightened. The vocal tones softened. The mood...calmer.

That day, he'd never forget.

CHAPTER 35

Having news reports about him on TV made him feel helpless. But, what could he do?

Segments on TV. Articles in the newspaper. Samples of his letters. All there for everyone to see. And to think this all started with a letter.

Yes.

That's it! The letter.

Herb scurried over to locate the letter. It laid right next to the envelope. He grabbed it and sat down on his couch. A lot had transpired since he was ordered to put the letter down and turn on his computer. He'd almost forgot about the damn thing. He flipped on his glasses and scanned to where he'd left off.

"Here we go, right where it said put down the letter and turn on your computer. I did all that."

His eyes focused in on the next paragraph.

Herb, I have a lot planned for us. Or, for you. You will soon see. Or maybe you've already seen some of my meticulous attention to detail.

Either way, know I have gone through a lot to make our time together special. A year's worth of planning and research have gone into this spectacle. From following your routines—inside and outside—to exploring the technology I needed to carry out the proceedings which you will be experiencing.

I hope you like my use of the em-dash. And if the use of the word 'proceedings' tilts everything into the legal realm, like you're on trial, well in a way, you are.

And I, ultimately will be the judge and the jury. Welcome to my court.

As you can see by my well written letter here, my muse was in full gear during the full tenure of this writing. So much of my heart has gone into this project. It has been a work of passion. All that you will experience has come out of me.

I hope your senses are heightened and fear is running through your mind like corrosive acid through a radiator, eating away at your soul and your obnoxious ass. My hope is to wear your arrogance down to ground zero. Make you see what's really important. Obliterate your snobbish ways by destroying the material things you hold with such significance. And after all of that, I might make you beg for your life. The next day or two will have lots of surprises. I have a special surprise near the end. And after all of that, then, and only then will I make up my mind whether or not I'm going to let you live.

Have a nice day!

The letter ended and Herb clenched it in his hands. Sweat culminating in his palms.

No signature.

He turned it over. Nothing on the back. No hint of who it might be. No reference as to what he might call himself. Even an alias would do. No final quip to rub it all in.

Just...have a nice day.

He'd already seen quite a bit from this madman. Surprises for sure.

And a *special* one near the end, what could that be? His heart fluttered.

He glanced at his watch. 12:02 pm.

What more could possibly lie ahead?

One thing came to mind.

Talk him out of this. But how?

CHAPTER 36

The stakes had now been raised. This could happen no more.

The son-of-a-bitch was across the street and there had to be a way to get to him. That was the goal.

Herb walked to the TV. "Hey! We need to talk!"

Nothing came out of the TV but silence. Herb waited a few more moments.

He looked around the room, cleared his throat and threw it at him again.

"Hey! You there?"

No response. However, an update came on with bright red headlines blasting out from the screen.

NEWS UPDATE.

The reporter said, "We have breaking developments in the case involving literary agent Herb Keeler and his ad in the USA Today apologizing for sending humiliating rejection letters to prospective writers. Several years ago he sent a letter to a college student with a history of emotional issues, eventually committing suicide. CNN obtained copies of the letter. I'll read an excerpt to you."

He looked down at the letter in his hand and began to read.

"What makes you think you're qualified to write about autistic kids? These kinds of people can't fit in the real world. Don't belong in the real world. And then you come along and make them think they can. Preposterous!"

The reporter looked up and said, "This is hard to read."

And then he continued, "If you think you have a career in writing, I might suggest writing the obituaries for a living where your writing is about as alive as the subject matters you'd be writing about."

The reporter looked back up at the camera and shook his head. "There you have it. Blistering letter! We have the mother of Randy standing by with my colleague, Jill Halosowski. Jill?"

The camera cut to Jill standing next to someone with a microphone in her face. "Yes. I have the mother of Randy with me, Leslie Young. Leslie, how'd you find out Randy received this letter?"

A stoic look covered her face. She took a few moments to gather her composure. It took everything in her to muster up the courage to speak. "It wasn't until weeks after his death we found the letter tucked away in his desk drawer. When we pieced together the time of his death with the date on the letter, we knew the letter played a large part in his suicide."

"Leslie, did Randy suffer from emotional challenges?"

"Randy had autism. He kept to himself for many years. After a year in his PEERS program at the high school we saw great strides in him being able to interact within a controlled environment. PEERS assigned him another student to help with his school work and to help him socially."

She had to stop to grab her composure.

"He grew more confident in his writing. In fact, so much, his teachers encouraged him to seek out an agent to represent him. And then he received this letter, which not only set him back, but eventually led him to take his own life."

Her voice began to crack and her eyes swelled with tears.

"When you say it set him back, what do you mean?"

"He went back to staying in his room. Secluding himself from the rest of the world. The PEERS program made him feel good about talking to people. Confident. But this jerk, this Herb Keeler, took it all away with one letter. One horrible letter."

The reporter held the microphone up close to capture every word. "Leslie, was there anything else derogatory in the letter?"

"Oh yeah. He said Randy was, and I quote, 'as qualified to tell a story as much as a baby learning to walk is as qualified to run a marathon. You should give up writing and take up knitting.' What kind of person insults others like that? He's some kind of sicko getting his jollies. I hold him responsible for Randy's death."

The reporter turned back to the camera. "One letter. One letter that led to the suicide of Randy Young. And the parents hold Herb Keeler responsible. Back to our desk in Atlanta."

The anchorwoman shook her head. "The more we learn about this guy the more we dislike him. It sounds like he had a good reason to apologize to the world. What could've been the catalyst to reach out to all the writers of the world he scorned and say he's sorry? Some event? We're desperately searching to speak to Herb Keeler in person. So many questions yet to be answered, and yet so many more to be asked."

Her eyes were drawn to the monitor next to the camera and she paused while she hung to every word dancing across the screen. The silence on air was uncommon and awkward.

Her brows grew stern and serious.

"I'm sorry. We have a new development. We have a story sent to our station manager telling about a woman who sent her memoir to Herb Keeler. The information we have says it was from a woman who'd been raped repeatedly as a little girl. The memoir was a way for her to purge her struggles. But, he shut her down. We have excerpts from his response to her."

The reporter donned her glasses. "Here's his response. 'What you have gone through is sad. I agree. But if you think your sniveling about it in a book is going to be of interest to John Q. Public, you're dead wrong. No one cares. These stories are a dime a dozen. Your story has been told a thousand times. Just because you were abused sexually as a child. Oh boohoo. Poor pitiful you. That's not enough, sister. I could go to any bookshelf in America and find another pathetic story like yours. If you want me to represent you. I need something substantial. Something different. Something with legs that will move. Yours I'm afraid, doesn't.'"

The reporter took off her glasses and continued.
"Our sources say she tried to call Herb Keeler and he told her to, "Suck it up and move on." This was someone crying out for help. Her depression eventually led to her death. It doesn't say how she died. We're trying to reach out and locate the person who sent this letter."

The reporter displayed a look of disapproval.

"We have more to this story. We're sending you to Oyster Bay, New York in front of the house of Herb Keeler with New York correspondent, Sheryl Hawthorne. Sheryl."

She yelled into the microphone to compensate for the loud wind blasting into her face. "Yes. Thank you. I'm standing in front of Herb Keeler's house. We've knocked on his door repeatedly and made numerous phone calls with no answer. We've also reached out to several of the publishing houses he's corresponded with and no one knows his whereabouts. This entire story is baffling. For someone to run a full page ad in a national paper and then to disappear with no explanation. It doesn't make sense. Although, maybe he evacuated because of the hurricane."

Herb paced in front of the TV. He strode up to his steel-curtain blinds and tried to pry them apart. He pumped his fists. Open and shut. Over and over. His toxic frustration filled every cell in his body. His breath quickened. His chest tightened. "I'm right here people. Don't you know? I'm right here." He yelled.

The voice from the TV responded. "I KNOW YOU WANT TO GET OUT OF THERE. BUT DON'T FORGET. YOU DON'T WANT THEM TO HEAR YOU. REMEMBER? I HAVE YOUR FRIEND. AND REMEMBER REESE'S COLLAR? AND LAST OF ALL, I CAN BLOW YOU INTO SMITHEREENS. ANYTIME I WANT."

Herb kicked the TV. "I don't care anymore! Do what you want with me. I don't care."

All the commotion brought Reese up to Herb. She whimpered as she tried to bring comfort to him, sensing he was stressed beyond all imagination.

He shook his head and bent down to hug her. She licked his forearm and her tail wagged. Her love radiated through to him and the timing couldn't have been any better.

While he soaked in the hug, his glare at the TV sickened him with the circus taking place right outside his door. News trucks and reporters scattered themselves in front of his house. He could hear the rain slamming against his siding. The wind moaned with each gust threatening to be stronger than the next. Like little bullies making up gossip about someone they didn't know. The scoundrels. They seemed to take great glee in knowing he was hiding. Or so they thought.

He wanted to yell out to them. *Yes. I said those things. But, I've done some good things, too. And while I'm ashamed of what I've done, I'm not hiding. Someone has trapped me. They're toying with me. And they're probably going to kill me.*

CHAPTER 37

Herb yelled at the TV, "You ass!"

The news babbled on. Talk of the stock market having an uneventful day. Description of a category one hurricane with sustained winds between seventy-four and ninety-five miles per hour. Able to cause damage to unanchored mobile homes and signs. Several shootings were reported. Just another news day in New York City.

"Wake up!" Herb screamed.

He plopped back onto his couch, staring blankly at the TV waiting for an answer. His mind swirling in fear. And numb with confusion. What to do? What could he do? What were his options? Did he even have options? Where'd his captor go?

His eyes closed as his head tilted up to the ceiling. His temples pulsed with every beat of his heart.

He popped his eyes open wide as the words coming from the anchor person assaulted his ears. "We have a new development in the Herb Keeler story. We received an unconfirmed call today from someone stating they were Herb Keeler. He said he was unavailable till further notice and after apologizing to all the writers he needed time to reflect and take his medicine like a man."

Herb grabbed a pillow from the end of the couch and threw it at the TV. "Bullshit!"

CHAPTER 38

Herb rolled over, and buried his face down into the couch. He held his hands over his head attempting to block this situation out from his mind. He'd need more than hands over his head to block this all out.

This couldn't be real. How could it. The worst nightmare ever. In all of mankind. Trapped in your own house. You couldn't make this stuff up.

He rolled back over and looked at the TV. More ramblings of news-bites. He only heard blah-blah-blah.

The voice from the TV returned. It overshadowed the news anchor voices. "HELLO HERB. HOW ARE YOU?"

Herb ignored him.

Silence followed, only filled by the anchor people carrying on with the day's events, flowing with their rhythmic cadence.

"I KNOW YOU'RE THERE. ARE YOU PLAYING HARD TO GET?"

He just stared at the TV. His emotions getting worn to the state of exhaustion. He said nothing.

"REMEMBER THE YOUNG ASIAN BOY IN BEIJING WHO HAD NO SHOES AND NO SHIRT, BEGGING, WHO YOU SNUBBED? I SNUCK A $100 BILL IN HIS HAND."

"What're you talking about?"

"DON'T YOU REMEMBER? WE WERE IN THE TEMPLE OF HEAVEN. THAT LARGE PARK WHERE ALL THE ELDER PEOPLE HANG OUT ALL DAY AND DANCE, PLAY MUSIC, GAMES AND GENERALLY HAVE A GOOD TIME."

"Of course I remember. But what about the boy?"

"YES. A GROUP OF ELDERS WERE PLAYING MUSIC WITH THEIR INSTRUMENTS. WEIRD CHINESE INSTRUMENTS. I THINK THERE WERE ABOUT EIGHT OF THEM. EIGHT PEOPLE. AND NEXT TO THEM, A BOY. PROBABLY ABOUT NINE YEARS OLD, HOLDING A CUP OUT. BEGGING."

"I remember. No shoes. No shirt. He looked kind of happy. Too happy to be begging. That's why I snubbed him."

"YOU FOOL. THAT WAS PROBABLY THE SMARTEST PERSON IN THE WHOLE PARK. HE UNDERSTOOD IF YOU SMILE, PEOPLE ARE MORE LIKELY TO GIVE YOU MONEY. I TOOK AN INTERPRETER OVER TO HIM AND ASKED HIM QUESTIONS."

"Like what?"

"LIKE WHERE ARE HIS MOM AND DAD?"

"And?"

"HE DIDN'T HAVE A MOM AND DAD."

"Did he know what happened to them?"

"HE NEVER KNEW. HE WAS ABANDONED BY THEM. ONLY ONE CHILD PER FAMILY OVER THERE. REMEMBER?"

Herb expressed genuine interest. "So, who was taking care of him?"

"NO ONE. NO ONE FAMILY. HE WAS BOUNCED AROUND IN A NEIGHBORHOOD FROM ONE FAMILY TO THE NEXT. THEY ALL PITCHED IN TO TAKE CARE OF HIM."

"Then what was he doing begging?"

"IT WAS HIS WAY OF CONTRIBUTING TO THE FAMILIES. HE BROUGHT MONEY BACK TO THEM. HIS WAY OF SAYING THANKS."

"And you got that all through an interpreter?"

"YES. IT WAS AMAZING. I WOULD'VE LIKED TO HAVE BROUGHT HIM HOME."

"Why didn't you?"

"BECAUSE MY LIFESTYLE WOULDN'T ALLOW THAT TYPE OF COMMITMENT."

"What lifestyle?" Herb's posture straightened up. Maybe his captor was about to reveal something useful.

"TOO BUSY. AT HOME AND IN OTHER AREAS."

"Like what other areas?"

"THAT'S ALL YOU NEED TO KNOW."

"What do you do that makes a commitment for a child impossible?"

"I'VE REVEALED TOO MUCH ALREADY."

His mind turned. Should he take the gamble? Would he upset his captor if he asked? Would another bomb go off in the house if he questioned? He had to roll the dice.

"Which one were you on that trip?"

"PLEASE DON'T INSULT ME. I'M NOT EASY."

"I had to try. You weren't the only one enthralled with that boy. I might have snubbed him with my money, but I felt something for him. I don't know if you recall, but I went back and bought him a steamed loaf of bread. He ate it immediately. The whole thing."

"I DON'T RECALL THAT. YOU HAVE A HEART AFTERALL?"

"Yes. And it appears you do too?"

"MAYBE WE'RE BOTH NOT AS BAD AS THE OTHER THINKS WE ARE?"

"Maybe not. But either way, you still have me locked up in my house."

"AND YOU STILL DROVE MY MOM TO DO THINGS WHICH LED TO HER DEATH."

Herb shook his head, and snorted a sniffle. "I don't know what else to say. I'm sorry for whatever role I played in your mother's death. I never knew that. And certainly never meant to do that."

"THAT'S OKAY. YOU'RE GOING TO PAY FOR IT."

CHAPTER 39

If only she were here now.

Katie.

She washed away all the torment within. Made him feel new. Gave him a sense of goodness. Eased away his stress. Cleansed the poisonous feeling that anxiety brought him.

She couldn't be here physically. But, she could be here in thought.

Herb's mind wandered back to their fifth date. That's when he finally took matters into his own hands. He brought Katie and Cooper to a Yankees game. Sat right along the third baseline. Ten rows from the field. Saturday afternoon. Hot dogs. Beer. And pizza.

The players were still taking their warm-up swings when they sat down. "You been to a Yankees game, Cooper?" Asked Herb.

"No, sir. My dad's a Mets fan. Once a year we go."

"Ah, so I'm leading you down a dark path."

"Yes. My dad wouldn't approve."

Herb grinned. "Sorry. I'm not much of a sports aficionado. But, I do appreciate the lore and history of both teams."

"Probably more of that with the Yankees."

"Yes. Probably. Maybe next time we could try a Mets game."

"Yeah. Maybe next time."

"Hear you're thinking about Harvard or Stanford?"

Cooper shuffled uncomfortably in his seat. "Yeah. Thinking about it." He looked right into Herb's eyes.

"Leaning toward one or the other?"

Cooper shrugged. "One or the other."

Herb glanced over at Katie. The look on her face sensed Herb's struggle for conversation.

"We're taking him for his school tours next month. California will be fun."

Herb nodded in approval. "California would be a nice place to go to school. No snow." He looked at Cooper for a response.

Nothing. He looked at Herb, than turned his gaze out towards the field.

Hmm. Playing hard to get.

The game started. Several innings went by. Conversation proved difficult. If this relationship was going to stand a chance, a rapport with her son would be critical.

"You play any ball, Cooper?"

"No. Sports aren't my thing."

"Me either. What is your thing?"

"I like to read."

Jackpot. Now, you're in my arena.

"What kind of stuff do you read?"

"Young Adult stuff. Books that have series."

"Like Dashner?"

"Yeah. I liked the Maze Runner series."

"James is a client of mine."

"That's cool. I heard you were some kind of big agent or something."

He nodded his head. "I represent writers. You do any writing?"

"A little."

"What kind of stuff?"

"Suspense. Young adult."

"Nice. You ever think of going to school for writing?"

He looked at his mother. She looked back at him. "Yeah. But, I'm told it's not the best way to make a living."

"Oh, really." Herb looked at Katie with a disapproving glance. "Well, I happen to make a very good living by being in the world of writing."

It was as if someone tore down a wall between Herb and Cooper. "See Mom. I told you it could be a good thing."

Katie responded. "All your father and I are telling you is to have something else to major in to keep your options open."

"Did you write before you became an agent?" Cooper asked.

"I did. But, I was no good. I saw a better use of my skills as an agent."

"What kind of stuff did you write?"

"I dabbled in romance, but I didn't have the knack for it."

"That's too bad."

"Not really. Cause it led me down the path to become an agent. Which has been extremely lucrative for me."

"Cool."

They barely knew a game of professional baseball was being played live right in front of them. They talked for the rest of the game about the world of writing. Katie rarely had a chance to intervene.

After the game they went out to dinner and Cooper went on to hang out with friends. In departing from Herb and Katie he said, "It was nice to meet you Mr. Keeler."

"Please. Call me Herb."

"Okay. Thanks for the ballgame. Nice to meet you."

"Same here. Have a good night."

When he left the house Katie gave Herb a look. "Looks like you won him over."

"He's a great kid. You've done a great job in raising him."

"Thanks. My ex gets some credit, too."

"Sounds like you two respect each other."

"We do. We just couldn't live together."

"I guess if you have to be split, that's the way to do it."

She nuzzled up under his shoulder, wrapped her arms around his waist, looked up and gave him a big kiss. A lengthy kiss. A take your breath away kiss. And when they both broke for air, she said, "He won't be back for quite a while."

"Oh."

Her eyes were wide. Wide with excitement. They said everything.

She grabbed his hand, led him up to her bedroom, and from there, they took their relationship to the next level.

CHAPTER 40

His mind snapped back to reality. Herb felt his stomach tighten up. Hell, his whole body tightened up. His breathing quickened. He could hear himself laboring. He swallowed hard. He drew in a deep breath.

"Oh God!"

He rocked back and forth on his couch. He rubbed his arm. Up and down. Again and again. His head felt dizzy. He looked all around the room. He held on to the couch with his right hand. *Steady.*

He directed his voice at the TV. "Can't you forgive?"

"I'D LIKE TO. BUT I DON'T THINK I CAN. MY MOTHER WAS MY WHOLE WORLD. YOU SNUBBED HER LIKE A FLY ON THE WALL. LIKE SHE MEANT NOTHING. MY MOTHER! I FIND THAT UNFORGIVABLE. MY INTERNAL TURMOIL TELLS ME I MUST BALANCE THE SCALES OF JUSTICE."

Herb ran his fingers through his hair. He clenched his fists. Open and shut. He stood straight up. He paced his living room. Fast quick steps. Back and forth. Turn. Again. He looked like the expectant father. Over and over.

He sat back down. Stuck his hands straight out. The shaking uncontrollable. "For the love of God. Can't you please forgive me?"

Silence was his answer.

Herb looked all around the room. Up towards the ceilings. Behind him. On to the floors. Looking for a sign.

Would another explosion be in the works? Another of his prize possessions to be destroyed?

"Oh, come on. What're you doing? Quit playing with me!"

His voice quivered. A look of helplessness overtook him. His breathing picked up and his eyes misted. Tears draped down his cheeks. His hands shook violently. He held his head down in his hands with his eyes shut and broke down into a deep cry. An emotional-deep-breath-all-out cry.

He rocked himself back and forth. Crying every tear, every regret, every imaginable sorrow, every disdainful comment he ever made toward anyone out into the river that flowed down his cheeks.

This was a broken man. By the laws of nature, he was meant to be broken. For far too long, he'd dished out vile disrespect, mean-spiritedness, condescension, belittling dialogue, humiliation. And no regard for others feelings. None whatsoever. He was far overdue for the reckoning he experienced.

His cry slowed. He caught his breath. He wiped the tears from his cheeks with the back of his hand. He opened his eyes and he couldn't help but notice something.

Like a lighthouse on a faraway shore.

CHAPTER 41

His booze closet.

He sauntered off the couch and poured himself a scotch. The slight burn going down took his mind away from his peril. It forced him into a deep breath which soothed him when he exhaled. He took another sip. Bigger than the first. "Ah." He licked his lips and savored the numbness which graced them.

He sat up and breathed in and out again. A subtle confidence arose within him. A non-justified self-assurance. What could he possibly be confident about at this point in time? Amazing what liquor can do.

His forefinger held up his chin. His head, high in the air. Potentially something stirring deep inside. A connecting of the dots if you will.

He jumped up with a sense of purpose, went to his closet in his bedroom and reached up and pulled down a box. He carried it with haste out to his kitchen table and tore it open with the same enthusiasm young children rip open their presents on Christmas morning.

He scooped out the envelopes of pictures. Each marked with where they were taken. This was back in the days before he had flash drives and computer folders to save his pictures on. That's okay. He never minded. Nothing better than holding a memory in your hands. The physical touch of that memory flowing from your fingertips through your heart and delivering you an emotion.

He sorted past the legions of systematized remembrances. It resembled a file cabinet of passion, sentiment, sensation, excitement and feelings. Italy. Lake Louise. Nantucket. Nevis. Yachting in the Seychelles. Augusta. Thrillerfest. Tahiti. French Riviera. Sri Lanka. Victoria Falls. New Year's Eve. Tanzania Safari. He paused while his eyes grew wide.

There it was. In his hands. The treasure that could be his key. The key to his release. His freedom. The envelope with *thee* picture in it.

At least he would know. He would know that one of the people in that picture was the same person stationed in the house across the street. The same person instrumental for this whole thing. The person who had mountains of angst against him. The person who wanted to toy with him and torture him.

Ritz Carltons of Asia.

"Ah. Here you are. Just what I'm looking for. Beijing, Kuala Lumpur and Bali?"

He held the envelope delicately. Like nitroglycerin. And carefully opened it up.

The first series of pictures, spectacular shots of the landscape. Terraced rice fields of Bali. The beautiful beaches. Lush mountains. "Mmm...." Herb mumbled to himself.

Then he came to Beijing. Pictures of him standing on the Great Wall. A beauty standing next to him, his arm around her waist. Both looking in love. A picture of them eating some fries at a McDonald's. Big smiles from familiar food. A good shot of her in front of one of the pagodas at the Summer Palace.

He had to laugh. The next one caught a close up of someone riding a bike along next to his rickshaw attempting to sell him a Rolex. Salesmanship at its best. The funny part. He bought five of the damn things. All for a hundred bucks.

The next feature even funnier. His exquisite travel partner scrunching up her face after sipping the snake wine from a jug with a dead snake coiled up inside of the bottom. Herb didn't even have the gumption to try it. He knew he liked that girl for some reason. She was like a strong dose of medicine. She was willing to try anything.

The next couple of pictures were a blur of the Beijing Opera, the Flying Acrobatic show, various poses next to locals or candid shots of thousands of people riding their bikes. A pleasant smile warmed his face. And then there it was...the shot he was looking for.

The group picture standing out in Tiananmen Square.

All twenty-two of them.

CHAPTER 42

He slowly looked at each one of them. Staring into their eyes. Searching for some kind of sign that would tip him off.

First, his natural beauty, the brunette. That's how he always referred to his women. Not by their name. It was either the red head, the big titter, or the one who gave great blow jobs. They were just objects to him. The brunette was adventurous with a capital T. Willing to do anything with a dare. Or try anything for the first time. And she loved to get mischievous in places she might get caught. Always kept Herb on his toes. And other body parts, too.

Next, the couple from Canada, north of Edmonton. Sandy and her husband, Don. Two teachers who took the chance and became successful pig farmers and real estate tycoons. He always referred to them as "the Canadian couple."

He took plenty of naps throughout the tour. Mostly on the bus. Seemed like retirement life agreed to him.

Sandy, extremely sociable. Talked with everyone. Spoke fondly and often about her kids and grandkids. Short in height, but a dynamite of energy bursting out. Loved to learn about everyone's families and their lives. And loved to learn about the cultures of the people on the trip. Wanted to dig deeper about their rituals. About their diets. Took copious notes about everything.

She constantly asked the guides for more information. Couldn't get enough. The guide almost had to drag her away when they went into one of the schools in Beijing. She kept talking about the cute kids, and the way tai chi was taught at such an early age. She even had Herb and his friend over for a round of wine before dinner one evening. Herb chuckled, recalling how he spilled some red wine on her new blouse she'd just purchased from the world's best silk producer. Rather than be upset, and knowing Herb felt terrible, she laughed it off. It's just the kind of person she was. The nicest people. Even invited Herb and his friend up for a visit to Canada if they ever had the chance. They were married for a long time. Older. A grandma so filled with love and involvement with her contented hubby.

Sandy reminded Herb of his mother. His mind drifted back to when she lay there in the ER bed, recovering from the electric shock given to her heart. He stood over her, looking down at her soft face. Kindness radiating from her.

"Mom. I'm here."

He grabbed her hand and held it. The crinkled fingers felt good in his hand. Just like when he was a young boy.

"It's me. Your boy. I could sure use a cup of your ginger tea. Get better."

He studied her, waiting for a response. Nothing. Not a blink. He squeezed her hand, hoping for a squeeze back.

No such luck.

Herb inhaled a breath. And swallowed. "I want to tell you something. It's important."

He reached over with his other hand and stroked the back of her hand. "I no longer blame you for the abuse Dad did to me. You never knew. How could you do something if you never knew? I should've told you. I know if I would've told you, you would've ended it. But, I was too scared. I'm sorry for blaming you all these years. No more. When you get out of here, its tea at my house. Hurry up, Mom."

He blinked, and looked back down at the picture of Sandy and Don. Herb couldn't imagine the pig farmer blowing up his Monet.

But, what about the next couple?

CHAPTER 43

The next couple, Frank and Brenda from New York City. At first when Herb met them, he thought, uh-oh, more New Yorkers. Going to be loud and obnoxious. Especially when he heard that tough Brooklyn accent. In fact, in the beginning of the trip he avoided the couple. But, overhearing some of their conversations he could tell they were the sweetest people. Had lunch together a couple of times.

Frank was proud of his New York City. "You come to my town. I'll show you a good time." At the farewell dinner Frank had a lot of wine and couldn't stop telling jokes. His bar-bill rose to well over five-hundred dollars. He did something to do with the oil business. Selling equipment or something along those lines.

She, on the other hand, did modeling in her younger years, and now ran her own modeling agency. Had to be in her upper sixties, but she still knew how to turn heads. Especially Herb's.

She wasn't afraid to challenge Frank about anything.

He, very opinionated, had a lot to say about the government regulations as it pertained to the oil business. Brenda quickly defended the regulations as necessary steps to insure the safety of the people using the equipment. As much as he hated to admit it, she was right. Not afraid to disagree, they still had a magnetism for each other that couldn't be broke.

It didn't make a lot of sense to Herb. There was no way one of them would blast a cigar in his face. If one of them had an issue with Herb, they would come right out and confront him right then and there. But, the ones next to them? That was a different story.

CHAPTER 44

Back row, on the left, Jason and Billy. Not used to being around gay men, Herb stayed away from them until the third day of the trip when the seating arrangements gave them no choice. Same table. Just the four of them. Jason a mortgage broker and Billy a commercial fisherman.

They traveled the world together. Loved their wine and were infatuated with food. In fact, Jason studied and became a sommelier as a hobby, just because he loved wine.

Billy, on the other hand, proved to be quiet. When Herb found out Billy spent several years commercial fishing in Alaska, he asked him if it was as tough as what he'd seen on the reality show depicting the life of fishermen up in that region.

Billy perked up and shared some tidbits of how he had endured stormy seas and high winds.

He even shared the rope burn scar on his forearm due to a mishap. The scar sat right below his tattoo of a beautiful gray wolf sitting on top of a rainbow.

Being in his comfort zone, it was the only time he spoke up. He never initiated a discussion, but if prompted, he'd respond.

Herb could see him possibly having some scores to settle. He picked up his pen. Only to be distracted by a loud cracking noise slam against his house. The howling noise outside grew louder.

He took his pen and wrote a note on a piece of paper. *Possibilities.* Underneath it, he wrote *Billy.* Pure speculation. But at this point, he had nothing else to go by. He had to trust his gut feelings.

Now he was getting somewhere.

CHAPTER 45

The next couple, next to Jason and Billy, Mike and Lisa. From Herb's stressed out memory, Mike was some kind of a computer geek at a large accounting firm. Claimed he ran his own business for some time before taking the job at the big firm.

His wife, Lisa, a real estate investor. They lived just outside of Nashville in the sprawling farmland community of Franklin. It was littered with country music stars and their mansions and ranches. From their dinner conversations, she'd built up a nice portfolio of properties consisting of both residential and commercial. She had a keen interest for property values everywhere on the trip. It was her primary question to the guides.

Her and Mike were always trying to break away from the group to get onto a golf course. Herb got to join them once. They didn't keep score. It was all about being out there. Fresh air. Beautiful scenery. A bevvy or two, indigenous to the area of course. They just wanted to be in the moment. Friendly couple. Gave each other a lot of ribbing back and forth. Respectful.

Herb couldn't imagine Mike being filled with vengeance, or wanting to blow up a lamp in his house. Just couldn't see it. No way!

But, who the hell could it be?

Just about to look over at the next couple in the pic when the lights flickered and the house went completely dark. Everything silent, except the blowing and the objects-turned-projectiles darting against his house. Just when fear, uncertainty and loneliness couldn't be any worse, he found himself at a deeper level.

CHAPTER 46

His survival instinct kicked back in, revived by a new challenge. He slowly felt his way over to his cigar cabinet and grabbed his lighter. He had to regain power. He wanted to continue to review the pictures. But, it was important to maintain communication with the voice. There was no way of knowing when the power would come back.

In his mind he started considering his options. He could review his pictures with a flashlight or a cigar lighter. But that wouldn't keep in touch with crazy-man. Then he remembered. The generator. How could he forget? He walked his way down to the basement using the lighter as a means for visibility and turned on his generator. As the engine fired up, so did his lights. He strode up the steps and turned the TV back on. He looked across the street and could see through the blowing rain that his captor also had a generator because his lights were on as well. The machinelike voice came out from the TV. "HERB. GLAD YOU REMEMBERED YOUR GENERATOR. I SAVED YOU A NEWS CLIP THAT CAME OUT AN HOUR AGO. I WANTED TO MAKE SURE YOU SAW IT."

Herb squinted as he studied the TV. A completely bald reporter stood outside a publisher's office in New York. It was either his gray mustache or his lackadaisical delivery that screamed at the camera, "When can I retire?"

Behind him, a group of protestors.

"We have a group representing literary agents called the Association of Authors Representatives. They're protesting against the standard royalty of 15%."

The reporter turned around and asked one of the protestor's if he could ask a few questions. "Your name, sir?"

"Garret. Garret Cisco."

"Garret, I understand an agent receives a 15% royalty for sales on a book. Is that correct?"

"Yes sir."

"What's your group protesting?"

"With the amount of work we do, between reading countless numbers of manuscripts, squabbling with writers about where their work needs improvement. And being the burden of bad news when no publisher will represent our clients. We're just not getting paid enough. We're looking to increase the standard to 20%. I feel it's reasonable. My colleagues feel it's reasonable. And it's time we made people aware. Without us, the reading world wouldn't exist."

"I see. I understand you have protestors at two of the other big publishing houses as well."

"Yes sir. We need to let the big houses know. And it's paramount the writers know about this. After all, they need to agree to the terms."

"Do you expect push back from the writers?"

"Of course. Whenever change is involved, there's always an element of push back. But, in the long run. It'll be better for them. The writers know the value we hold for them. We can negotiate better contracts. And we act like readers when we read their work. We can tell them where they need to improve. Our value is priceless."

The reporter nodded. "That makes sense. Thank you for your time. I wish you and your colleagues the best."

"Thank you."

The agent walked back to his place in the picket line.

The reporter continued. "There you have it. The literary agents are asking the industry for a raise in pay. You haven't heard the end of this story. Stay tuned."

Herb stared blankly at the TV, trying to absorb all he'd just seen.

The TV blurted out, "WHAT DO YOU THINK?"

Herb rubbed his chin. "I think they're absurd."

"WHAT DO YOU MEAN?"

"They're demanding more money? The way the industry is going. Writers are trying to step around the agents and go directly to the publishers. This is just going to encourage them to do it faster. This will hurt all of us."

"REALLY?"

"Yes. And here I am trapped in my house and can't do a thing about it. Someone needs to tell them. Stop!"

"TOO BAD YOU'RE TRAPPED."

Herb mumbled under his breath as he turned away from the TV.

"Son-of-a-bitch."

"SORRY?"

Herb scowled. "You have anything to do with this?"

"I PLEAD THE FIFTH."

He shook his head in disgust.

CHAPTER 47

Herb sat back down at his table and continued scanning the picture further. He barked at the TV, "Can't believe you're messing with the industry while I'm trapped in here." He waited for a response. But, none came. He looked down, squinted and leaned in to see the picture better, middle row, far left, George and Kelly.

Interesting couple. George owned his own software company. Dealt mainly with building firewall protection for large companies. Whatever the hell that meant. Kelly, a superintendent for a large school system in Naples, Florida.

They predominantly talked about two things. Their daughters. Two beautiful, smart and funny college girls. One at the University of Southern California and one at the College of Charleston, South Carolina. Couldn't have been any further apart from each other. Hugging both coasts.

It struck Herb as odd that he was able to recall so much of the minute details of all of these people. Funny he thought, he'd only spent a week and a half with these folks, and yet they became so close. The other thing George and Kelly talked about, their boat. Although, by the pictures Herb had seen, he came to realize it was no ordinary boat. It was a full blown yacht.

Just the kind of friends Herb liked. They hit it off well. In fact, Herb had been down to visit them for a two day excursion six months ago.

There's no way George could have any animosity towards Herb. He would have sensed it. Who would invite someone on their boat if they had intentions of holding them captive in their house?

Wait a minute! Herb paused for a second. What if that was a ploy to get to know him a little better? Have someone case his house while he was gone and find his weak spots? Discover things he could destroy in the spirit of revenge. Train his dog, or wire his TV.

But, George and Kelly were so personable. So likeable. Herb liked them a lot. Could they really do something like that? At this point, all possibilities had to be considered. Herb's sense of human nature is what got him to be successful. Despite his instincts telling him, no way, these people would never do it, he had to write them down. Under *Possibilities, George* and *Kelly*.

Herb mumbled to himself, "Don't be you. I like you guys."

CHAPTER 48

Standing next to George and Kelly, Vince and Susan. How could he forget this high octane couple? Vince, a famous automotive consultant. Herb had seen his face in the news many times. Both on TV and in the papers. Whenever something big was going down with the car companies, usually Vince was involved. Had that rugged handsome thing going. Herb was rubbing shoulders with famous people here. In the right place baby!

And Susan? What a knock out. Herb glanced down at her. Studied her features. From that alluring face to the appetizing body. His eyes scanned up and down her entire frame. Taking her all in. He felt they connected. He couldn't put a finger on it. The couple seemed happy. Why would she emit signals towards Herb? Probably just some harmless flirting. That's okay. He didn't mind.

She didn't allude to having any type of a career. Yet, she seemed way too confident and accomplished in her demeanor to not have a career. She was able to have great one-on-one conversations and at the same time she could speak to many of the folks as a group. When Herb inquired as to what she did for a living she simply said, "took care of the household." He couldn't help but sense there was much more to her.

But, no way could he see either of them blowing things up in his house. They had way too much going on in their life.

The other thing that caught his recall, he didn't have any idea where this couple lived. He remembered them responding to the question of where they lived with something vague like, "in between places."

Herb didn't think anything of it at the time, but then again, he didn't think he'd be trapped in his house by one of these people. Now, things took on a whole new relevance. Leaving no stone unturned, Herb took out his pen and under *Possibilities,* jotted down *Vince* and *Susan.*

Out the corner of his eye he caught a glimpse of the next couple. A smile ran across his face.

CHAPTER 49

Middle row, far right, Dan and Kathy. Here was a couple to be jealous of. He owned a large travel company in New England. Family business. Kids were in it. Brothers and sisters. Parents. Nieces and nephews. They'd traveled to all seven continents. Had lots of great travel experiences to share. Averaged six trips a year together, plus all the trips he did for his business. Herb had serious travel-envy here.

Cathy ran a Foundation which supported kids around the world, plus she wrote as a columnist for a local newspaper. Herb remembered their daughter did some kind of writing for the company, too.

He looked closer into their eyes. Looking for a sign. His antenna perked up. Way up! That's two writers in the family. With writing as a possible trait within the family. Maybe one of them were scorned by Herb's response to their query letter. If they'd written him one. Or, maybe it was one of their mothers who'd written him a query.

This all made sense. A good possibility here. Serious consideration had to be given.

On the lighter side, Dan was Herb's scotch drinking buddy on the trip.

Only problem, he had to listen to endless hours of mindless discussion about his beloved Patriots.

Thank goodness for the scotch.

But, was all this, "scotch buddy" thing an act?

A way of getting close to Herb to explore personal things about him? To learn about his routines? To find out when he left his house?

He remembered Dan bringing up his own pets which transitioned into Herb talking about Reese. And now Reese is walking around with an explosive device around her neck. This all seemed too coincidental.

Could he have the aptitude for revenge? He had to think. Dan had this intense stare that made Herb wonder what he was thinking. Like he was looking through him. He found it intimidating. Maybe he was imagining ways to torture Herb. Looking back. That could be a possibility. He grabbed his pen and put *Dan* and *Kathy*'s name down under *Possibilities*. And he marked it with a star.

Then circled it.

Excitement grabbed him. He was getting to the last row.

The bottom.

CHAPTER 50

Bottom row, far left to be exact, Duncan and Peggy. Lived on St. Simons Island in Georgia.

He a financial planner and entrepreneur who created businesses and sold them off.

He reeked with all things Irish. He might have even pissed green. Probably little shamrocks poured out of his penis. But he sure carried the aura of friendliness around him.

Peggy, a charmer from the start, developed her own line of clothing. Delightful couple. Peggy with her infectious laugh. A great conversationalist. The kind you wish all of your people were. She was a true lover of people.

Both of them transplants from the Detroit area. That probably explained why he looked like he always had a sunburn. Irish, from Michigan, and moved to Georgia. He could have been the posterchild for the local dermatologist.

Thinking hard for any other snippets about this couple, Herb remembered them spending their summers up at their cottage in northern Michigan.

Wait! The captor said something about being a professor at a university up in Michigan. This could hold some weight.

They had such a sense of compassion about everything in life. And, he really liked them. But, the coincidence here couldn't be ignored.

Whoa!! Maybe this was it. Duncan with the big smile. All the while dying to torture Herb in his own home. He thought he smiled a bit too much.

A gentle confidence swelled up inside of Herb. A sense of finding a buried treasure, or at least another clue to its location. This, stronger than anything else thus far. It's the smiley ones you have to look out for sometimes. *You never know what's going on behind that smile.* Herb leaned into the picture talking right into their faces. "Duncan, if it's you, I'm onto you."

Herb grabbed his pen with vigor and scribbled *Duncan*'s name down under *Possibilities*. And he noted it with a little shamrock right next to it. And he bit his lip as he put the finishing touch on the shamrock, then poked it with his pen for emphasis.

His eyes glanced back to the photo.

"Next!"

CHAPTER 51

Next couple, bottom row, far right. Lynn and Skip. Herb liked these folks.

A loud crack of thunder exploded outside. Shook the house. Felt like it hit the house. Reese whimpered and scurried over to Herb. He reached down to her and stroked her head. "It's okay, girl. It's going to be okay." He wrapped his arms around her and pulled her in towards him. The wind howled louder. "This is crazy. I have to stay focused."

He patted her head and directed himself back to the picture. Lynn and Skip. An interesting mix. He, a retired newspaper man. Used to own the Tampa Times, eventually sold it for a handsome profit.

Lynn, a former principal for a Catholic High School in Tampa. Now, ran a thriving travel company out of her house. They both lived on Marco Island. They both liked their wine. In fact, so much they produced their own batch every Christmas to give to friends and family.

The one thing Herb remembered was they had a son who was an investigator up in Lansing, Michigan. The thought ran through Herb's head, what if they used his professional capacity to research Herb? Having a family member with those capabilities was priceless. Especially if you had a score to settle with someone.

Herb reached back, deep back in the recesses of his mind to recall any conversations about either of their childhoods. Nothing surfaced about abuse in any way or form. Still, if one of them had a mother who'd been scorned by Herb, they had the perfect resource at their fingertips.

Trying to calculate who would have had a rough upbringing would be difficult to pin-down indeed.

Herb tapped the pen on his desk and then jotted *Skip* and *Lynn* down on his list under *Possibilities*. You never could tell. Someone in this picture was making his life a living hell. Maybe it was a newspaper man, or the retired Catholic principal.

Anyone was possible.

Looking down at the photo, one last couple. Last, but not guilty.

Or were they?

CHAPTER 52

Bottom row, third and fourth from the right, John and Danielle. This couple couldn't have been for real.

They claimed they got married in Newport and had the reception at The Rosecliff Mansion. Sure that's nice and all, but they said it was covered by Oprah Winfrey on her O network. Sure, doesn't everyone have their wedding broadcast across the country's airwaves?

He an MBA from Harvard and Danielle an undergrad from Harvard. He stated he started and sold two businesses for millions of dollars. The first by the time he was forty. Quite annoying.

And if that wasn't enough, he said he was developing a sports website for kids for all kinds of sports throughout the world because he's tired of having to explain erectile dysfunction to his kids during commercials. Come on, who makes this shit up?

Supposedly, they lived in Cambridge and had a place on Nantucket Island, too. And if that wasn't enough, he also owned a place in Colorado and another in New York City. Manhattan no doubt.

The irritating part, they're young, beautiful and obviously have money.

But, do they have to go to such great lengths to make up all of this other stuff? This is ridiculous.

Could he have this inner angst to make Herb feel jealous? Could he be the person across the street peering at Herb through his binoculars toying with him? Maybe his bullshit story of his life was a peek at his twisted animosity towards Herb.

Herb grasped his pen and scribbled hard the name under *Possibilities. John.*

And he underlined it. Twice.

Now he had a list.

Who could it be?

CHAPTER 53

Herb looked at his list. Under *Possibilities* he followed his pen down alongside each name. Tapping it on each one as he read out their name.

"Billy. You angry young man." Herb massaged his head, squeezing his hands back and forth on his forehead. His mind scanning his memory, searching for a conversation they may have had regarding Billy's mother. Any iota of a discussion. Nothing.

"George and Kelly. I hope not." A smile warmed his face. The yacht experience touched his heart. No recollection of a mother-discussion ever surfaced. Not that he could remember.

He rubbed his hands together to keep his train of thought in gear. He remembered his writing professor say, "A body in motion is a mind in motion."

"Vince and Susan." Herb licked his lips. "Girl, you're a looker." Herb indulged the view in front of him. He shook his head in admiration. "Such a natural wonder."

When Herb thought of this couple, mother discussions weren't even on the radar. Car companies were the main topic of conversation with them. Except when they spoke of the deluxe products coming out. Herb found most of it a bore.

He poked his pen on the next one. "Dan and Kathy. Hmm..." He glared at them. "A family of writers. If it's you, you're all mine."

Herb paced back and forth. His head faced down in thought.

Then upward to the ceiling. And back again. "Banter about his mother. Come on. Think. A fond memory. A brief mention."

His mind ticked. He thought of where they sat. Where they stood. Where they drank. What they talked about.

Nothing.

His pen trailed down to the next one. "My Irish friend, Duncan. Don't think that pretty smile is going to fool me." Herb recalled discussions of his seven brothers. Every story had a brother in it. The thing about it, they were good stories. Always interesting. Many times, funny. Made you want to meet his brothers. But, no recollection of him mentioning his mother.

Then smacking his pen sideways like a drumstick he gave it a strong thwack onto Lynn and Skip. "Mrs. Principal and Mr. Newspaper man. I know you have the resources."

Herb remembered her saying she was from some place called Ecorse. The only reason he remembered that was because it sounded like *'of course.'* It struck Herb as kind of funny. But, no mention of Skip or Lynn's mother.

And jabbing his pen at the last name several times and one final poke for emphasis, he dug into the last name on the list, John.

"And you, wonder boy, with the unbelievable life. What is your real story?" He remembered long discussions of Nantucket Island, but not much else. No discussions of family with a troubled background.

He took his pen and tapped each name as he counted them going downward.

He let out a sigh of frustration and mumbled to himself, "Eleven. Eleven out of twenty-one. One or two of you are across the street right now. Playing scare-the-shit-out-of-Herb. And enjoying it way too much."

He looked up towards the ceiling in deep thought, pursed his lips, blinked several times and stood up. More like he jumped up.

A thought was born. And it was time to get to the bottom of this.

Herb screamed at the top of his lungs, "Wake up TV boy! We gotta talk!"

CHAPTER 54

Silence screamed back at Herb. He stood eagerly. Awaiting a response.

Nothing.

The stillness in the room made his skin tighten. The only other noise, the screaming wind outside. This was the first time during this whole affair he desperately wanted to hear the voice from the TV. Craved it. So bad he was willing to fight for it.

At the highest capacity he could muster, he yelled, "TV boy, where the hell are you? Wake up you son-of-a-bitch!"

He let out a slow breath. And waited.

A flicker of sound crackled from the speaker. Evidence Herb's efforts were fruitful.

The first sound, a yawn. Obviously to demonstrate the captor wasn't the least bit rattled by the show of emotion displayed by Herb. As casually as humanly possible the voice asked, "YOU RANG?"

Herb could see right through the sound of the voice. *Okay. Hold your composure. No need to feed his indulgence.* "Ah, yeah. I haven't heard from you. I'm lonely. What've you been up to?"

"MISS ME?"

"What do you think? What've you been doing?"

"GRABBING A SNACK. HANDFUL OF PEANUTS TO TAKE OFF THE EDGE. WHAT ABOUT YOU?"

"Been looking into your eyes."

Silence sailed across the air. This gave Herb a sense of control. His captor stopped in his tracks. Another first.

Herb wanted to say something witty like, "what's the matter? Cat got your tongue?" But instead, he used his negotiation skills. He said nothing. *He who talks first, loses.*

The silence lingered. Good. Time to get in his head. And stay there. Keep him back on his heels.

Herb took one step closer to the TV and waited. Nothing.

Okay. Take the next shot.

"You hear me?"

"YES. YOU WERE LOOKING INTO MY EYES?"

"Yes."

"HOW?"

Herb had his hands on his hips. Standing upright and confident. "How might you think?"

The voice chuckled. "OKAY HERB. YOU MADE AN INTERESTING STATEMENT. I'LL GIVE YOU THAT. DON'T THINK YOU HAVE ONE UP ON ME. REMEMBER, I HAVE *YOU* TRAPPED IN *YOUR* HOUSE. I'M IN CONTROL HERE."

And he laughed again for emphasis. Obviously attempting to shrug off any sign he was alarmed.

Not to be startled easily. Herb shot back. "That's right. I'm looking into your eyes right now. And I see a disturbed person."

"OH REALLY? AND HOW THE HELL ARE YOU LOOKING INTO MY EYES? NO WAY YOU CAN BE LOOKING AT ME. NO WAY."

"You sound so sure of yourself. You didn't sound so sure a moment ago. I sensed a touch of uncertainty."

"HERB. HERB. HERB. YOU CAN PLAY YOUR LITTLE GAMES. BUT, YOU'RE FORGETTING, I'M THE MASTER GAME-PLAYER HERE. I HAVE YOU. IF YOU'RE LOOKING INTO MY EYES, YOU MIGHT AS WELL SHARE WITH ME WHAT THE HELL YOU'RE TALKING ABOUT."

Herb swallowed. It frustrated him to give control back to his captor. He had to keep playing the voice. Keep it concerned.

"All right. I'm looking into your eyes. I've got a picture of you."

The voice scoffed. "REALLY? WHAT DO I LOOK LIKE?"

Herb paused. Here was a chance to put it on alert if he had the right response. What could he say? What would give the voice reason to believe it had the right picture of the right person?

He looked at the picture. Studied it closely. What blanket statement could he say that would apply to everyone? *Quickly.* He had to respond soon.

Aha. "I have a picture of you standing in Tiananmen Square."

Another round of silence ensued.

Herb waited. *Let's see how the voice responds. I've got the hand in play.*

Herb looked around the room. He felt an ounce of control flow back through the house.

"TV boy, I'm looking into your eyes. Standing in Tiananmen Square."

Before he could finish pronouncing Square, a question shot out of the speaker. "WHAT AM I WEARING?"

Damn. Good question. Steady. Calm. Breathe.

He studied the picture. All had long pants on. Some white jeans. Some slacks. Others, khakis. Some with sweats.

"You have a pair of long pants on."

Immediately laughter broke out of the TV. "HERB. HERB. HERB. YOU PLAY ME FOR A FOOL. YOU'RE INSULTING. NOW, I KNOW YOU'RE GUESSING. BECAUSE WITH THE WEATHER WE HAD, EVERYONE WAS WEARING PANTS THAT DAY. UNLESS YOU CAN TELL ME WHAT ELSE I WORE THAT DAY. YOUR GIG IS UP. YOU DON'T KNOW WHO I AM. DO YOU?"

Damn. The voice is smart.

Panic surged through his heart. *I have to make my best guess.* Herb looked at all of them and keyed in on Dan and Kathy, the ones with two writers in the family. *Okay, here goes.*

"You have a blue jacket on and a Red Sox baseball hat."

Laughter erupted through the TV. "GOOD GUESS. BUT, NOT EVEN CLOSE. WHAT MADE YOU THINK THAT WAS ME?"

Herb felt like a fool. He hated being played. "How do I know you're being honest? I wouldn't expect you to fess up even if I did pick you."

"ARE YOU LOOKING AT THE GROUP PICTURE IN TIANANMEN SQUARE? BECAUSE THAT'S THE ONLY PICTURE I REMEMBER BEING TAKEN OF ME. YOU MUST BE LOOKING AT THE GROUP PICTURE."

Herb didn't answer. He couldn't. It hurt to be exposed. The voice was right.

Herb's brain danced with vigor reviewing all the pictures he'd taken. Bali rice fields. Strictly scenery. Octopus for dinner. Splayed nicely on a plate. Everything visual that ran across his memory bank was scenery and historic buildings. Monuments. Oceans. Lakes. Only one lousy people-picture. But, for some reason, the only one with pictures of others.

Only moments earlier Herb couldn't wait to hear from the voice. Now, the gloating sound emanating from the speaker irritated him to no end. "HERB. JUDGING BY THE SOUND OF NOTHING COMING FROM YOU, IT APPEARS I HIT A NERVE."

Herb said nothing.

"THE ONLY PICTURE YOU HAVE OF ME IS THE GROUP PICTURE, ISN'T IT?"

Herb didn't have to respond. He knew he'd been caught.

"ANY GUESSES WHICH ONE IS ME?"

Herb squinted his eyes and tightened his lips.

The robotic voice continued to grind the victory in. "GO AHEAD. TAKE A GUESS. WHAT'S IT GOING TO HURT?"

Herb scanned the picture. He wanted to guess. He wanted to pick one out and see what the response would be. But, he knew. He knew even if he guessed the captor wouldn't fess up.

Taking a few steps and pacing for confidence, Herb spoke into the TV, "I have some questions for you before I go making careless guesses about who you are."

A cough emerged from the TV. And then, "SORRY, *MY DEAR FRIEND*, AND I USE THAT TERM WITH JUST A TINGE OF SINCERITY."

"Sincerity? You have me holed up in my house. You have an explosive device around my dog's neck. And you're on the verge of blowing me and my house into smithereens. How could there be even a tinge of sincerity? I don't find this funny. At all!"

"WHILE I CAN APPRECIATE YOUR PREDICAMENT, I AM SINCERE. I'M ENCOURAGED THERE MIGHT BE A GLIMMER OF A HUMAN BEING INSIDE OF YOU WITH YOUR WORK FOR THE ANIMALS. THAT IMPRESSED ME. BUT, YOUR TREATMENT OF MY MOTHER AND HOW THAT AFFECTED HER HAS BEEN RAGING UP INSIDE OF ME FOR YEARS. YOU HAVE NO IDEA. THIS ANGER HAS GOT TO BE DIRECTED. IT MUST BE CHANNELED. AND YOU, MY FRIEND, IS EXACTLY WHERE IT IS AIMED. I REFER TO YOU AS A FRIEND BECAUSE YOU HAVE BEEN IN MY THOUGHTS FOR COUNTLESS YEARS. BECAUSE OF THAT, I REFER TO YOU AS A FRIEND. BUT, IN NO WAY DOES THAT MEAN I LIKE YOU."

Herb sat in silence. The comments resonating inside of his soul. Of course it made sense. The motivation on the other side of the TV was real and strong.

The line of questioning Herb would need to uncover the identity of his captor would have to be clever and well thought out. And that still might not be enough.

This would be nothing short of a miracle to escape from.

He looked at his watch. 1:37 pm.

CHAPTER 55

Escape.

The word his hottest new writer, Daniel Beard used often. "That's why they read my books," he said. "To escape." Young Adult maestro. Herb recalled taking Cooper and Katie to his book signing at one of the local bookstores.

Cooper was star-struck. He got to shake hands with a real life writer. Not just any writer. A popular writer, whose books turned into movies.

Herb set it up so they could meet prior to the event. One on one.

"I've read all your books, Mr. Beard."

"Thank you. Which one's your favorite?"

"John Has A Long Mustache."

"Ah, you're a war buff I see."

After the first bit of conversation started, he felt comfortable. "Yes. D-Day always fascinated me. I like how you wrapped your characters around real life history."

"Thanks. The war stuff always got me. Ever since I was a kid."

"Me too."

"Obviously, you like to read. You write?"

He looked over at Herb as he asked the question. Herb, careful not to get caught by Cooper, winked back.

"I do."

"What kind of stuff?"

"Young Adult. Same as you."

"No kidding. I'd love to see some of your stuff."

Cooper's eyes bulged, "You would?"

"Sure. Send me your work and I'll give you some feedback. I love helping people perfect their craft. I'm thankful for the folks who helped me."

Cooper looked at Katie like he just received a corvette for Christmas. The lines from his smile engulfed his entire face.

"I will, Mr. Beard. I'll send it to you as soon as I get home."

Mr. Beard glanced out the corner of his eye at Herb, and then back at Cooper. "Oh, there's no hurry. Make it your best, and then I'll take a look at it."

"You got it."

"Say, would you like to help me out with my signing and stand next to me and hand out books? It would be a big help."

"Oh man. Sure!"

Herb and Katie had lunch in the coffee shop while Cooper assisted Mr. Beard.

"I think it's fair to say you've won him over. Thanks for being so good to him. "Katie said to Herb.

"He's a great kid. I'd like to help him out any way I can. If anyone can help him be a better writer, it's Daniel Beard."

She looked him straight in the eye. "You're so different from what I initially thought. You really can't judge a book by its cover."

He smiled. "I'm glad you looked inside the book. There's a lot to see."

If only he could go back to that time. That place.

When life was good.

CHAPTER 56

Instead, here he sat. Trapped. He had some serious figuring to do.

He pondered. Where to start? What did he know about the voice?

Lived in Michigan. Was a professor. Had two kids. Lived somewhere between Detroit and Lansing. "Wait. Wait a minute. Michigan. Duncan. That Irish son-of-a-bitch. Duncan. It's you. Isn't it?"

As an authoritative figure the robotic voice asked, "AND WHY DO YOU THINK I'M DUNCAN?"

"Because you're a professor in Michigan and Duncan was from Michigan."

"SURE. BUT DIDN'T HE LIVE IN GEORGIA?"

"Yes, but maybe you go back and forth between both places."

"YOU'RE FUNNY. FIRST, YOUR TONE IS ASSUMING I'M DUNCAN. I APPLAUD YOUR ASSUMPTIVE APPROACH. BUT, IF THAT'S TRUE, DO YOU THINK I WOULD'VE TOLD YOU I WAS FROM MICHIGAN WHILE I WAS ON THE TRIP? IF I'M DUNCAN?"

"You're trying to throw me off. Aren't you?"

A laugh came over the speaker. "YOU MAKE A GOOD POINT. I COULD BE. BUT, ON THIS ONE, I'LL BE STRAIGHT. I'M NOT DUNCAN. ME GOING ON THAT TRIP WAS NO COINCIDENCE. MY PURPOSE FOR THAT TRIP WAS TO STUDY YOU. I STALKED *YOU ALL THE WAY*. CAPICHE!"

Herb thought about it. If he's not Duncan, then out of thirteen that left twelve still possible.

He looked at his list. Bunch of rich misfits. He hated them. Walking pompously around these iconic sights. As if the world owed them. Strutting themselves as if these land formations were put here by God himself just for their viewing pleasure. The arrogant bunch.

Part of him liked them. They all had a flare for the exotic. Savoring the cuisine. Delighting over the delicious scenery. The silky sensation of the wine. Rubbing shoulders with accomplished people in their respective fields.

Padding their egos of self-importance. *I did this and I did that. I'm worth so many millions. I own this company. I run this division. I wrote this many books. I ran this many marathons. My kids did this and that. I've set foot on seven continents. I've traveled to this many countries. I drive this car. Blah, blah, blah.* With each glass of wine their self-worth elevated. Each brats in their own right. Maybe that's where Herb could relate.

However, the things he liked about them—were also the things he hated about them.

How could that be?

Was Herb changing?

He shook his head to clear his thoughts. Enough contemplating, time to systematically flush out the nut-job. Smoke his ass out.

Herb grabbed his list. Sat straight up.

Player number one. Billy. The quiet gay Alaskan fisherman with the scarred arm with the wolf tattoo over a rainbow.

Eager. Hesitant, and anxious, Herb started. "You're a fisherman."

"YOU'RE RIGHT."

"I knew it. You're Billy!"

"WHAT?"

"Billy's a commercial fisherman in Alaska. That's you."

Laughter ensued. "OH BOY, YOU'RE FUNNY. I LIKE TO FISH. BUT, I DON'T DO IT FOR A LIVING."

"You have a tattoo on your forearm?"

"I DESPISE TATTOOS. ON MEN ANYWAY. I LOVE THEM ON A WOMAN. ESPECIALLY WHERE YOU CAN'T SEE THEM WITH CLOTHES ON."

"You don't have any tattoos?"

"NO. YOU THINK ONE QUESTION AND YOU HAVE THIS WHOLE THING FIGURED OUT?"

Herb ran his fingers through his hair. "Just getting started."

"KEEP GOING. I FIND THIS EXTREMELY AMUSING. IN FACT, I'M SORRY I DIDN'T THINK UP THIS LITTLE GAME MYSELF." The voice rose with excitement.

Herb winced. "Damn." He crossed out Billy's name on the list.

"Eleven to go."

CHAPTER 57

Next up, George and Kelly. Herb mumbled under his breath, "Please don't be you."

The voice from the TV came out, "SORRY, I COULDN'T HEAR YOU."

"Good."

"DO ANOTHER ONE. THIS IS FUN."

Herb shook his head in disgust. "Okay. George and Kelly. Let's see, what do we know about them?"

He rubbed his chin. "Owner of a software company. She, a superintendent. Own a kickass boat. Live in Florida. Two daughters. And if this is you, you invited me to hang out on your boat for almost a week."

"I DID, DID I? AND DID I HAVE A GOOD TIME?"

"You did all right. Do you remember the fresh fish we ate?"

"REFRESH MY MEMORY. PLEASE."

His words were fast. Excited. "We went deep sea fishing. Caught a bunch of snapper. You cut your finger bad from the hook. I cleaned it and bandaged you up. Kelly cooked the fish up—ceviche style. Squeezed loads of lemon and fresh ginger over the snapper. I've never seen a grown man moan over food so much."

"BOY, SOUNDS LIKE I MISSED A GOOD TIME. I WISH I WERE GEORGE."

"How's your hand doing?"

"WHAT?"

"From the fish hook."

Laughter came from the TV. "YOU'RE GOOD. TRYING TO CATCH ME SLIP UP ARE YOU?"

"Well?"

"MY DEAR BOY, I HAVE SORRY NEWS FOR YOU. I'M NOT GEORGE. BUT, I HAVE TO SAY, I LIKE YOUR STYLE. THIS IS FUN."

"What do you like to do for fun?"

"FOR STARTERS, I LIKE TO COUP PEOPLE UP IN THEIR HOUSES WITH THE IMMINENT THREAT OF BLOWING UP. IT'S MY FAVORITE WEEKEND ACTIVITY."

A look of frustration panned over Herb's face.

"I think we've already established that. What else do you like to do?"

"YOU ALREADY KNOW ABOUT VOLUNTEERING AT THE ABUSE SHELTERS."

"Yes. It's such a contrast. Nice guy volunteer to women. Trap men in their house. It doesn't add up."

"WE'LL JUST HAVE TO WRITE IT OFF AS, I HAVE ISSUES."

Herb sucked on the corner of his lip. "We're in agreement there." He had to ask again. "Your hand healed?"

The voice laughed again. "OKAY. YOU CAN QUIT. I'M NOT GEORGE, EITHER. NO HOOK SCARS TO SPEAK OF. BUT, I KIND OF WISH I WERE GEORGE. SOUNDS LIKE HE HAD A LOT OF FUN."

Herb went back to his paper. Crossed off George and Kelly. Okay. That left nine.

CHAPTER 58

Herb yelled over to the TV, "If I guess which one is you, are you going to tell me?"

"THAT'S A GOOD QUESTION. I REALLY DON'T KNOW. IF I DO DISPOSE OF YOU, IT'S NOT GOING TO MATTER IF YOU KNOW ANYWAY."

Herb interrupted. "You have a problem saying the word *kill*, don't you?"

"MAYBE. AND HERE'S THE THING. IF I DO DECIDE TO LET YOU LIVE, THEN IT'S NOT IN MY BEST INTEREST TO LET YOU KNOW WHO I AM."

This was music to Herb's ears. There was hope. "That's true. And if that's the case, I don't even want to know who you are. We can quit playing this game right now. Just let me go and we can both go on our merry ways."

"NOT SO FAST. I HAVEN'T DECIDED IF I'M GOING TO DELETE YOU OR NOT. I LIKE TO KEEP MY OPTIONS OPEN."

"Delete me? You really struggle with the word *killing*, don't you?"

"MAYBE."

"That's okay. You don't have to do that. You don't have to make yourself a killer. Once you do, you can't go back. That's who you become."

"LOOK, YOU DON'T TELL ME WHAT TO DO OR NOT DO. I'LL DECIDE FOR MYSELF WHEN THE TIME IS RIGHT."

"When will that be?"

"WHEN I SAY IT IS." The voice took on an authoritative tone again. "LET'S GET BACK TO THE GAME."

"No. I don't want to play anymore."

"HERB, YOU DON'T HAVE ANY CHOICE. I SAID WE PLAY."

Herb's posture stiffened. "Not if I don't want to."

"YOU'RE FORGETTING. I'M IN CHARGE. AND I SAY PLAY."

"No. I don't want to. I'm done."

"HERB...YOU'RE NOT BEING SMART." And the captor dragged the word *smart* out as if it were one long sentence.

"What do you mean I'm not being smart?"

"I'M THE BOSS. IF I SAY PLAY, WE PLAY."

"You can't make me."

"ARE YOU SURE YOU WANT TO DO THIS?"

"I'll do it anyway I want."

"WE'LL SEE ABOUT THAT. REMEMBER THE LITTLE WOODEN BOX YOU BOUGHT IN HONG KONG MADE OF TEAKWOOD WITH INLAID JADE AND PEARL?"

Panic rushed over Herb. He looked up at his shelf against the wall. The one that showcased all his souvenirs. The Murano glass from Venice. The painted oxcart from Costa Rica. The hand-carved figures from Tanzania. And there, in the middle of them all, the wooden box. He took a step toward the box and...

Bam!

The blast sprayed pieces all around the room, peppering Herb across his chest and splashing wood fragments across his face.

He blocked his eyes with his hands and hit the floor.

He looked up at his shelf. Shattered to kindling wood.

Other pieces were knocked onto the floor.

His Murano glass piece, nine thousand dollars-worth of glass, destroyed.

Carved figurines strewn around the room. And his teakwood box with inlaid jade and pearls, reduced to splinters. The pearls and jade scattered somewhere throughout the room.

Anger boiled up inside of Herb. From his position on his chest, lying on the ground, he yelled, "If you think this is going to make me play your game. You're fucked! I'm done! I'm not doing anything!"

Silence filled the room. The only noise to be heard, the earsplitting wind outside.

CHAPTER 59

Herb rolled over and sat up. Resting his arms on his knees. He looked around the room. Smoke still smoldered from the shelf. Like unwelcome company, destruction made its presence once again in his house. It permeated every room of his home. Frustration seeped into his bones.

The trauma of every infraction tortured his emotional well-being. Extreme fear followed by layers of complete quiet. Up. Down. Die. Live. Boom! Ah.

It exhausted him.

This voice, this son-of-a-bitch. It liked to pull the trigger. The mean streak, there, no doubt. The intense intellect, crawling to be entertained. Starved for a challenge. A mind too bright for its own good. Dangerous.

Herb stood up and looked around the room. What other objects had been booby trapped? What other destruction did he have in store?

How could he harness all that he knew into a plan to get out of this? He massaged his chin with his thumb and forefinger. *Starving for a challenge. Crawling to be entertained. Too bright for his own good.*

These must be the elements to play on. Maybe he did have to continue this game of guess-the-psycho-traveler. Keep the voice engaged. Keep it busy. At least it's not blowing something up. At least it's not getting closer to Herb's demise. The longer he stalled, the better chance of a change in heart. A slip up. Or a chance to escape.

You want to play? Then let's play.

CHAPTER 60

Herb dusted the debris off his chest. Shook the dust out of his hair, and rubbed the remains off his face. Hard to succumb to defeat, but knowing it could be the path to freedom, Herb grabbed his list with a new zest and sat back down in front of the TV.

With the sound of submissiveness in his voice, Herb called out, "Okay TV man. You win. Let's play this game."

With an eerie calmness to his cadence, the robotic voice spoke, "ARE YOU OKAY? I DIDN'T WANT TO HURT YOU."

"I'm okay. But my shelf and my objects are destroyed."

"I'M SORRY. I KNOW HOW MUCH YOUR OBJECTS MEAN TO YOU. BUT, I BET AT THIS POINT THEY MEAN VERY LITTLE TO YOU, HUH?"

Herb thought for a minute. The voice was right. It was just a box. Someone out there in the world designated jade and pearls as objects worthy of a high dollar value. Just shiny rocks. Somehow, the objects didn't mean as much to him anymore.

The only thing he thought about was his life. The ability to continue to walk on the face of this earth. Breathe its air. Taste its treasures. See its beauty. Do and feel an act of kindness. And to be with Reese. Snuggle up to her warm fur. Let her lick him in the face. Walk together and feel the wonder of being alive. And his friend. He wanted to see his friend again. And Katie. To have her in his arms again. "Yeah." He confirmed. "They don't mean much."

"WHEN YOUR LIFE COMES DOWN TO THE RAW BASICS, WHAT'S REALLY IMPORTANT RISES TO THE TOP, DOESN'T IT?"

The wisdom of the voice proved evident. Shaking his head in the affirmative, Herb said, "Yes. You're right."

"I'M GLAD YOU'VE COME TO YOUR SENSES. SOMETIMES WE NEED A TOUGH LESSON TO TRULY LEARN."

The voice allowed it's last comment to marinate into Herb's mind. Let it meander into the tiny recesses of his cranium.

After several minutes passed, the voice came back, "OKAY. BACK TO WORK. WHO ELSE DO YOU THINK I AM?"

Herb looked down at the list and smiled. "Vince and Susan."

"THIS OUGHT TO BE GOOD."

"Why do you say that?" Herb's eyebrows grew serious.

"I DON'T KNOW. I CAN'T WAIT TO HEAR WHAT YOU HAVE TO SAY."

"But why particularly for Vince and Susan?"

"BECAUSE THERE WERE SO MANY DIVERSE PEOPLE ON THIS TRIP. I CAN'T IMAGINE YOU COULD REMEMBER SO MUCH ABOUT EACH OF THEM. I CAN BARELY REMEMBER THEIR NAMES, LET ALONE WHAT THEIR LITTLE LIVES WERE ABOUT. I FIND IT AMUSING YOU REMEMBER SO MANY THINGS ABOUT THEM. I CAN'T WAIT TO HEAR WHAT YOU REMEMBER ABOUT THIS NEXT COUPLE. I HONESTLY FORGOT THEIR NAMES."

"Maybe it's because I pay attention when people talk."

Barely finishing the word *talk* and the voice exploded from the TV. "PAY ATTENTION WHEN PEOPLE TALK? YOU DIDN'T PAY ATTENTION TO MY MOTHER'S LETTER–DID YOU? IF YOU HAD, WE WOULDN'T BE HERE RIGHT NOW."

Herb stared into the TV screen. And sat dazed. The insight–profound. The anger received through the TV. "You're right. I'm sorry."

How could he blame the voice? The passion. The frustration shooting from the speaker into his ear.

Keeping the momentum of the game going, the voice continued. "ALL RIGHT. ENOUGH ABOUT ME. LET'S SEE HOW MUCH YOU REMEMBER ABOUT THIS NEXT COUPLE."

"Vince and Susan." Herb stated.

"YOU KNOW, IT SOUNDS LIKE YOU'RE ANNOUNCING THE NEXT BATTER UP IN A BASEBALL GAME. THIS IS FUN. I SHOULD HAVE TAKEN UP KIDNAPPING PEOPLE EARLIER AND HAVE THEM TRY AND GUESS THEIR WAY OUT. THIS IS LIKE A SPORT."

"What do you know about sports?"

"I KNOW A THING OR TWO."

Herb's antennae went up. Could be an enlightening moment. "What sports are you into?"

"I'M INTO TWO. SWIMMING AND ARCHERY."

"So, you've dabbled in those?"

"NO. I'M GOOD. VERY GOOD."

"You swam in college?"

Now we're getting somewhere.

"LET'S JUST SAY I'VE SPENT SIGNIFICANT TIME IN THE POOL."

"And archery?"

"WHEN I SHOOT, I DON'T MISS."

Herb's brain went into overdrive. High gear all the way. Who talked about swimming and archery on the trip? Who does he remember spending time in the hotel pools? Or swam in the oceans? He tried to remember swimming himself, or hanging out at the beach. But the trip had limited beach time. He couldn't remember seeing anyone in a pool or on the beach swimming. Damn. Just when he thought he was onto something.

"If this is you. You're some type of big-shot auto consultant. I don't remember where you live. You have a beautiful wife. I don't remember if you have kids or not. And I don't know what she did for a career. And I don't know if I ever found out where you live."

"THAT'S PRETTY GOOD. I DON'T EVEN REMEMBER THAT MUCH. I DIDN'T FIND THEM VERY INTERESTING MYSELF. BUT, YOU'RE RIGHT. HIS WIFE WAS A LOOKER."

"How do I know you're not Vince?"

"BECAUSE I'M TELLING YOU I'M NOT."

"That doesn't mean anything."

"YOU KNOW, WE'RE GOING TO HAVE TO GO THROUGH THE GAME AND SEE HOW IT PROGRESSES. THAT'S ALL I CAN SAY. IS THAT ALL YOU REMEMBER ABOUT THEM?"

"Yes."

"ME TOO."

CHAPTER 61

That left seven.

Herb looked down at his list. "Dan and Kathy. The man who owns the travel company. And his wife, a writer. If you're Dan, maybe it's your wife, the writer who I upset. Maybe it's not your mother who I scorned."

A chuckle trickled out from the TV.

"What's so funny about that?" asked Herb.

"I LIKE YOUR LINE OF REASONING. I FIND IT AMUSING."

"If you're indeed Dan. Can you please tell me? Is it your wife I upset? If it is, it would give me the chance to personally apologize to her for my wrong-doing. Are you Dan?"

"I CAN'T JUST BLURT OUT THE ANSWER. YOU NEED TO DO SOME DIGGING. SOME FURTHER QUESTIONING."

"If you're Dan, you're a scotch drinker. You know I like scotch. When I drank my scotch here in my house you booby trapped my cigar. I believe I shared with you how I like to smoke a cigar with my scotch. That would make you a viable suspect."

The voice scoffed. "HOW RIDICULOUS. JUST BECAUSE DAN DRANK SCOTCH WITH YOU ON THE TRIP DOESN'T MEAN HE BOOBY TRAPPED YOUR CIGAR."

"How 'bout this? If you're Dan, I believe your daughter was a writer. Could I have wronged her?"

"IF I WERE DAN, I WOULD SAY THAT'S A POSSIBILITY."

"Are you saying you're Dan?"

"I'M NOT SAYING I AM AND I'M NOT SAYING I'M NOT. WHAT ELSE DO YOU HAVE ON HIM?"

Herb glanced around the room. He looked down toward the ground and his thoughts turned inward. "What about Reese?"

"WHAT ABOUT REESE?"

"I remember talking about her with Dan on the trip. We discussed our pets. If you're Dan, you knew enough about her to plant an explosive on her. For that I despise you."

"I HAVE TO ADMIT. THAT, I'M NOT PROUD OF. REMEMBER, YOU HURT MY MOTHER WITH THE ULTIMATE LACK OF COMPASSION. THAT FURY HAS MADE ME DO THINGS I NEVER THOUGHT I WAS CAPABLE OF."

"Is it you? Are you Dan?"

"YOU HAVEN'T MADE A GOOD CASE WITH ANYONE YOU'VE TALKED ABOUT. ESPECIALLY DAN. NOTHING YOU HAVE SAID LINKS ME TO HAVING YOU HOLED UP IN YOUR HOUSE. NOTHING. AND YOU'RE NOT GOING TO FIND ANYTHING. BUT, JUST TO MAKE SURE I HAVEN'T LEFT A CLUE, WE'RE GOING TO CONTINUE THIS PROCESS AND MAKE SURE. BESIDES, I FIND IT SHEER ENTERTAINMENT."

"You're a fucking monster."

"IT TAKES ONE TO KNOW ONE MY FRIEND. IT TAKES ONE TO KNOW ONE."

CHAPTER 62

That whittled it down to five left on the *Possibilities List*.

Herb checked off Dan and Kathy. He looked up. "You know, just because we talked about a couple of people already, doesn't mean you're not one of *them*."

"OF COURSE IT DOESN'T. BUT, WE'RE GOING TO SEE HOW CLOSE YOU CAN GET BY GOING THROUGH THE WHOLE LIST."

The complexion of frustration warmed over Herb's face. He ran his hand over his head, rubbing the back of his neck for comfort.

"Are you just wasting my time?"

A true gut busting laugh jumped out from the TV. He carried on until he couldn't laugh anymore. After he laughed himself out, Herb could hear him catch his breath. "OH, YOU'RE GOOD. THAT'S FUNNY. AS IF YOU HAD SUCH A BUSY SCHEDULE ON YOUR HANDS. AS IF YOU HAD THE WHOLE DAY IN FRONT OF YOU WITH A TO-DO-LIST A MILE LONG. OH, THIS IS GOOD STUFF." He continued to laugh some more and it ran into hysteria again. He could hardly contain himself. Losing his breath in and out.

"I LOVE YOUR LINE OF QUESTIONING. YOU SHOULD HAVE BEEN A DETECTIVE INSTEAD OF A LITERARY AGENT. IF YOU HAD, YOU WOULDN'T BE IN THIS PREDICAMENT."

"Am I right? Is this thing over? Have I identified you?"

A big sigh rolled out of the TV. "HERB MY DEAR BOY. YOU DID A GOOD JOB OF QUESTIONING. BUT, YOU STILL HAVE THREE MORE PEOPLE TO REVIEW."

Herb groaned.

Like a teacher to his pupil, the TV gave another command.

"ALWAYS BE THOROUGH."

CHAPTER 63

Herb looked at the list. Three more to go.

"Lynn and Skip."

"WHO?"

"Lynn and Skip. The Catholic Principal and the Newspaper man."

"YES. WHAT ABOUT THEM?"

"There are a couple of things about them that raise my awareness."

"SUCH AS?"

"I know they live in Florida, but I remember her saying she had a son that was a detective in Lansing, Michigan. This is real close to you. To me, this is a big reason."

"HOW?"

"First, there's the Michigan connection. Not just any connection. Close to you near Lansing. And second, with her son a detective, they could use him to do a lot of research on me. Real detective work."

"LIKE WHAT KIND OF DETECTIVE WORK?"

"You know, background checks. Find out where I live. Bank accounts. All the stuff you probably used to track me down."

"YOU KNOW THERE ARE OTHER WAYS OF GETTING INFORMATION WITHOUT BEING A DETECTIVE."

"Like what?"

"GOOGLE."

"Yes. But, I'm sure there are other resources that surpass Google that the detectives use."

"YOU'RE RIGHT. I GOTTA GIVE YOU FLYING COLORS FOR THIS ONE. IT ALL MAKES SENSE. CASE CLOSED. YOU GOT ME."

"You serious?"

"YEP."

"I knew it. Are you Skip?"

"I DON'T KNOW. WHICH ONE DO YOU THINK I AM?"

"I think a guy would have to be the one to do all of this."

"THAT'S A BIT CHAUVINIST. WHY CAN'T A WOMAN BE CONDUCIVE TO PLANNING ALL OF THIS? IF THEY KNEW WHAT YOU'D DONE TO ME, THERE'S A LOT OF WOMEN THAT WOULD BE GLAD TO FRY YOUR ASS AND FLIP YOU SEVERAL HUNDRED FEET IN THE AIR WITH A NICE LITTLE EXPLOSION."

"I'm sorry. Are you Lynn?"

"I COULD BE."

"Are you?"

"YOU KNOW, YOU HAVEN'T TOTALLY EXHAUSTED EVERYONE."

"I don't need to. It's you, either Lynn or Skip. I don't need to go any further."

"YOU THINK SO?"

"You said so."

"WHICH AM I? LYNN OR SKIP? AND DON'T FORGET, YOU HAVEN'T EXPLORED JOHN. REMEMBER? JOHN AND...WHAT WAS HER NAME? I THINK IT STARTED WITH A D."

Herb responded. "Danielle."

"YES. THAT'S IT. YOU HAVEN'T STUDIED THEM."

"I don't need to. You already admitted you're either Skip or Lynn."

"SURE I DID. BUT, DO YOU REALLY BELIEVE ME?"

Herb sat down. His breath went out of his lungs like air out of a balloon. He felt deflated.

"You're just playing me, aren't you?"

Laughter came out of the speaker. Devious laughter. Mean spirited and contrived laughter. With intentions to hurt and deceive.

Herb barked at the TV. "You're not Skip and Lynn. Huh?"

"YOU'RE NOT DONE EXHAUSTING ALL THE POSSIBILITIES. CONTINUE."

"What are you? OCD?"

"I SAID, CONTINUE. IF I SAY, CONTINUE, YOU CONTINUE."

"What if I don't?"

CHAPTER 64

Herb braced himself. He had to stand up to this menace. This monster. He had nothing to lose. He waited for the response.

The voice rumbled out from the TV. "YOU MUST. THE GAME CAN'T STOP. IT MUST BE PLAYED ALL THE WAY."

Herb made mental note of this. The voice had a mental pattern that mandated finishing things through. All the way. No matter what.

"All right. You want me to finish through? We'll finish through. The last one is John."

"WHAT?"

"I said John."

"YOU MEAN JOHN AND DANIELLE? EVERYONE CAME IN PAIRS. REMEMBER? ARE YOU INSULTING THE FEMININE CAPACITY AGAIN? YOU DON'T THINK DANIELLE COULD HAVE THE MENTAL APTITUDE TO PLAN AND EXECUTE A SCHEME LIKE THIS?"

"What's with defending the feminine regime?"

"JUST MAKING SURE ALL OPTIONS ARE BEING CONSIDERED."

"Okay. Now that the womanly concerns have been met, can we move on?"

"IT'S YOUR SHOW."

Herb shook his head in frustration. "Okay, we have John and Danielle. If what they told us is true, they're highly educated. Have the financial backup to make this all happen. And were extremely standoffish with the group on the trip. Avoiding any chance they might expose themselves with too much information."

"MAYBE THEY DIDN'T WANT TO SOCIALIZE WITH ALL THE OTHER UPPITIES ON THIS TRIP. EVER THINK OF THAT?"

Herb rubbed his chin in thought. "Could be."

"LET ME ASK YOU THIS? WHAT'S YOUR MAIN REASON FOR PUTTING THEM ON YOUR LITTLE LIST?"

Herb thought about it for a moment.

"The fact they didn't really engage with anyone on the trip. I believe they were there to observe me."

"GEEZ...JUST BECAUSE SOMEONE DOESN'T HAVE THE SAME SOCIAL APPETITE AS YOU DOESN'T MEAN THEY'RE SOMEONE WHO HAS A SCORE TO SETTLE. I'M DISAPPOINTED IN YOU, HERB."

"Well, we've gone through every person on the trip. You tell me, who the hell are you?"

"I'M NOW YOUR FRIEND FOR LIFE. I'M THE DEMON IN YOUR EVERY THOUGHT. I'M THE MONSTER ON YOUR SHOULDER. I'M THE FEAR IN YOUR GUT WHEN YOU AWAKE. EVERY DAY. I'LL BE THE ANXIETY THAT GNAWS AT YOU AS YOU TRY TO SLEEP AT NIGHT. I'LL REPRESENT THE REMORSE YOU *SHOULD* HAVE FOR EVEN THINKING OF INSULTING THE SCORES OF PEOPLE YOU BELITTLED."

The enjoyment of the delivery could be heard in every syllable.

"YOU CAN'T ESCAPE ME. I'M THE REGRET YOU CAN'T OUTRUN. THAT'S WHO I AM! THE BIGGER QUESTION IS, WILL THIS INNER TORTURE END IN JUST A FEW HOURS? OR WILL I LET YOU LIVE WITH ME INSIDE YOUR HEAD FOR YEARS AND YEARS?"

Herb didn't say a thing. He sat down in his chair–staring at the TV. The bigger question wreaking havoc inside his head.

He looked at his watch. 2:13pm.

CHAPTER 65

He had to escape. If he couldn't escape physically, he had to escape mentally.

His heart took him back to Katie. Back to four weeks since their first date. He'd met Katie's son. Won him over. Had sex with Katie. The best sex he'd ever had. Maybe being in love made the difference. Was he really saying that? Being in love?

The fifth week–the trouble started.

"When will I meet your mother?" Katie asked. "She sounds like a doll."

"She's great. And she'll love you."

"When do I get to meet her?"

"She's going through physical therapy right now. Had a fall in the bathroom. As soon as she's done, we'll get together."

"When will that be?"

"She's got about four more weeks to go."

A skeptical "Okay," came out of her mouth.

Four weeks came and went. Another week followed.

Katie and Herb strolled through Central Park. It was their thing. Holding hands. "When do I get to meet your mother?"

Herb licked his lips with discomfort. "She's had a setback."

Katie looked concerned. "Oh no."

"The therapy's progressing, but not fast enough."

"When will she be done?"

"Should be a couple more weeks." Herb let go of her hand and pulled a couple of nuts out of his pocket and stooped down to feed the squirrel that approached them. "Here boy." He clicked his tongue.

"You just don't want to introduce me? Do you?"

"No. No. No. That's not it at all. She just needs a little more time. We'll see her."

"Therapy is only for a couple of hours. Why can't we take her to dinner?"

After his last nut went to the squirrel Herb stood up, he paused before he answered. "She's tired after all they put her through."

"Maybe we could bring her a bowl of soup. It would keep her from having to cook."

"I've already offered. She just isn't in the mood for company."

"Even from her son's new girlfriend?" She looked at Herb, penetrating his eyes.

He paused before he answered. "Even from her son's new girlfriend."

She stared into his gaze. Daring his response. Challenging his basic integrity. She bit the side of her lip.

"You don't want to introduce me, do you?"

"No. That's not it at all."

She turned and walked away.

"Katie. Stop."

He ran alongside her. "I swear. You'll meet her. It's just not the right time."

She didn't look at him. Kept walking at a brisk pace. Didn't say a word.

"Look, when it's right you'll meet her."

"Are you ashamed of me?"

"No."

"Is it because I have a son?"

"No."

"Am I not up to your mother's standards? Not sophisticated enough?"

"No! That's not it at all."

She stopped. Her face inches from his face. "Then what is it?"

He hesitated. His head bowed to the ground. He looked up at her. "It's just not the right time."

"You're stringing me along." She started walking again.

"No. I'm not."

"I can feel it in my bones."

"Katie."

"My instincts tell me you're full of shit."

"Katie, when the time is..."

"Right now, I have to go." She picked up her pace and started jogging.

Herb stopped. And watched her run.

Away.

Chapter 66

The stress from that day snapped him back to his current situation. One stress to another. Herb attempted to suck in a big gulp of oxygen. But his passageways wouldn't let air flow down his throat. It felt like he couldn't get enough air. Like he was choking. Struggling to catch another breath. Like all his air-passageways were squeezing shut.

Anxiety traveled through every pore on his skin. He ran his fingers through his hair. He rubbed his arm up and down. Over and over. He pulled his shirt down, straightening it out. Several times.

He looked around the room. His home. His castle. Now it felt like prison. Trapped in a cage. He wanted nothing more than to get out. How did this all happen? He crouched down onto the floor and curled up like a ball. The fetal position the only one that delivered comfort.

Reese walked up and licked him in the face. Showering him with love. Herb reached out and pulled her in close, snuggling her, feeling the warmth and softness of her touch. Reese forever the recipient of his unconditional love.

"Reese, how'd we ever get to this place?"

She licked him back on the cheek, as if she acknowledged the question as a good one. Hell, she had an explosive collar around her neck. She couldn't agree more.

"What if I'd have been nice? Droves of people wanted me to be their agent. What a privilege. Me. They wanted me, Herb Keeler to be their agent." He stroked Reese's head with his fingers, soothing the both of them. "And what did I do with that privilege? I abused it. I had to be nasty. I kicked them down. I made them feel less than worthy. As if I was the only one that could feel superior."

A look of disgust started to take over his face.

"Why'd I do that? What would compel a person to take someone who has the courage to step into a new arena like a newborn baby taking his first steps and knock the living shit out of them? Why? What's wrong with me?"

Reese looked at him with admiration. Oblivious to his inner turmoil.

A crackle wafted out from the TV. "YOU'RE ASKING GOOD QUESTIONS."

"Shut up!"

"HERB."

"You've been listening to me?" Herb sat up, still stationed on the floor. The air starting to flow back in his lungs.

"YES. I TOO WONDER WHAT MAKES SOMEONE SO MEAN TO OTHER PEOPLE. I UNDERSTAND MY OWN MOTIVES FOR BEING NASTY TO YOU. REVENGE. BUT, WHAT ABOUT YOU?"

He rubbed Reese's belly. Bit his lower lip and said, "I'm not sure."

A few moments went by. In a slow easy tone the voice asked, "WHAT WERE YOU LIKE IN COLLEGE?"

"What was I like in college? I wasn't a great student. I was a decent student. I held a 3.0 grade point. I studied..."

The voice interrupted. "I DON'T GIVE A DAMN ABOUT YOUR ACADEMICS. DID YOU HAVE A GIRLFRIEND? DID YOU USE WOMEN FOR YOUR OWN NEEDS AND DISCARD THEM? WERE YOU MEAN IN COLLEGE?"

"Well, I..."

"BE HONEST."

"I, ah, I...dated lots of girls."

"EXACTLY WHAT I THOUGHT. A HEARTBREAKER. HUH?"

Herb hesitated.

"YOU PROBABLY ENJOYED STRINGING THEM ALONG. EVENTUALLY, THEY'D REALIZE YOU HAD ANOTHER GIRL OR TWO ON THE SIDE. HUH?"

He didn't respond. He couldn't.

"THEN WHEN THEY CONFRONTED YOU, YOU SHOWED YOU DIDN'T CARE. EVEN ENJOYED THE HURT IN THEIR EYES. DIDN'T YOU?"

He stood silent.

"I'M GOOD. HUH? IF THERE'S ONE THING I KNOW. IT'S HUMAN NATURE."

He said nothing.

"WHAT ABOUT FRIENDS IN COLLEGE?"

"Sure. I had friends. We'd go to the bars. Study a bit."

"ARE YOU STILL IN TOUCH WITH THOSE FRIENDS?"

"What are you, a psychologist?"

"JUST TRYING TO FLUSH OUT SOME OF THE OBVIOUS ABOUT YOU."

"I don't know what staying in touch with college buddies has to do with anything."

"PEOPLE LIKE YOU DON'T HAVE FRIENDS. THEY LOOK AT PEOPLE AS VEHICLES TO GET WHAT THEY WANT. THEY DON'T TREASURE THE CLOSENESS OR SHARING OF EACH OTHER'S LIVES."

Herb stopped stroking Reese's belly. He sat there. Thunderstruck. No one had ever spoke about him in such an accurate manner. The voice was spot-on.

Stillness filled the air.

"WHAT'S THE MATTER? YOU'RE AT A LOSS FOR WORDS?"

"No. You've said enough. You're right. I did womanize. I hurt many girls. I objectified them. They were just things to me. Not people. Not friends. They were there for my amusement."

"OKAY. WE'VE ESTABLISHED THAT. YOU WERE A SHITHEAD. WHAT ABOUT YOUR FRIENDSHIPS?"

A lump rose in his throat. Admitting the truth wasn't easy.

"You're right there, too. I didn't nurture my friendships and maintain them. We were friends during that time during school and then we all went our separate ways."

"DON'T YOU HAVE ANY FRIENDS? THERE HAS TO BE SOMEBODY."

He licked his lips. Took in a deep breath, "I have Reese. And I have Joe. Joe Mathews. My editor friend. Er, actually, *you* have Joe." A short pause hung in the air. "Is he okay?"

"YES. HE IS OKAY. YOUR DOG AND YOUR EDITOR. THOSE ARE YOUR TWO FRIENDS? YOUR DOG CAN'T DISAGREE WITH YOU AND TELL YOU YOUR SHORTCOMINGS. TELL YOU YOU'RE MEAN. TELL YOU YOU'RE NOT NICE. AND YOUR EDITOR, YOU PAY HIS BILLS. YOU SUPPORT HIM FINANCIALLY. HE RELIES ON YOU. SO HE ACTS LIKE HE'S YOUR FRIEND. YOU'RE HIS MEAL TICKET. WHAT A GREAT BASE FOR A FRIENDSHIP. HE PROBABLY DOES WHATEVER YOU ASK OF HIM. HUH? ALWAYS CATERING TO YOU. RATHER THAN YOU ASKING WHAT HE WANTS TO DO OR WHEN HE'D LIKE TO GET TOGETHER, I BET YOU DICTATE EVERYTHING IN THE WHOLE RELATIONSHIP. AND HE KISSES RIGHT UP TO YOU, HUH?"

Herb sat there in thought. Everything the TV said resonated with him. It sank in deep to the bone. If he'd been any more accurate the voice could be accused of being Herb. This voice, this person on the other end of the TV knew human nature. Knew it scary.

"HERB. ARE YOU STILL WITH ME? I DON'T HEAR ANYTHING FROM YOU."

"There's not much to say. You're right."

"THE FRIENDSHIPS YOU HAVE REALLY DON'T HAVE MUCH TO STAND ON, DO THEY?"

Herb's spirit and body returned to the deflated balloon status. He didn't have much to be proud of. His breath slowed. His posture sank. He buried his head down into his hands.

And he cried.

Here this man, this gargantuan of a literary giant, who stood on top of the world in his chosen field. He, who held the envy of his peers. This icon who every writer wanted him to represent them. It took years and years to build up to this stature. And now, here he was, broken, lonely and begging for his life because of the way he treated people.

Herb cried. And cried. His body shook. His face wrenched in red. He had no one to turn to. No one to comfort his loneliness. All of his accolades couldn't console him. Nothing could tell him, *you're okay Herb. It's going to be better tomorrow. Hang in there. You'll see.*

There was no one. And that was the worst part.

As he hugged Reese, his mind drifted. Maybe he did have someone. Maybe he really wasn't such a bad person. Maybe he really did care. He just hadn't allowed himself to do that. Care for someone. He soothed Reese's soft chin, and whispered in her ear, "Maybe I have Katie."

The loud voice bellowed from the TV. "HERB. I HAVE A QUESTION FOR YOU. A VERY IMPORTANT QUESTION."

CHAPTER 67

"HERB. HAVE YOU EVER KILLED ANYBODY?'

This stopped Herb cold in his tracks. He quit crying. His head shot straight up. And a look of puzzlement covered his face. "Have I ever killed anyone?"

"IT'S A VALID QUESTION. YOU'VE HURT SCORES OF PEOPLE RIGHT TO THE INNER CORE OF THEIR BASIC EXISTENCE."

"Not true. I hurt many. Yes, by chastising their writing. I'm ashamed to admit I belittled them. But, I haven't hurt them to their inner core."

The volume blasted out from the TV. "YOU DID WHEN IT CAME TO MY MOTHER! YOU FUCK!"

Herb took it in. He breathed hard. The echo from the TV bounced around in his brain. Like a pinball darting around ricocheting off of his skull. Over and over.

He cried again. "I'm sorry. I'm truly sorry. I don't understand why I did what I did."

"WELL THEN, ANSWER MY QUESTION. DID YOU EVER KILL ANYONE?"

"No. Of course not."

"WRONG ANSWER. YOU DID KILL SOMEONE. YOU KILLED MY MOTHER."

"I'm sorry, but I didn't kill your mother."

"YOU DID. YOU LED HER DOWN THAT DARK PATH THAT STEERED HER TO HER DEATH."

"I would never want to kill her. You've got to believe me. I'm sorry for your mother."

He cried and sobbed. Grasping hard to catch his breath. He turned to the TV, and cleared his flem-filled throat. He took a breath. A breath to gain his courage, and asked, "Have *you* ever killed anyone?"

Calmness hung in the air. Like a thick fog blocking any noise from the TV.

"I said. Have. You. Ever. Killed. Anyone?"

Stillness filled the air. Then a subtle reply trickled out. "NO."

Herb looked at the TV. The answer giving him an element of hope. If his captor never killed anyone before, then maybe he wouldn't kill Herb. Maybe. This was good.

"Had you ever thought of killing anyone before?"

"YES. LOTS OF TIMES. BUT, YOU'RE THE FIRST I'VE CARRIED THROUGH THIS FAR."

Herb scratched his head. "Lots of times?"

"YES. WHEN DIFFERENT MEN CAME INTO MY MOTHER'S HOUSE. WHEN I HEARD THEM WITH HER, IT DROVE ME MAD."

Herb felt a lump of empathy swell from within his heart. "Was it a few, or lots of men?"

He could hear the voice let out a heavy sigh. "A LOT. TOO MANY. I FELT ANGER TOWARDS THEM ALL."

"Was it *just* anger? Or, did you want to kill them?"

A moment of thought took place and then, "BOTH. I WAS ANGRY. *AND* I WANTED TO KILL THEM."

"Like physically end their lives?"

"YES."

Herb responded. "Wow!"

"YES. I EVEN FANTASIZED HOW I'D DO IT."

"No."

"I THOUGHT IF I LINED THREE OF THEIR HEADS UP NEXT TO EACH OTHER I COULD SHOOT THEM ALL WITH ONE BULLET."

"Did you have other fantasies about killing them?"

"OH YEAH. I THOUGHT ABOUT SHOOTING THEM WITH ARROWS. RUNNING MY CAR INTO THEM AT SIXTY MILES AN HOUR. MY MIND WENT NUTS HEARING THEM WITH MY MOTHER."

"I'm sorry you had to hear all of that. It had to be the worst."

"THE ONES THAT DESERVED IT THE MOST SLAPPED HER AROUND. SOME EVEN PUNCHED HER. IF I'D HAVE HAD A GUN AT THE TIME I WOULD'VE KILLED AT LEAST THREE OF THEM. AND I WOULD HAVE EMPTIED THE WHOLE ROUND ON THEM."

"Voice? I wish I knew your name."

"NOT GOING TO HAPPEN."

"That's okay. I understand what you went through."

The voice cleared its throat. "YOU DO?"

Herb drew in a large breath and began. "Yes. My father. He was a son-of-a-bitch."

The voice slowed his rhythm down. Easy, conversational. "TELL ME MORE."

Herb swallowed the big lump in his throat. "First, I have to say, I've never told anyone what I'm about to tell you."

"GO ON."

It was evident it took courage for what he was about to say. "As a child, I was a good student. Actually, I was a real good student. But, when I brought home the occasional A minus or a B plus, there was hell to pay."

"WHAT DO YOU MEAN, *HELL TO PAY?*"

"It was various things. Punishments. Sometimes I'd be grounded for weeks at a time. Secluded in my room, only to come out for meals, bathroom, and to go to school. No friends. No playtime."

"BASTARD."

"I remember one time I brought home my report card to show to my mom and dad. All A's and an A minus. One A minus. I was proud. I came into the kitchen. My mother hovering over the stove. My father reading the paper with his dinner in front of him. And I had the biggest grin of pride on my face and I shoved the report card right in front of his newspaper, expecting a response of pride and adulation from him. He reviewed it slowly, turned it over, and rearing his head up, roared with the ferocity of a lion, 'You're not good enough! What's wrong with you? A minus? I expect perfect.' He stood up quickly, the chair flying out from beneath his bottom and he grabbed me by the neck and pulled me in closer, and slapped me back and forth with both hands, using the palms of his hands, as if I were a punching bag. Over and over. Sickens me to this day. I pleaded with him. 'I'm sorry, Dad. It won't happen again.' And he continued to yell at me, 'You're not good enough! You're not good enough!'"

"TRUE BASTARD."

"And I sank to the floor, crying, sobbing to him, 'I'm sorry. I'm sorry, Dad.' And then he just stood over top of me like a prize fighter over his knockout opponent."

"WHAT ABOUT YOUR MOTHER?"

"She tried to stop him, but she couldn't. He was too strong. Too big. He slapped her. Punched her. Eventually, they divorced. The worst part, somehow he had an in with the judge and was granted visitation where I could stay with him every other weekend. Lucky me, eh?"

"THAT'S BAD."

"No, it was an appalling situation. Like being thrown to the school bully every other weekend. Only the bully is ten times bigger and a hundred times meaner. And the bully loves to beat up on you, only he's your dad."

"HOW COULD THAT BE ALLOWED?"

"Fucked up state of affairs. He'd make me play checkers with him. He always won. He'd belittle me verbally. Tell me how much of a loser I was. I'd never amount to anything. My mother doesn't love me. Blah, blah, blah. Then he'd lock me in this closet for three hours at a time. No light. No food. No water. And he'd stand outside the door yelling insults into my brain. I had to listen to this shit, over and over again. Crying my brains out. Begging him to stop."

"HE WAS A BAD DUDE."

"I remember weekends where he made me watch porn with him."

"SICKO."

"Messed up."

"HOW OLD WERE YOU?"

"This happened from the time I was..." Herb looked up towards the ceiling doing some figuring in his head. "Let's see I was seven when it started and it was up until the time I could drive. So, I was sixteen when I stopped visiting the son-of-a-bitch."

"WAIT A MINUTE. I THOUGHT YOU SAID HE LEFT YOU WHEN YOU WERE TWELVE."

"I'm sorry. I lied."

"WHY?"

"I don't know. This was a bad chapter in my life. I never admitted to anyone it really happened. You're the first."

"YOU'RE TELLING ME HE MADE YOU WATCH PORN WITH HIM FOR NINE YEARS AND YOU WERE A KID?"

"Yes."

"DID YOU TELL YOUR MOTHER?"

"No way. He said he'd beat me with boxing gloves on to hide the body shots. Just so nobody could see the marks. And he knew I had a penchant for motorcycles. He threatened to take my motorcycle away if I told anyone. Anyone! Those two threats were enough for a young kid to comply. Fear drives you. I was petrified. Tired of being beaten. You know?"

"I DO."

"You wonder why I don't have close friends. I never wanted to have anyone over my house with all of this shit going on. This stuff lingers in your head. Can't get rid of it. There's this anger with the world rumbling inside and I can't make it go away."

"THIS IS A WEIRD QUESTION, BUT I HAVE TO ASK."

CHAPTER 68

Herb pondered this line of questioning. He was engaging this nutcase. That was good. Maybe he could find a point of leverage. Something that could change the mind of this voice. To allow him to live.

"IF YOU COULD KILL YOUR DAD, HOW WOULD YOU DO IT?"

"Look, I'm not planning on killing my Dad."

"I THOUGHT YOU HAD ALL THIS INNER ANGER."

"Killing him for it isn't going to make it go away."

"HOW DO YOU KNOW? MAYBE IT WOULD. EVEN THE SCORE. YOU KNOW?"

"No."

"WOULD YOU WANT TO DROWN HIM?"

"No."

"OR WHAT ABOUT FIRE? THAT WOULD BE SPECIAL. BURN HIS HORNY LITTLE ASS."

"No. I don't want to do this."

"WHAT ABOUT FREEZING HIM TO DEATH?"

Herb started pacing. "Knock it off."

"WOULDN'T IT BE GREAT TO LOCK HIM IN A BIG FREEZER AND WATCH THE SON-OF-A-BITCH FREEZE? SEE HIM BEGGING YOU TO LET HIM OUT. BEGGING *YOU*, HERB. YOU WOULD BE IN CONTROL. OVER HIM. YOU TELLING ME YOU WOULDN'T WANT TO HAVE CONTROL OVER HIM?"

"Stop! I don't want to talk like this anymore!"

"LET ME ASK YOU THIS. IF I COULD BRING HIM TO YOU, WHAT WOULD YOU LIKE TO SAY OR DO TO HIM?"

Herb stroked his chin with his forefinger and thumb. His gaze lost in thought. A sigh of reflection left his abdomen. "Hmm...What would I say or do to him? That's a good question."

"THIS WOULD BE YOUR CHANCE TO EVEN THE SCORE WITH HIM. TO FIGHT BACK AGAINST THE DEMONS HE PLACED IN YOUR SOUL."

The words he heard swirled inside of Herb's mind. *Even the score. Fight the demons in my soul. Even the score. Fight the demons.*

Herb awoke from his spell. "What're we even discussing this for? You can't bring my Dad here."

Loud laughter roared from the TV. "HERB. HERB. HERB. YOU HAVE NO IDEA WHO IS MESSING WITH YOU."

Herb pondered the thought. *What would he do if his father were in front of him? Over thirty years had gone by since he'd seen him. He tried to block out his voice. Erase what he looked like. The sound of him screaming at him outside the closet haunted Herb every day. Would pounding on his face cure Herb of these visions? Would his voice go away?*

Would inner-peace follow?

CHAPTER 69

Thoughts of inner peace took Herb back to the library. With his mother. Reading her mysteries. Scanning the back covers to discover a new book. Whenever she tripped over something good, she'd run over to Herb to share. "Look at this one. Two young boys, witnesses to a murder. The bad guys are after them, and the police don't believe them. You want to read it first?"

This played out countless times.

The best part, sitting in the farthest corner of the library in a table hidden by tall bookshelves. They provided a private cove. The coziness back there, just the two of them, made him feel so special. Like no one else in the world existed.

During the winter months after school, she'd buy them a hot cocoa on the way and hunker down and read for an hour before coming home for homework. In the summer, they'd sneak in an occasional ice cream cone or a cold lemonade. Every visit felt like a special treat.

Sometimes, they'd walk behind the library along the small pond and throw rocks in the water. "What do you want to be when you grow up?" She'd ask.

"I want to be rich."

"And what do you want to do to get rich?"

"I don't know. What can I do to make lots of money?"

"You could be a writer. And make up your own stories."

"Can it make me rich?"

"Maybe."

"Then I want to be a writer."

He'd throw a few more rocks in the water and they'd saunter home. This routine carried on for years. To think back made Herb feel safe. Comfort.

And love.

A far cry from where he was now.

CHAPTER 70

Herb stirred in his seat. He rubbed his fingers together with his thumbs. On both hands. He swallowed hard. Inner peace is what he needed. He had to question the wacko. To hold court. Find out what this piece of shit was about. And to maintain a dialogue that might lead to his escape. That was most important.

A strong crash boomed from the other side of the steel curtains. The sounds of glass shattering vaguely could be heard. A protrusion pushed its way inward near the top half of the curtain. Looked like some type of branch or a board had lodged itself through the window anchoring itself against the curtain. The curtain still holding off the water and the wind. But, the sound still raging. By all accounts, the storm appeared to be gaining strength.

Herb shook his head back to the present and gathered his thoughts. Picked up a sheet of paper. Jotted a few notes. Ran his fingers through his hair. Smacked himself in the face, and mumbled to himself, "Let's go."

He looked up into the air and let 'er fly. "Since I don't know your name, I'm going to get right to the question. What's your biggest reason for holding me captive with eminent destruction your end goal?"

"YOU ALREADY KNOW THE MAIN REASON. REVENGE. REVENGE FOR THE WAY YOU TREATED MY MOTHER. DID YOU HAVE TO ASK?"

Herb shuffled in his seat again. Licked his lips. "I'm sorry. I wanted to warm up the interview. Get some basic questions laid out."

"WARM ME UP? GEEZ, WHAT DO YOU THINK THIS IS, ROLLING STONE MAGAZINE?"

"Sorry. Work with me. I'm in a precarious situation. A bit nerve racking. As you can imagine."

"GO ON."

"Okay. We know revenge. What other reasons do you have a subject locked in his house, ready to blow his ass sky high?"

"FOR FUN!"

"I beg your pardon?"

"YEAH. FUN. BY THE TONE OF YOUR VOICE, I LOVE HEARING YOU SQUIRM. MUST BE SHITTING BRICKS. HUH? THIS IS GREAT."

Trying to sound professional and keep his objectivity, keep emotion out of it, as if he were referring to a third party rather than himself, Herb continued. "Okay, we have revenge. We have fun. What other reasons do you have for breaking the law and kidnapping me?"

"MONEY. YOU WIRED FOUR HUNDRED AND FIFTY THOUSAND DOLLARS INTO MY BANK ACCOUNT. YOU WIRED A MILLION INTO THE STUDENT'S FAMILY'S ACCOUNT. MONEY FOR ME IS ONE REASON, BUT THERE'S A SENSE OF JUSTICE PLAYING OUT WITH YOU SENDING THE MONEY TO THE FAMILY."

Herb winced. This person wanted revenge, but there was also an element of righteousness. Maybe he could appeal to the conscience of this individual. Maybe.

"You feel you're helping society?"

"NO. I'M HELPING THE FAMILY OF THE PERSON YOU WRONGED. AND I'M BALANCING THE SCALES OF JUSTICE."

Herb bowed his head. "I understand. I've already conceded. What I did to that young man was wrong. I don't understand why I did what I did."

"THE MONEY FOR THE FAMILY WAS TWOFOLD. TO MAKE YOU PAY AND TO COMPENSATE THEM FOR THEIR LOSS."

"I understand. That was money well placed. I know this sounds weird, but thank you for making me pay. I feel the family is owed and it's the least I can do."

"YOU'RE DAMN RIGHT."

"Okay. Money. Revenge. What other reasons made you plan this long ordeal to kidnap me?"

"YOU FORGOT FUN."

"Okay. Fun. What else?"

"IT'S LIKE THIS. I CONSIDER YOU AN ENEMY. YOU WRONGED MY MOTHER. THEREFORE CONSEQUENCES MUST BE FACED."

"You got me there. I'm definitely facing consequences."

"ENEMIES BECOME ENEMIES BECAUSE OF THEIR BEHAVIOR. THE BEHAVIOR MUST BE CORRECTED IN ORDER FOR THE ENEMY TO PAY RESPECT. UNDERSTAND?"

"Yes. I do. I respect you. You have my utmost attention. Is there anything else that motivated you to carry this plot out?"

"YES. POWER!"

"Power?"

"YES. THE POWER OVER YOU. THE POWER TO CONTROL YOUR ENTIRE ENVIRONMENT. THE POWER TO CONTROL YOUR FINANCIAL POSITION. THE POWER TO MANIPULATE YOUR EMOTIONAL CONDITION. AND THE POWER TO BREAK YOU. AND ULTIMATELY, THE POWER TO DECIDE IF I WANT TO LET YOU LIVE OR NOT."

"I see. You like the power."

"HOW OBSERVANT. YOU HERB KEELER, THE HIGHLY REGARDED LITERARY AGENT ARE UNDER MY POWER. AND YOU CAN'T DO A THING ABOUT IT. THIS FEELS GOOD."

Herb rubbed the back of his left hand with his right, letting the words roll through the air waves floating in the room.

"I imagine we covered it all."

"WHAT?"

"We discussed all the reasons you locked me in my house?"

Laughter rippled from the TV. "NO. THERE'S ONE MORE."

Herb waited. No response. "Okay, you're going to make me ask?"

"OF COURSE."

"Okay. I'll bite. What other reason did you do all of this?"

"SEX."

CHAPTER 71

Herb's brows furrowed. He looked around the room. He ran his hands through his hair. He sniffed for a burst of air.

"What?"

More laughter flew from the TV. Herb's eyes darted around, his head turning in deep thought. His mind searching for understanding.

"What?"

"THAT'S RIGHT. SEX."

Herb bit his lower lip. "Explain." This didn't contain logic.

"NOPE. YOU'RE GOING TO HAVE TO CHEW ON THAT ONE."

"What does sex have to do with anything?"

"YOU WILL SEE."

None of this made sense. Herb's heart raced. Fear ran through his body like poison through a syringe.

"How will I see?"

"YOU'LL SEE."

"When will I see?"

"IN DUE TIME."

Herb's throat felt dry. He walked over to his sink and poured himself a glass of water. The wetness renewed his sense of now. Of being in the present.

"I need more than that. When is *due time*?"

"IT WILL MAKE SENSE WHEN I WANT IT TO MAKE SENSE."

This latest factor gave Herb momentous concern. Things were getting weirder. He needed to learn more about this person's psyche. Find one weak point. One thing he could play on that might lead to release. He needed something. Something to arm himself with. Questions. Yes. Questions. He needed more questions.

"Who inspired you the most in your lifetime? Either as a child or as an adult?"

Silence glided into Herb's conscience. The stillness provided him a sense of peace. No verbal attacks. But, he knew he had to stay one step ahead of this force. What would be the next question? How could he expose an opening into this mind? No time for reveling in inner peace.

And then, a question was asked of Herb. "WHO INSPIRED YOU?"

Herb caught himself off guard. He didn't expect a question.

"YOU THERE? WHO INSPIRED YOU TO BE THE PERSON THAT YOU ARE?"

Herb thought about it. It didn't take long to answer. One word. One name. It hit him immediately.

"Hitler."

Surprise emitted from the mechanical voice. "HITLER?"

This was the most inspirational person in Herb's life? The man responsible for masterminding the murder of millions of Jews? Could things get much worse?

With certainty in his voice, Herb responded, "Yes. Hitler was the most inspirational person in my life."

"REALLY? BUT, HE KILLED MILLIONS."

"I know. But, he wanted to make the human race stronger."

"BUT, HE MURDERED PEOPLE. LOTS OF PEOPLE."

"But, he believed he was making the human race stronger. Don't you get it?"

"NO. BOTTOM LINE, HE MURDERED MILLIONS OF PEOPLE. THAT'S NOT RIGHT!" The voice's anger shot through the TV.

"I don't condone his mass murdering. That was wrong. It's that he believed he was making the human race stronger."

The voice shouted out from the TV. "AND HOW DO YOU RELATE? HOW DO YOU GET INSPIRED BY SOME LUNATIC LIKE HITLER?"

"Because, in my world, I wanted to make the literary world stronger."

"MAKE THE LITERARY WORLD STRONGER? UNBELIEVABLE! YOU JUSTIFY YOUR RIDICULING OF BUDDING WRITERS AS YOUR WAY OF MAKING THE WRITING WORLD STRONGER?"

"Exactly."

"ABUSING THEM DOESN'T MAKE THE WRITING INDUSTRY STRONGER."

"How do you know?"

"COMMON SENSE."

"Bullshit. You don't know how many people went back and became better writers after receiving my criticism. Do you?"

"WELL, I, UH..."

"You don't. The strong ones don't give up just because someone belittled them. They persevere. They move on. Those are the ones I want. The strong ones. They come back."

"IT'S STILL NOT RIGHT. IT'S NOT RIGHT."

Herb fell back into his chair. Exasperated. Proud of his honesty. But, he still didn't find out who inspired his wacko.

CHAPTER 72

He felt this same primal frustration when he tried to get Katie back. Deep want. And a desperate desire to change the situation. Despite hopelessness pervading.

After Katie bolted from Central Park, Herb called her cell. No answer. He tried again before he went to bed. No pick up. Tomorrow he'd try. He'd talk to her then. Regain her confidence. Make her see she just needed a little more time. It would be all right.

The next day came. He left a voice mail. "Katie, this is Herb. Please call me. I know I upset you. It's not you. It's not your son. You have to believe me. Please call me."

No response.

He called again at the end of the day.

And the next day. And the day after that. And, the day after that. Before he knew it, a week had passed.

Herb's heart ached. For the first time in his life, he cared for someone. Respected someone. Looked at her as an equal. Wanted her opinions. Valued her feelings. And woke up every morning eager to see her.

And he may have already blown it.

CHAPTER 73

Herb leaned his head back in his chair. The sweat dripping down his temples. His bare feet warmed by the heated floor. The emotional toll of this questioning-game wearing him thin. Add to that, it was obvious his heated floors had been turned up. Another hand played by the force.

And if that wasn't enough, a burgeoning hurricane assaulting his house. Would the old farmhouse even be able to stand up to hurricane winds? How long could this all go on? And how would it end? The manipulation, the questioning, the toying with his environment, and the mental torture it all evoked. He found it maddening.

He sauntered over to the sink and refilled his water glass. He yelled out towards the TV. "I see you turned up my floors again. Go ahead. I don't care anymore! You hear me? I don't care. Set your snakes loose on me. Rearrange my refrigerator. Do whatever. I don't care! Blow me to smithereens. I don't care anymore!"

Veins popped out of his neck. He walked over to his thermometer for the floors and pressed the down button, poking it hard with his finger. Over and over. No effect on the gauge. It held at ninety-two degrees. The light blinking with each poke of the finger. He turned towards the TV and yelled, "Blow this whole fucking house up into the clouds. Right now!"

He broke into a laugh. A psychotic laugh. Madness taking over his face.

The voice evoked a chuckle from the TV. "HERB, I SEE THIS SITUATION IS TAKING YOU TO A NEW PLATEAU. ANOTHER PSYCHOLOGICAL DIMENSION."

Herb laughed. "You have no idea. I don't even know who I am."

"IT CAUSES ME TO WONDER. TO WANT TO ASK *YOU* A QUESTION."

Herb stared at the TV. A mean stare. Daring the voice.

"You're there. You've done anything you wanted to me. You've blown up my personal things. Embezzled my money. Humiliated me in front of millions of Americans in the newspaper. Blew up stuff in my face. Kidnapped my friend. Wired my dog. Put me under imminent threat of death. And now, you have the audacity to act like you want permission to ask me a question. Why start asking now? By all means...ask. What question is troubling your warped little brain so much you have to build it up–to ask?"

CHAPTER 74

Herb topped off his full glass of water, walked over to the front of his couch with a deep sense of purpose, not caring whether water spilled onto his floor and plopped himself down. He took a big swig, and with eyes wide opened, he waited. He waited for the big question. The question that demanded permission.

A garbled noise trickled out from the TV. The captor cleared its throat and in a slow rhythmic cadence, said, "WHAT'S YOUR BIGGEST REGRET?"

That was the question. The one with the build-up. A great question. Had it been asked three days earlier he'd have had a different answer. But, after this ordeal, Herb had changed. His values realigned.

He tilted his head back, his eyes following a spider walking upside down on the ceiling. The poor little guy exploring the landscape in Herb's house.

"What's my biggest regret? That's a good question."

He webbed his hands together and tucked them behind his head. His right leg crossed over his left knee...and he thought.

Feeling important ruled his actions. Believing he stood supreme to every living soul. That's what directed his course of every thought and action.

His impression of himself is what concerned him most when he addressed others. He had to make them look less than he. Had to. No one could stand taller than he. In anything. Clothes. Cars. Money. Women. His opinion of himself had to be premier to anyone else. It was beneath his ability to applaud someone else's accomplishments. That would involve conceit they were better than him at something. That couldn't happen. No way.

"I DON'T HEAR AN ANSWER. DOES THAT MEAN YOU'RE THINKING?"

"Quiet. Let me think."

"THINK AWAY."

Herb sank in his chair. He'd been belittled in front of his entire industry. From the man on top of the mountain to the joke on the news. He couldn't get any lower.

His personal things he cherished so much, his clothes, his motorcycle, his precious paintings and wooden boxes, all destroyed or ruined. He looked around at those things. They were just things. Who placed such a high value on them? It seemed silly the vast sums of money he spent. They didn't matter anymore. He felt shameful for the weight of importance he placed on them.

He looked at Reese. The electronic collar locked around her neck. The innocent look of love staring up at him. Pure unconditional love. He fell to the floor and wrapped his arms around her and pulled her in and held her tight. At that moment she was the most important thing to him.

He looked up at the picture on the wall of his friend Joe standing next to him on the golf course at Pebble Beach. One of the few people who befriended Herb. The only one who understood him. It was a one-way relationship, but it worked. Herb missed him. And he feared he would be harmed. He cried out to the TV, "Please don't hurt my friend. I beg you."

"IT SEEMS MY QUESTION IS CAUSING YOU TO EVALUATE WHAT'S REALLY IMPORTANT."

"Joe means so much to me. Please don't hurt him."

"I MUST SAY, YOU TALK LIKE A CHANGED MAN."

"All I ask is please don't hurt Joe, and please don't hurt Reese. They aren't responsible for my actions. You must let them go. Please! I beg you!"

"HERB. I'M STARTING TO LIKE YOU. YOU'RE TALKING LIKE A HUMAN BEING."

"My friends mean so much to me. If you want to kill me, so be it. But, please let them go."

"I LIKE WHAT I SEE, HERB. I LIKE YOUR THINKING. NOW, BACK TO THE QUESTION. WHAT IS YOUR BIGGEST REGRET?"

Herb swallowed. His voice shaky. His mind churned. He inhaled a deep breath. A wave of emotion enveloped him. And all at once he felt—calm. Inner peace. As if a spell had been cast upon him. "I have several biggest regrets."

"SEVERAL?"

"Yes. Several. First, I regret humiliating all those people."

"THAT'S GOOD. AND..."

"I regret talking down to them. Making them feel like losers. I should have had more empathy towards them."

The words came out slowly and effortless. As if they'd been there all along and were finally set free.

"WHAT ABOUT THE STUDENT?"

Herb bowed his head in shame. "If I could do it again, I wouldn't have been so mean. Maybe tried to give him some positive feedback to his writing. Let him know he had potential."

"WHAT ABOUT YOU TRYING TO MAKE THE WRITING WORLD A STRONGER WORLD?"

He wiped his upper lip with the back of his hand. "I believe I could have done that with encouragement rather than belittling."

"BRAVO. LIKE THE PART IN A GOOD NOVEL WHERE THE CHARACTER EVOLVES. THE READER SEES THE CHANGE. THE ELUSIVE ARC. YOU HAVE GROWN, HERB."

He looked at his hands. He turned them over. For some reason they looked different. He felt different. He felt the transformation throughout his being. He sat up straight.

"HERB. ANY OTHER REGRETS?"

"Yes. I regret not introducing Katie to my mother."

"KATIE? WHO'S KATIE?"

"She's the first person who ever cared enough about me to show care for my mother. Without ever meeting her. We just started going out six weeks ago."

"SOUNDS LIKE A QUALITY GIRL."

"You have no idea. I may have blown it."

"IF YOU CAN SHOW YOU'VE CHANGED, THERE MIGHT BE HOPE."

"I hope you're right."

"IS THERE ANYTHING ELSE YOU REGRET?" The tone in the electronic voice hinted there was something else. Something gravely overlooked.

He stopped. Thought. Something obvious. *What could he be missing?* Then, like a lightning bolt hit him, he uncoiled. He exasperated a gust. "Oh, I'm sorry. One of my biggest regrets. I wish I never would've responded the way I did to your mother. That was horrible. Mean."

"THOUGHTLESS."

"Yes. Thoughtless. I should've reached out and tried to send her help. Showed I cared."

"SOMETIMES HERB, THAT'S ALL PEOPLE NEED. TO KNOW SOMEONE CARES.

Herb meshed his hands together in the prayer formation and held them up to his mouth. The transformation sank in. The events of this spectacle impacted him.

He looked up and addressed the TV. "Those are my biggest regrets. I don't know if I'll feel this way tomorrow or in a month, but right now, I do."

Five minutes went by before the TV responded. Maybe it was ten. Maybe thirty. Herb reveled in the self-discovery. The quiet of the moment. It had been a turbulent time in his house up till now. The silence wrapped around him and he savored it.

"HERB. YOU HAVE EXCEEDED MY EXPECTATIONS. I APPLAUD YOU. I DIDN'T KNOW HOW YOU WOULD REACT TO EVERYTHING. AND WHETHER YOU WOULD'VE ACTED DIFFERENTLY OR NOT, I STILL HAVE THE SAME THING IN STORE FOR YOU. LIKE THE FINAL ACT IN A GOOD NOVEL, THERE WILL BE A TWIST. A SURPRISE. SOMETHING YOU DON'T EXPECT.

CHAPTER 75

"OKAY, IF YOU'RE STANDING, SIT DOWN. IF YOU'RE SITTING, RELAX. I WANT YOU TO FEEL AT EASE WITH THIS NEXT CHAPTER. NOTICE HOW I KEEP FOLLOWING THE LITERARY THEME?"

Herb sat down. A concerned look consumed his entire body. He looked all around him, not sure if something else within the house may erupt.

The TV came on, static covering the screen. In three seconds a strong visual of an attractive couple covered the screen. Nothing but flesh. Kissing. Grinding. Moaning. Close ups. And, oh, totally nude.

An expression of puzzlement washed across Herb's face. Why was a porn video being played for him? Of all the things he'd been subjected to since he'd been trapped in his house, this one didn't connect. What could this possibly have to do with revenge? Or with transforming someone? No sense. None at all.

He found himself aroused. After all, he was a man. He thought it peculiar, here he was held under captivity, a stressful event, and yet still stimulated by the visuals. A self-observance, like a professor studying a subject, only he was the subject.

The video played for twenty minutes. If the voice were attempting to apply revenge and paybacks to someone who'd caused harm, how would porn be used to accomplish this? His brain went into overdrive. All the people who'd wronged him–he couldn't think of one instance where he'd used porn to even a score or hurt them in some way. It just didn't add up. Herb's curiosity couldn't wait any longer. He spoke towards the TV. "Excuse me, what's the purpose of showing this? This doesn't make sense."

This evoked a slight laugh from the TV. "YOU WILL SEE."

This went on for another ten minutes. He didn't see the point in allowing himself to be aroused. He stood up and started pacing. Twelve more minutes and finally the video ended. Herb squared off with the TV and braced himself.

What's next?

Like an MC at a party the voice spoke. It suggested a feeling of friendliness. As if everyone in the room were in this adventure together. And willingly.

"HERB. YOU READ YOUR LETTER. HOWEVER, THERE IS ANOTHER. IN A BOOK. ON THE BOOKSHELF. HINT. AUTHOR'S INITIALS...JP. I NEED YOU TO RETRIEVE THAT LETTER AND READ IT. I HAVE A LITTLE SOMETHING FOR YOU."

CHAPTER 76

Herb hurried over to the bookshelf and stepped directly to the section alphabetized starting with the P's. Herb ran his fingers along the books, looking at the names. "What do you know? First one." He looked at his shelf and he had two rows of books from one of his favorite authors, James Patterson. "Mr. JP." He grabbed his first book. *Beach House.* Opened the front and back panels and shook the book. Nothing came out. He flipped through two more books. Nothing visible. The next book had an orange cover with red lettering, *Sail.* Shook it vigorously and the pages flapped carelessly. Nothing in there. His eyes scanned over to the next one. *Judge & Jury.* One of his favorites. Co-authored by Andrew Gross. Something caught his vision protruding from the pages at the top of the book. He grabbed it like a young boy opening a gift at Christmas. Cautiously, he opened the book. Can't have the damn book exploding on him. He grasped it with anticipation. Flicked through the pages and what do you know. An envelope fell out.

He guardedly picked it up. "HERB" was typed on the outside. It was not sealed. He slid his fingers under the flap opening the envelope which revealed a letter inside. Careful no surprises would greet him, he drew the letter out deliberately. Slowly. Unfolded it and began to read.

Herb,

We've come a long way, baby. Sorry for the cliché. I couldn't resist. It's been a pleasure to get to know you. It's been a long journey. Longer for me. Since I started planning this over a year ago. You've been the recipient of all of this attention. I hope you appreciate the effort. All for you.

By now we should have shared a lot of experiences. We may have dabbled into the world of self-discovery. Or we may have simply applied fear and pain for your past discretions.

Either way, the journey is coming to a close. After all, all good things must come to an end. Sorry for sounding cliché again. I know you agents frown upon clichés. This one just seems to fit.

But, yes, the final chapter is nearing. In case our game of Hangman never occurred, this letter is a back up to inform you, your house is going to blow up at 10 PM tonight. If we did play, then it serves as a reminder. Yes, that's right, the bomb is set to go off at ten o'clock this evening. I know you don't like the inconsistencies in usage of time—numeric versus words. Too bad.

Herb looked at his watch. A little after three o'clock in the afternoon. Less than seven hours left. He mumbled to himself, "Shit!" And continued to read.

At this particular time I have to ask for your utmost cooperation. For your sake and for mine—I demand it.

You're about to see something disturbing. This will awaken your senses. And I want to grab your attention.

After that, simply follow my requests and hopefully our little adventure will flow in the right direction. For you. And for me.

The End?

CHAPTER 77

Herb held the letter in his hand but looked away. His insides rumbled with two diverse feelings.

One, glad this nightmare was about to end...finally.

Two, how would it end? Would this be the end of his life? Would he die in his house? What did the mastermind have in store? Either way, he was about to find out. He wanted to get on with this torture and end it. One way or another.

He walked right up to the TV and squared off with it. As if facing the bully, eye to eye. "All right, let's see what you got! I'm ready!"

He braced himself. He looked straight into the TV. Nothing happened. He glanced around the room. Looking for any movement. He crouched his knees. In the ready position. Any type of something that could serve as a projectile towards him, or might explode. He surveyed every object, wall, ceiling and piece of furniture.

Nothing.

Five minutes went by.

"Hey, Mr. Voice! Where are you?"

"I'M SORRY. HAD TO GRAB A HAND FULL OF PEANUTS. A LITTLE SOMETHING TO TAKE OFF THE EDGE."

Herb looked perplexed. Lost in thought. He murmured to himself. "Peanuts. Peanuts."

He marched to his table and looked at the group picture again.

His eyes scanned every person in there. Staring right into their eyes.

Under his breath he mumbled, "Peanuts. Peanuts. One of you, always ate peanuts. At the bar. Usually late afternoon. Come on. Come on. Which one?"

He ran his finger over their heads as he smoothed it back and forth, across the picture. "Come on old memory. Don't let me down."

The TV voice broke in. "DID YOU WANT ME?"

"I'm sorry. I have to go to the bathroom."

Herb took the picture and ran inside the bathroom.

The voice called out. "DID YOU FIND AND READ THE LETTER IN THE ENVELOPE?"

Herb yelled back to the TV. "I've got it. I need to go to the bathroom. That's where I do most of my reading. I'll let you know when I'm done."

He ran in. Shut the toilet lid. Plopped down and glared at the people. The intensity could have burned a hole through the picture.

"Is it you? Billy? Jason...Mr. Fisherman? Or the Canucks...Sandy and Don. No. Don't remember you stuffing peanuts in your mouths."

He stared at Frank and Brenda. "Are my New York friends the peanut heads?"

He moved his head closer to the picture.

"How 'bout Mike and Lisa? Nah. Cigars were his thing." On to the next.

"George and Kelly. I had nuts on their yacht. But, all the time? I don't know..." Hearing his own voice felt good. Herb hadn't talked to a live, normal voice in some time.

Looking down into their eyes. "Duncan and Peggy. Love your beer, don't you? Nuts go with beer. Don't remember you eating them all the time. Hmm."

Come on. Batter up. Who's next?

"Dan and Kathy. My scotch man. Ate everything. Healthy eater. No peanuts."

Onto the next ones. "Couple number...whatever, John and Danielle. Liked wine. Nibbled on cheese. Don't remember peanuts. Someone definitely liked their peanuts."

He scanned the group. Eyes keying in on the next couple. The man, strong. Movie star looks. The woman. Beautiful. Striking. His eyes grew wide. His mouth fell open. It hit him like a train. His heart stopped.

It couldn't be.

CHAPTER 78

He remembered peanuts going into that beautiful little mouth. Almost every night during happy hour. No way.

The voice yelled out. "ARE YOU WITH ME HERB?"

He walked out from the bathroom and stepped in front of the TV. "Yes. I'm with you. Are you..."

"DID YOU READ THE LETTER?"

"Yes. I read the letter. Are..."

"GOOD. THEN YOU KNOW THE BOMB IS GOING OFF AT TEN TONIGHT?"

"Yes. I have to ask you a..."

"NO TIME FOR QUESTIONS. TIME IS OF THE ESSENCE. PLEASE FOLLOW. I DEMAND YOU."

A stoic expression graced Herb's face. He listened. "But, I need to know something. Are you who..."

The voice interrupted. "YOU ARE GOING TO SEE A VISUAL. THIS IS NO RECORDING. IT'S A LIVE FEED."

What could this be?

When the screen came up, Herb couldn't believe his eyes. An old man stood in a barren room, shackled to a brick wall, standing next to a chair. He wore gym shorts and a golf shirt. High white socks and tennis shoes. He looked frail and distraught.

The voice chimed in. "GO AHEAD."

Herb didn't understand. Was that meant for him?

The old man began to speak. "Herb? I want to tell you, I'm sorry for everything I did."

He screamed back at the TV. "Dad!" Herb's eyes began to moisten. "Leave him out of this! What's he to do with any of this?"

"HERB. DON'T YOU SEE? THIS IS YOUR CHANCE TO BALANCE THE SCALES OF JUSTICE. YOU CAN MAKE RIGHT ALL THE WRONGS YOUR FATHER DID TO YOU."

Herb looked at the old man. Frail and scared. He looked weak and harmless. Hard to believe he was responsible for all the mental anguish Herb had endured. For years.

He'd fantasized many a night of how he might get even for how he'd been treated. Feeding him to gators in the Florida swamps. Tying him to a chair and pummeling his head with a sledgehammer till there was nothing left. The amount of anger that welt up inside him was more than any one person should have to feel in one lifetime. But, it was there. Full to the brim.

Funny, he'd not thought of his Dad for quite some time. At least that's what he told himself. But, when the opportunity to belittle someone came up, thoughts of his father rumbled around in his head. In some small way, belittling others was his way of getting back at his Dad.

He never realized that until now.

"WOULD YOU LIKE TO DO SOMETHING TO YOUR DAD? TORTURE HIM? MAKE HIM SAY UNCLE AS YOU SAW OFF HIS FOOT? I CAN ARRANGE THAT."

He let out a sobering breath. "No. I don't need to do those things. Let him go. Please. Can he hear me?"

"LET HIM TELL YOU HIMSELF."

The old man said, "Herb. I hear you. I can't see you, but I know you're there."

The voice spoke. "AMAZING WHAT VIDEO CONFERENCING CAN DO, ISN'T IT?"

Herb swallowed. And stared at the man. This frail being who tormented his psyche for so long. Looking helpless and pathetic.

"You okay?"

"Scared, son. Don't know what's going on."

Herb pleaded. "Let him go."

"DO YOU HAVE ASPIRATIONS TO RECONNECT WITH YOUR FATHER?"

He pondered the question. The man was not worthy. He mistreated Herb beyond what should be forgiven. He just got older. Still the same old man.

"No. I don't. But, he doesn't deserve this."

"ARE YOU SURE?"

"Yes. I'm sure."

"MAYBE YOU WANT TO TELL HIM SOMETHING. SOMETHING YOU'VE WANTED TO SAY TO HIM FOR YEARS. SOMETHING YOU WANTED TO SAY TO HIM WHEN YOU WERE A CHILD. WHEN YOU WERE WEAK. WHEN HE WAS BIGGER THAN YOU. STRONGER THAN YOU. NOW'S YOUR CHANCE TO LAY IT ON THE LINE."

Herb sat down. These were good questions. What an opportunity?

Herb took a moment. Thought about it. Realized the opportunity. An opportunity he dreamed about for much of his life. Mostly when he himself was helpless. The anger. The inner angst to want to lash out. To want to deliver pain and mental suffering. The desire to even the scores of abuse.

It surprised him. All that build up. All that emotion.

Gone.

"No. I'm good. Let him go. I don't want to reconnect. But, I don't want harm to him."

The man's posture slumped with relief. He sat in the chair, staring at the camera. Herb felt as if their eyes connected. Those mean, cold hearted eyes. His father said, "Thank you, Herb. Thank you."

The voice spoke, "IF YOU WISH NO HARM TO COME TO YOUR FATHER, THEN YOU MUST FOLLOW MY INSTRUCTIONS. AND FOLLOW THEM WITH NO HESITATION. EVERY THING I SAY. AND I MEAN EVERYTHING! UNDERSTAND?"

Herb looked at his Dad. And nodded his head to himself. It felt like the right thing to do. For himself.

"Yes. I understand."

"GOOD. THIS NEXT CHAPTER IS AN EXCITING ONE. I'VE BEEN WAITING FOR THIS. A LONG TIME."

A puzzled look splashed across Herb's face. "Okay. Can I ask a question first?"

"NO. YOU'RE ABOUT TO RECEIVE A VISITOR. THE BOMB SENSOR WILL BE TEMPORARILY DEACTIVATED. WHEN THE DOOR BELL RINGS. OPEN THE DOOR AND LET THE PERSON IN. IMMEDIATELY."

ACT 3

COMPANY'S HERE

CHAPTER 79

The doorbell rang.

Herb's palms felt clammy. He pumped his fists at his side. He rubbed his thumbs against his forefingers. He didn't think he'd ever be able to open his front door again. Ever. And now that he could, the mere thought of it scared him beyond belief.

Was this all a ruse? Just to get me to blow my own house up? Is the mastermind somewhere far off watching with binoculars ready for good laugh?

Who cares? Let's just get this over with. Now.

The bell rang again. The impatience of the second ring causing Herb to take his first step towards the door. He wasn't ready. His second step, like dragging a leg drenched in a bucket of wet cement. He had to get to the door.

He trudged forward.

Upon arriving, he looked at the edges of the door. From the floor to the top, where the hinges followed along. No sensor or anything unusual there. On the opposing side, where the knob resided, he looked for any hint of a sensor. Nothing to be seen. Had to be on the top. Upon further examination, nothing could be seen. "Hmm."

Pounding on the door startled him. Loud, obnoxious pounding.

That addressed one of his concerns. Someone was there. They couldn't be miles away ready for a display of explosions.

Little by little, Herb reached for the knob. His hand shaking uncontrollably. Finally touching the knob, he grasped on. Lightly at first, and then he clenched it firmly. *What if it blows? It won't. Someone's there.*

He turned it deliberately, braced himself, took half a step back, and pulled it tentatively.

First, half an inch. Rain and a strong blast of warm air rushed in. The pressure on the door, strong from the hurricane.

No explosion. He blew out a gust of breath.

A presence from the other side could be felt flowing through the opening. And a scent.

Perfume.

He pulled it open with full force. And there it was.

The voice.

The mastermind.

The person responsible for making his life a living hell for the past day and a half.

A look of shock and complete disbelief covered his face.

There stood a woman. The most striking woman. Donning white short shorts. A red V-neck t-shirt, overflowing with cleavage. White tennis shoes. Everything accented by her long brown hair. And a small leather purse. All drenched in hurricane rain. Her t-shirt clinging to her for annunciation.

The final garnishment, both hands grasping a nine-millimeter hollow point semi-automatic pistol aimed right at his forehead.

Herb's mind raced. It was her. The one who ate the peanuts.

As a man, his natural lust from within surged. As a prisoner, and as someone whose friend, dog, and father were being held hostage, he wanted to strike out. The two contrasting emotions battling it out within.

He wanted to strangle her.

"You fucking bitch! If it's the last thing I do I'm going to kill you!"

Before he could think, in one fluid motion she pulled up her leg and kicked him in the chest, knocking him back six feet into the house. She slammed the door behind her. Locked it. And stormed past him and pulled the trigger on the gun.

Herb hit the floor and covered his head.

The bullets sprayed his red cedar chair at his reading desk. Drenching it with bullets up and down, disintegrating the chair into splinters. Herb covered his head. The noise earsplitting. Seemed like the shooting would never end. Up. Down. Sideways. Around. Back and forth.

Overkill indeed.

When she finished shooting, smoke filtered up from her gun. Herb raised his head and looked at the chair, splinters of wood protruding from all sides.

He glared up at her.

She flipped her wet hair over her shoulder. Hand on her hip. Rain drops dripping onto the floor. And stared straight into his eyes, "Good to see you. Herb." The voice. Soft. Feminine. So different from what he'd heard from the TV.

He didn't move. "You like to make an entrance. Don't you?"

She held the gun, pointing it at him. She didn't say a word. Her eyes, wide, filled with exhilaration. She let the silence play on his mind.

He stared into her gun. His Adam's apple swelled as he tried to swallow.

She spoke. Slowly. Deliberately. "Yes. It's kind of my thing."

He started to lift himself from the ground. "You're not going to get away with this." He said.

She stepped up and stomped her wet foot on his back, pressing her full weight onto him, pressing him back to the ground. "In case you didn't know. I already did." And she pressed more weight onto his back. Raindrops dripping from her clothes onto him. He groaned in pain.

A whimpering sound could be heard coming from the bedroom. Obvious, the shooting kept Reese from coming out to explore the new visitor.

She called out, "Reese. It's me."

Reese walked out. Tentatively at first. Upon seeing her, Reese ran up to her. She barked with enthusiasm. Her tail wagged with intense strength.

"Reese. It's good to see you, too." She kept her eyes squarely on Herb, not to give him a chance of making a move. She poked the gun into his back. "I'm not forgetting you."

She pulled a dog treat out of her pocket and shared it with Reese, petting her on the head while Reese scarfed it down, not taking her eyes off of Herb for a second. "Good girl, Reese. Good girl. I missed you, too."

"You even thought of Reese?" He said, his head facing down to the floor.

"Like I've been saying all along. I prepared."

"It's you. The auto executive's wife."

"Yes. How observant of you." She said.

"Susan, I believe."

"Yes. I wondered if you'd remember me. Or, at least my name. I knew you'd remember me. The way you made eyes at me on that trip." She flipped her hair away from her face.

"Don't flatter yourself."

"Please. I was embarrassed for your companion the way you looked at me. If my husband would have caught wind of that, he'd have let you have it. Deservedly."

"You can't say you didn't feel some small connection between us?"

She laughed. "I was just playing you. Getting to know you a little better. The start of my plan before I started stalking you a year ago. A girl's got to have a little fun before she decides to right the world of its wrongs."

"Playing me, huh?"

"Sure. I learned a lot about you on that trip. That you had a dog. That you lived in a remote area out in the country. I got a good sense of your personality. Your pompous arrogance. Your superior attitude. All of that made me even hungrier to get even for the way you treated my mother. I feel I'm not only doing right by her, but I'm doing the world a favor."

"Well, you've done quite a bit. Embezzling my money. Belittling me in front of the whole world in the USA Today. Ruining my reputation. You've been busy."

"Thank you. It's good to be appreciated."

"Whatever you have in store for me, please allow my dad, my friend, and Reese to go. Please. They aren't responsible for my actions. If I must pay, okay. But, please let them go."

She took her foot off of his back. "I applaud your character here. This isn't something I would've expected at the beginning. I do believe this experience has made you evolve. Wouldn't you agree?"

Herb coughed. The facedown position into the floor was proving difficult to talk with the bend in his throat. "Yes. Maybe I have." He cleared his throat. "Excuse me. Is it okay if I sit up?"

She stepped back. Pulled him up from the back of his collar. The end of the gun still poked in his back. He stood up. His legs wobbly. She pushed him away with the end of the gun.

He turned around. And for the first time they stared at each other. Like prize fighters sizing up the opposition. Judging who would outfox the other. Asking themselves who would be standing at the end of the bout. Who would have the physical stamina and out-persevere the other? Who would sneak in the most shots? Or, who would make the final knockout blow?

Only time would tell.

He looked at her. Admired her cunning. Respected her ability to carry out such a grand plan. Revered the courage it took to not only plan and execute this plot, but applauded the attention to detail it took to do all the things necessary to make it a reality.

This was some woman. This would be the type that could change his life. If only she were his.

He stared into those glacier blue eyes. Those captivating marbles, alluring him in. Pulling him into her spell.

She tilted her head, her long brown hair hanging to one side, smiled, and said, "I have something to show you, Herb."

CHAPTER 80

A look of bewilderment danced across his face. What could she possibly have to show him? In his house? Everything up till now had been a complete surprise. *What's one more?*

He arched his eyebrow as if to say, *okay, show me.*

She motioned him towards the kitchen with her gun. He took the hint and walked in that direction.

"You don't have to keep that gun on me. I'm not going to do anything stupid."

"That's right. You're not. That's why the gun will remain on you. Keep walking." She poked him in the back to keep his attention, and to let him know who was in control.

She said, "Stand over there. By the refrigerator."

He did as he was told.

She bent down in front of the sink where a throw rug lay. It had a landscape mural weaved into it of Guilin, China. Large pinnacle rocks covered in lush vegetation with the Li River winding through them, with a fisherman pushing himself along with a bamboo pole. Only the mountains were wine colored throughout over a white backdrop with the fisherman sporting a light blue shirt and donning a Chinaman's hat.

She kept her eyes on Herb, the gun pointed at him the entire time. She pulled the rug back, her hands sliding across the warm floor.

"I forgot, I still have your heat on." She leaned on one knee and pulled out her cell phone and started pushing buttons. Looking up at Herb every two seconds. "Need to hit the override on the temp."

"Good." Herb motioned his hand for the refrigerator door.

"Don't move! Don't! Fucking! Move!" She shot up to her feet. The gun pointed right at him.

Startled, he stopped in his tracks.

"What're you doing?" She yelled.

"I was going to get us something cold to drink."

"No. You don't move! Unless I say. Understand?"

He put his hands up in surrender. "I'm sorry. It won't happen again."

Her eyes seared through his. The message—she meant business.

"I'm sorry."

"You're damn right, you're sorry. Stand still."

She finished pressing the numbers on her phone. "There. That ought to bring the temp down."

She bent back down to the floor, her eyes squarely on Herb. She pulled the rug completely back. Took out a key from her pocket and inserted it into a crack along the dark oak wood floor. All by feel. Her stare not wavering for a second. Her eyes, cold and focused. With the key she flipped up the edge of the board. In one motion she slid her finger under the board and pulled an entire panel up. She slid the 15" x 12" panel of connected boards off to the side.

She glanced down in the hole. The bomb and its digital timer, displaying six hours and seventeen minutes, and descending with every second. She looked back up at Herb and his eyes were as big as quarters.

"Wondered where your friend was, huh?"

He rubbed his chin. "I didn't think to look under the rug. Damn!"

"Wouldn't have mattered, Herb. Even if you'd have moved the rug away, you wouldn't have noticed any difference in the wood floor. I had it beveled to perfection."

"Who did your dirty work?"

"I hired the best wood guy around. Told 'em it was for a small safe. Old coins and stuff. He thought it was kind of cute."

"You put a lot of thought into this, didn't you?"

"You have no idea."

A concerned look consumed his expression. "Why're you showing me this?"

"Good question. I want you to know the bomb is real. And we have less than seven hours before your house is history."

"What're we going to do next?"

"You will see."

"That's your favorite line, isn't it?"

She said nothing. Walked over and pulled out the chair from the kitchen table and said, "Sit." All while keeping the gun aimed directly at him. Her eyes zeroed in on him.

He did what any right-minded guy would do with a wild eyed woman with a gun on him would do. He sat. His eyes studied her every move. *Would she relax for even a second where he could overpower her? Take the gun away and end this? What could she possibly have up her sleeve next?*

His eyes stayed on her as much as hers remained on him. Like chess players trying to read their opponents minds.

He, curious as to what she would do next.

She walked to the top shelf cabinet and pulled two glasses down. It was obvious she knew her way around this kitchen. In fact, she opened the door and reached in for the glasses all while keeping her eyes honed in on Herb. To most, it would look like she lived here.

She positioned herself between Herb and the glasses, so he couldn't see them. She pulled a small vile from her purse and emptied the powdery blue contents into one of the glasses. She threw the vile back into her purse quietly so he wouldn't notice. She grabbed the gun with both hands and walked over to the refrigerator and retrieved one of Herb's lemon flavored sports drinks, keeping the gun pointed at him the whole time. She back-pedaled over to the glasses and filled each one up with the lemon flavored drink. When the liquid hit the bottom of the glass, the powdery blue substance dissolved upon impact. You couldn't tell one glass from the other.

She took the one with the powder in it to Herb and said, "Here."

He put his hand out and grabbed the drink from her. "Thank you."

"You're welcome. I know this hasn't been easy on you."

He took a sip. His thirst, strong. His eyes answering her. *Damn right it hasn't been easy!*

She raised her glass and said, "Here's to seeing you again." And she downed a gulp of the cold liquid.

He didn't toast. Simply took another swig. Half the glass empty now.

"With the heat down, that should help make it a little more comfortable in here. I imagine you must be dehydrated."

He nodded in the affirmative. And drank another long mouthful. And came away for a big breath and an, "ah."

She took another big swill and said, "I really like your sports drink. It says on the label it's great for dehydration."

"Yep. I drink it with every workout.

"That's good. You look in great shape. You take care of yourself." She said.

"I try."

"How can someone be so scarred mentally and yet still be so great physically?" She asked.

"Hey. I've got problems just like anyone else. Most people have mental scars from their upbringing. Mine are a little more intense."

"That's an understatement. Here's to mental scars." She raised her glass. He stared blankly. He downed the last sips.

"Mmm. That was good." She slammed the glass down and looked at her watch. 6:43 PM.

Perplexed, Herb looked at her and said, "What now?"

She smiled at him and said, "We wait."

"Wait for what?"

"You'll see."

CHAPTER 81

Susan pulled the other chair out from the table and dragged it over near the refrigerator so she distanced herself twelve feet from Herb. She plopped herself down. Kept the gun aimed at him. And they stared at each other. An awkward silence hung in the air.

He tapped his foot on the ground out of nervousness.

She flipped her hair to one side.

Herb's eyes scanned the gun. "You seem pretty comfortable with that thing."

She nodded the affirmative. "Thank you. I love shooting it. I'm one of the few at the gun range that has an automatic weapon. When I'm shooting it I get the looks."

"I'm sure they're looking at more than the gun."

She smiled. "I'm flattered. I'm glad you feel that way."

Again, more uncomfortable silence fell over the room. She crossed her right leg over her left. Maintaining the gun's direction at him.

His eyes assessed the features of his captor. Long athletic legs, emphasized by her short shorts. Her tee-shirt accentuated her upper attributes in a fine manner. And her face, stunning. This gal had the smarts and the looks to own the world. And at that moment, she owned *his* world.

Several minutes passed. She couldn't contain herself any longer. "So. Herb. Let me ask you. Who did you think I was? Did you have any idea it was me?"

He raised his head high into the air, contemplating how to answer. His intellect and pride on the line. Of course, at this point, he'd learned none of that really mattered. Pride. Self-importance. At the end of the day, no one really gave a damn. Way overrated. Why'd it take all of this to learn that?

He dove right in.

"This really was tough to figure out. There were a lot of strong personalities on that trip. Many of them had an aspect about them which made them viable candidates to be you."

She shook her head in agreement. "True. But we discussed them already, didn't we?"

Herbs crossed his arms and nodded back. "We did."

"After all that discussing was done, who did you think I was?"

Herb pursed his lips. Looked down towards the ground, and said, "I didn't know."

A smile ran across her face.

He continued. "That is...until you mentioned you needed peanuts again. Then it came over me like a wave of realization."

She laughed. "The peanuts gave me away?"

"I remember you eating peanuts frequently on the trip. But, I still couldn't believe you were capable to do all of this. No way."

She flipped her hair aside again. It was starting to dry. And flashed a forced smile.

He just gazed back at her. Expressionless.

"You know what this is really all about don't you?"

Herb dipped his head up and down. "Yes. Your mother."

She shot back at him. "More than that. It's about my *love* for my mother. Understand? Love."

He nodded in agreement. "I understand."

She looked at her watch. Almost an hour had gone by. "Good. Time to get up." She motioned with the gun. "Into the living room."

A flood of concern took over his face. He stood up and walked into the living room.

She barked her orders. "Your new ottoman. Grab it and pull it over in front of the TV."

"Did you buy this?"

"I did. Where'd you think it came from?"

"I thought my mother ordered it. The note said it was from her."

"Sorry. It came from me. I didn't want to freak you out too much in the beginning. Just another little detail of a long list. Now, pull it over. Now!"

Herb grabbed the peculiar wooden handles on the side and pulled it over to the middle of the room where her gun had pointed. He grunted as he pulled it over.

He looked at it with an inquisitive expression. "What are these weird handles doing on the ends?"

"You will see." She smiled.

Each side of the ottoman had two large wooden dowels protruding from them about seven inches out, and about three inches round. Each with holes drilled in them. They sported beveled ends and were stained with a dark color and covered with a clear polyurethane. Stylish.

"I've never seen an ottoman of this size." He said. It stretched out six feet long.

"I had it custom-made. Just for you."

With her purse still slung over her shoulder, she reached her hand in without taking her eyes off of him, and retrieved four pairs of handcuffs. She laid them out onto the floor, careful to make sure each one was in the unlocked and open position. On each side.

His heart started racing. His palms grew sweaty.

One look at him and she knew fear was back in his system.

"Okay, Herb. I need you to relax. I'm not going to hurt you. It's important you relax. Settle down. Take small slow breaths for me. Will you do that for me?"

He looked at her with comprehension.

"Go ahead. Small slow breaths. In slowly. Then, out slowly."

He did what he was told.

"What are you going to do to me?"

"You will see."

CHAPTER 82

"Okay. Sit." Susan said.

Herb obeyed.

"Here." She slid the first pair of cuffs over to him with her foot. Positioning it within his reach. Her gun squarely pointed at him. Right in his face. Then, she took four steps back.

"Pick it up."

He reached down, not taking an eye off of her or her gun.

"Click the one end around your right ankle."

He took his eye off of her to see the hand cuff. Picked it up and clicked it around his ankle. He swallowed hard. And looked back up at her. "Okay."

"Good. Now take your foot, slide it into position and take the other end of the cuff and click it into the hole in the dowel. Securing your right ankle to the ottoman."

His eyes squinted with protest, but he followed her orders. His right foot securely attached to the ottoman.

The wind blared outside. Something big slammed against the side of the old farmhouse. Shook it even. It distracted their attention for a second.

She glanced at the direction of the sound, then came back to Herb. "Right foot secured. Good."

She slid the next set of cuffs over toward his left foot. And took four steps back. Careful to keep the gun squarely aimed at his head. "You're a smart guy. You know what to do."

She could see by the look in his eyes his mind was swimming for a way out of this mess. His flight or fight response conflicting inside of him.

She screamed at him. "Now! Put the damn thing on your other foot. Hurry!" She waved the gun from the hand cuff to his left foot. And back. And back again. "Now!"

Surrendering, he did as he was told. He clicked the other cuff around his left foot, and then secured it to the dowel on the ottoman.

"Click it in!" She shouted.

She'd come a long way to get this far. Couldn't afford him to get skittish and weasel his way out of this now. She had to maintain the upper edge. Keep him under her control.

He clicked it in. Now, both feet were secured to the ottoman.

"Okay. Good." She bent down and picked the next cuff off the ground and tossed it to him.

"Put this one on your right wrist." He glared at her. His only show of resistance. His desperate attempt at maintaining his dignity.

She took one step closer. Her gun aimed direct at his left eye. "Now."

He clicked it around his wrist.

"Good. Lay yourself down and reach your hand up over your head and secure your wrist to the dowel."

He looked two parts bewildered. And four parts humiliated. He didn't move. May have been part confusion, too.

"You heard me. Lie down on your back and reach your hands up. You'll notice this thing is big enough to handle you laying all the way back. Your feet will hang over a little. Take your left hand and click your right hand into the dowel."

He looked behind himself, peering over his right shoulder first, and then his left. He lowered himself down onto his back. And then stretching his right hand up over his head, he secured his right wrist to the dowel with his left hand.

Click!

"Okay. Good. Now, I'm going to secure your left wrist to the dowel. You try something and this whole game will end early. And it won't be pretty. Understand?"

He shook his head in the affirmative. Anxiety clearly overwhelming him.

"Relax Herb. Relax. It's going to be okay. Breathe."

His wide eyes looked up at the ceiling. Worry consuming him.

"I intentionally left your left wrist for last as I know you're right handed. This should deem you less likely to try something with your weaker side. That's my wish. I strongly urge you to comply."

"How did you know I'm right handed?"

"Easy. I watched you smoke your cigars on news reels. I prepared. I tried to think of every little thing."

She put the last hand cuff in his right hand. "Here."

He grasped it.

"Good. Now pull your left hand over to it. Click the cuff onto your left wrist."

He took a moment. Then followed his order.

"Good Herb. Very good. Now bring your left wrist back over and stretch it up over your head and position it near the dowel above your head."

He followed the last order. His body started to squirm. The imminent realization he would be tied down starting to overwhelm him with anxiety.

"Easy Herb. Easy. It's going to be okay. Please breathe slow breaths. In. And out. In. And out."

He took his breaths. As she had asked.

"That's it. In. And out. Everything is going to be okay. Close your eyes and imagine you're on a sandy beach. The ocean lulling you to sleep. Go ahead."

He closed his eyes.

"Imagine the palm trees bristling in the wind." She spoke with smooth soft words. "The breeze calming your senses."

She could see his breathing starting to slow down. She stepped right up to him and grabbed his left cuff and clicked it into the last dowel.

His eyes shot open and he recognized he was totally tied up and trapped. Unable to move his arms and unable to walk, move or anything else under his own freewill. The anxiety forcing him to wriggle and squirm to no avail. "Agghh! Please! Let me out! I'll do whatever you want me to do! Just let me out! Please! Agghh!"

She stepped up to him, peering down at him, directly below her gaze. Eye to eye. Nothing he could do. They looked at each other studying each other's features. Contemplating when and what would come next. She bent down and put her lips two inches from his right ear.

She spoke softly. "It's okay, Herb. You're going to be all right. I understand you're a bit anxious. It goes with the territory. Can you imagine what my mother must have felt like when she tried to reach out to you for counsel? For validation she would be okay after what she'd been through. That she could get through to the other side of her life and move on? Only to be belittled and stepped on with your cruel words. Sure, she was weak. Sure, it didn't take much. But, she was a broken woman. A timid soul. Maybe with the right words of encouragement she could have dug herself out. Maybe. And it was all in your hands. And you blew it!"

She stepped away. Laid the pistol down flat on the floor next to the TV. She grabbed a small pillow off the couch and tucked it under Herb's head, propping it up so he faced the TV.

"How's that? Are you comfortable?"

He nodded. Her fragrance touched him. Drawing him into her spell.

"Herb. It's okay to talk to me, you know. Is that comfortable?"

"Yes." From his peripheral vision, he could see a piece of his teakwood box lying on the floor.

"Good. I want you to be comfortable."

She looked at her watch. 8:17 PM.

"Okay. Now for a little entertainment."

She turned the TV on. Pushed a couple of buttons on the remote. The porn she had on earlier picked up where it had left off. An inquisitive look consumed Herb's face. Understandably.

"Herb, I can tell by the look on your face, you're wondering, what the heck is going to happen next?"

He said nothing.

"Come on. Aren't you going to say, yes, you're right?"

Reluctantly, he said, "Yes. You're right."

"I'm glad you asked. Yes. I have a little porn on for you. I know how men are stimulated by the visual. That's what they say. I think that's all rubbish. I think women are, too. I know I am. This is as much for me as it is for you."

His confused look stayed on his face.

"Okay. I'll cut to the chase. You and I are going to have a little fun. That lemon drink you gulped down had a ground up Viagra pill in it. One hundred milligrams. Time should be just about right for it to be kicking in. A little porn for added measure. And we're going to see what we have going here. In planning, I had to account for the stress factor. How could a guy fuck who is held against his will? Whose house may blow up? Whose friend is held captive, and who has a nine millimeter aimed at him."

"Thanks to modern medicine and modern technology, add in Viagra and a porn video, and I'm willing to bet, despite being held against your own freewill, you're going to be able to step up to the plate and make this happen."

Herb stared with intense focus.

"If you can pull this off, I may even write in to the company and let them know the results as an endorsement for their product. You could even be famous for this experiment. How about that?"

Herb didn't look the least bit amused. Under any other circumstances, he'd have jumped to the opportunity to be with a creature of such beauty, of such raw sexual energy. Her mere eyes were enough to draw his loins to their primal purpose. But, under these pretenses, his mind processed a million other things. Like basic survival.

And of course, Katie.

"I don't care about being famous. This is not going to happen. I have a girlfriend."

"Herb. Herb. Herb. Have I not shown you the strength of my will? The lengths of what I will do when I put my mind to something. Believe me, this is going to happen. You will see. And as to you having a girlfriend. Too bad."

She smiled her smile at him. A smile he'd never seen from her. Directed to him. Devious. Suggestive.

She walked over to her purse and retrieved a long sharp knife. As she pulled it from her purse the light reflected off the silvery blade into Herb's eyes. The glare blinded him temporarily. When he opened his eyes back in focus, they widened with concern.

Observant, she attempted to ease his worries. "It's okay. I'm not going to hurt you with this."

"What are you going to do with it?"

"You will see."

"Yes. Of course."

She walked over to him and slid the side of it along his right cheek. His body stiffened.

She looked down at him and said, "Letting the metal slither against your skin is giving me the ultimate sense of power. How does it feel for someone else to have power over *you*?"

He didn't say a thing.

She slid the knife under the top of his shirt at the neckline and ran it down along his midsection, splitting his shirt right down the middle. Obviously, an extremely sharp knife. She took her left hand and ran it down his chest to his belly pushing the shirt aside, on both sides, exposing his chiseled chest and rippled abs. She shook her head back, revving up her excitement.

She laughed. "Time for me to get a little more comfortable here." She lifted her sticky wet shirt up from her waist and pulled it up over her head and threw it off to the side, leaving her standing there with her black bra on.

"Ah. I feel much better. This okay by you?"

He didn't say a word.

"Don't forget. You've got porn to watch, and of course, me."

She took his shoes off and tossed them aside, oblivious to where they landed.

"One for you, one for me."

She looked down at him. His expressionless face staring at her. His mind trying to figure this all out.

She tucked her hands behind her back and unclasped her bra. Her breasts fell out, free.

"You like what you see so far?"

He didn't respond.

"Come on, Herb. You know you wanted me on that trip. Now's your chance, big boy. Just you and me."

She ran her fingers down his chest over his abs and against his shorts and alongside his inner thigh.

He arched his back in protest. Obvious to her, she hit the right spots.

"Hmm. Someone is feeling something."

He looked away from her gaze.

She unzipped her shorts and slid them down over her hips and shimmied them to the floor, then stepped out of them with one foot and flipped them over the TV with the other.

"Herb. I'm over here. Look over here."

In protest, he didn't turn his head.

"Did you forget who's in control here? Did you forget I have your friend under my power?"

She ran her hand alongside his head and turned it toward her. Directing his eyes toward her breasts. He could now see she was down to her maroon silk panties. He swallowed a gulp of saliva.

"Herb, we're down to our last article of clothing. A moment I know you dreamt of while on our vacation. Your eyes told me that every day. And a moment I've dreamt of ever since I knew you led my mother to her death. All the planning. The detail. We're one step away. All this time. All this build up. And here we are."

She walked around him. Slowly. Seductively. Looking down on him. Running her fingers across his face. Letting them rumple across his features. His tan cheeks. Rubbing his ears between her thumb and forefinger. Brushing her breasts against his thick head of hair. She walked around him some more, letting him breathe in her intoxicating fragrance, driving him into delirium.

"Are you liking what you see, Herb? Are you feeling anything?"

His breathing clearly visible. His chest rising and falling with each second. His thoughts?

Speechless.

She raised her right leg and stepped up and over him, straddling his chest. Her bottom on top of his belly. She leaned down, her face to his. Her hair hanging into his face. Her aroma blowing his mind. And she slowly slid her butt back across his shorts. Obvious to her he was awake.

She reached down to the floor and picked up the knife. Raised it up to where he could see it. His eyes grew wide.

She stood up, still straddling him and slid the knife under his waistband on his shorts and in one strong fluid motion slit his shorts in half. Underwear and all. She grabbed them both and in one tug, jerked the remaining cloth from his mid-region and raised it above her head ceremoniously. The long, sought after prize.

He laid there motionless. Frozen.

And erect.

She threw the cloth out of sight.

"Hmm. Hmm. Hmm. What have we here? Looks like the drink and the porn were effective. Aay? I'd like to think I have a little to do with that."

He said nothing. With no influence as to what would come next, who could blame him for staying quiet.

"All right. For this all to work out, I'm demanding you be verbal during this process. If you say nothing else, I at least command you to moan or groan. Got it?"

He picked his head off the pillow and looked down at himself. "Okay."

She crossed her left leg up and over him and stood directly over his head. Her pelvis directly over his face.

"It's time, Herb. Time to pay. And time to play."

Their eyes studied each other over. His wondering what was about to happen. And hers, savoring the anticipation.

She reared her right hand back and with full force smacked him across his face. His look was one of surprise. And she did it again. His cheek blossomed pink.

"That's just to get the party started."

A startled look completely covered his face. He looked up at her eyes with a resistant stare. Defiant.

"Herb, I could take the side of my hand and tomahawk your throat, causing you to choke to death. With one strong blow." She placed her hand around his Adam's apple and ran her fingers over it and gently tapped it with the hard side of her hand. "One chop. Done."

He shot up an alarming stare. One of anger. One of fear.

"Good boy. Now I've got your attention."

She methodically slid herself back and positioned herself above him. In-line to complete this long awaited event. She slid her hand below his belly to make sure he was still ready. Oh boy, everything according to plan.

"Are you ready, Herb? Huh?"

He proved verbally unresponsive.

"You're not used to following orders, are you? I like ordering you around. Telling you what to do. Correction. I *love* telling you what to do. You don't have a choice. Nothing like a revenge fuck to cap off the day."

She paused, assessing his reaction to her last comment. He lay there unresponsive. "Nice to see you do as you're told."

And in one graceful motion she slid herself above him. But not on him. The anticipation driving them both to places they'd never been.

For him. Having someone else influence the direction. To let them lead. Do what they chose to him. Different. Exhilarating. A delightful shock. Liberating. And all against his will. Bizarre.

For her. Something new awoke from within. A revelation she'd never had before. Extreme control meshed with sex, power and complete dominance. His actual life in her hands. For her to make the ultimate decision as to whether he lived or died. And to tell him what to do. And to have him there for her to ride at her discretion. This way and that. For as long as she wanted. To tease him, if she wanted. To stroke him if she wanted. To slap him if she wanted. It was all up to her to decide.

However, she couldn't contain herself much longer. After all, she'd waited for this moment for over a year. And now, here he was, right beneath her. Here to be taken.

She found it–the ultimate. The pinnacle. The quintessential power trip.

And now, he must pay.

CHAPTER 83

"You're mine, Herb. You're just for me. Your total purpose? For me to do anything I please to you. If I want to run that knife along your throat and cut you, I could. If I want to beat you with a baseball bat in the head, a hundred times. I could. It's all up to me. But, what do I want to do to you?"

His look was one of fear and disdain. For her.

"And to revenge your misdeeds to my mother." She looked up towards the heavens and said, "Mom, this one's for you."

She positioned herself as if she were going to straddle him. Staring intently into his eyes. An inch away. Nose to nose. Scanning. Searching. Intimidating the hell into him.

"What do you think I'm going to do to you, Herb?"

He said nothing.

"You think I want to fuck you?"

He just stared into her eyes.

"You want me. Don't you?"

The intense look from his face. Frozen.

She leaned over his face, her breasts slowly canvassing back and forth in front of his eyes. They followed like soldiers marching to orders.

She swung them down closer to his cheeks.

She moved her lips into his left ear. And whispered. "Too bad. You get nothing."

She studied him closely. "Not so bad, huh, Herb?"

He didn't respond.

She sat up. Reared back and slapped him hard across his left cheek.

He reared his hip upwards trying to buck her off.

"Oh boy, making a cowgirl out of me. I think I like this."

She reared back again and gave him another slap. And another. And another.

He surrendered the struggle.

She looked at him. Pinned his arms down hard and screamed, "What you did to my mother was wrong! You don't deserve to live, Herb! You understand?"

She leaned over, still on top of him, her hips upon him. But, no penetration. No sex.

The planning. The attention to detail. The risks. The research. The investment of money. The outlay of time. And the supreme commitment. All of it brought together to lead to this.

She'd humiliated him. She'd tortured him verbally and physically in his own home. Embezzled his money into her own bank account. Sent much of it to people he'd wronged. Humiliated him to the public through the news. And now, humiliated him in private.

And finally, her body, skin to skin to his, she screamed in his ear, "Argh! How does it feel? How does it feel to be controlled by a woman?" She panted hard, trying to catch her breath. "And to come to this. The ultimate tease."

She looked him over, his eyes in a glaze. He looked away.

She rolled off of him and knelt down next to the ottoman.

The emotional high liberated every cell in her body. Her mind wishing she could carry this moment with her every second from here to eternity.

Her glance up caught something. Something interesting.

He lie there engorged. Full of blood. Veins popping on all sides. She shook her head and said, "Hmm, unfulfilled, huh?"

He didn't respond. The intensity plastered all over his face.

"Too bad...this is for all the women of the world who don't get satisfied by their men."

She'd reached the summit of *her* mission.

Now, she had to decide...what she would do next?

CHAPTER 84

She gathered all of her clothes and stepped into her panties and shorts. She glanced at her watch.

9:02 pm.

She barked. "Time's a runnin."

She pulled up a chair, right next to Herb's head.

"I don't know, Herb. I'm still not sure what I should do. Should I let you live? Or should I let you blow up in your house? This is tough."

He looked up into her eyes and said, "If my vote counts. Let me go."

"On what grounds? Huh? Tell me."

He took in a deep breath. This would be the biggest sales pitch of his life. Hell, the biggest pitch *for* his life.

"You've humiliated me to the world. Ruined my reputation."

She broke in. "All I did was reveal to the world what you're like."

"Okay. But, now everyone knows. Plus, you've embezzled my money."

"Whoa! Whoa! Whoa! I sent some of it to people you screwed over. And, I sent a little my way as compensation for what you did to my mother. A jury with sound mind and body would probably adjudicated more. It was justified."

"Okay. If I'm lucky to get out of this alive, I will have to rebuild my reputation."

"You're right."

"I assume my house is going to blow up? Is it possible to save that?"

She shook her head. "No. No. No. The house goes."

His chest bellowed. His brain craving oxygen to negotiate the chance to live.

"Okay. My house goes. If I live, I'll find a new place to live. But, if that wasn't enough, you've turned the whole industry upside down. You have agents protesting against our royalties. The writers won't go for it. You're messing with our livelihood."

She scoffed. And flipped her hair back. "I must confess. I had nothing to do with that. Pure coincidence. Timing was perfect."

"Hmm...I thought you were that good."

She smiled. "I'm flattered."

He threw her a serious gaze. "My friend Joe, and Reese. Two important things to me."

"What about them?"

He swallowed hard.

"I know I deserve whatever fate you have for me. I'm sincerely sorry for what I did to your mother. If I die right now, it's the biggest regret of my life. I should've been compassionate to her and tried to help her. My self-absorbed mind didn't think about others."

Susan listened intensely. And nodded.

Herb continued. "I apologize to you. And to the world. If I live past this day, I'll commit the rest of my life to bring good to others. To repay my debt to your mother and to the world."

"Great speech. How do I know you're not just saying this so I spare your pathetic life?"

Herb held his head down, his mind deep in thought. He drew in a deep breath.

And began slowly..."Because. Because of you. You made me realize my father made me feel small. And whenever I was in a position to make myself look big, I did so, but in a way that belittled them. I never realized that. You made me see that. For that, I thank you."

She pursed up her lips. And nodded.

"Good speech. I might even believe you."

"It's true. You've freed me."

"This is great. Here's my dilemma. I let you live. You know enough to have me arrested. I've had you kidnapped. I've embezzled your money. I kidnapped your friend and have destroyed your property. These are all crimes. Felonies. Probably enough to put me away for life. A smart person would say I *have to* kill you. If I don't, it's life behind bars, or running as a fugitive."

He shook his head in agreement. Then responded. "I don't care about the money. I can make more. Even with a basic existence. I don't need all this *stuff*." He motioned with his head for emphasis. "My main concern is Joe and Reese. And my father."

"You sound sincere."

"I am. Please let us live."

"I have good news. If I did let you walk out of here, you don't think I'd be so careless and not insure myself from you calling the police, do you?"

A questioning look ran across his face. "What do you mean?"

"I've imagined every possible scenario that could develop from abducting you. And that includes where we are now. Don't you think I'd have some way of making sure you don't run to the police?"

"I guess so."

"Good. But, just so you know. I've paid twenty-five-thousand dollars to a special friend. If I'm ever arrested, I'm allowed one phone call. That phone call would be to my special friend. His instructions are to take you out. Any way he pleases."

Herb looked at her straight in the eye.

She continued, "And after he kills you, he has another fifty-thousand to be wired to him. But, mostly because he owes me a favor. I got him into a work-release program from prison and used my connections to get him into a top hotel resort property and he worked his way up to where he's now a leading chef in the resort industry. I changed his life. He's married. Three kids. Nice home on the coast. But, he'd do one last favor for me. If I needed it."

A look of hope graced Herb's face.

"You'll never have to make that call. I may have made some bad choices in my life, but looking for you will not be one of them. You'll never have to make that call. I promise."

She looked at him. Bit her lip. And in one quick motion she threw on her tee shirt and stepped into her shoes. The sense of urgency in every move she took. She dove into her purse and retrieved a key.

She picked up her gun and unlocked both of his ankles. Next, she disengaged his wrists from the dowels above his head.

She stepped back and aimed it at him and said, "Find yourself a pair of underwear and grab a pair of shorts. Quickly."

She followed him into his room. He walked awkwardly because he was still erect as he hurried into the room, literally running for his life. She shook her head.

He slipped on a pair of underwear and stepped into some shorts. "Grab a tee shirt and put something on your feet. Hurry! We have thirty-eight minutes. And counting!"

He stared at her. His expression receptive. She appeared to be letting them both out of the house. This was good news.

He grabbed a pair of running shoes and slipped them on. No time for socks.

He looked over his shoulder. The gun still aimed at him. "You don't have to keep aiming that at me, you know."

"Yes I do. We've come way too far to get sloppy now. Just follow orders."

"Okay."

At that moment a loud crack could be heard from outside. They both looked at each other startled. And in the next instant, a large tree came crashing through the ceiling, knocking them both to the floor.

Numb from the hit to his head, Herb shook himself alert.

He found himself on the floor. Looking up he could see a large opening in the ceiling, split apart from the tree. Rain poured in and the wind intensified everything. Loud roaring wind.

Looking around he could see the tree had fallen on top of Susan. The tree's circumference had to be about three feet at the part lying on top of her arm. Branches were sticking out in all directions. Leaves made it difficult to see each other and assess the situation. Her head bled from a gash just above her right eye. She yelled over to him. "Herb. Help! I can't move my arm."

He noticed her gun lie just beyond her reach. He caught her gaze making that same assessment.

He struggled to get up. Dizziness caused him to pause. He gained his balance.

She yelled out to him, trying to out-scream the wind. "Can you get this tree off of me?"

He stepped up to the tree, squatted down and wrapped his arms around it. Pausing, he took a second to catch his breath. Anguish covered Susan's face. She'd lost the cockiness in her eye. He held his breath and threw all his weight into the tree. The wind muffled his loud grunts.

It didn't budge.

Something had to be done. He needed a rod or bar, or something to use as leverage.

Rain water trickled into the side of his mouth. The wetness welcome.

He scanned the room. Looking for anything.

Kitchen chairs. A table. In one corner a waste basket. In the other, a cane. Yes. A carved cane from Peru. Hard, dark wood.

Susan caught his glare zero in on the cane. "Hurry!" She said.

He grabbed it. Lodged it under the tree. And in one fluid motion, he pulled against the tree.

It moved.

Barely.

But, just enough for her to unlodge her arm from the tree. He picked her up. Stood her up on her feet. Wobbly, she took a step. "Thanks," she muttered.

She stepped past him, leaned down and picked up the gun.

His eyes questioned her.

He just saved her life. Would she use that thing on him now?

She stared back at him. Raised it with both hands up to her chest. And tucked it behind her back-belt.

She spoke with urgency. "Out the door. Quickly."

Herb ran to the door. As he reached for the knob, he stopped to look at her. He'd been trained up till now not to open it. His hesitation understandable. "Is it okay?"

She nodded. "Yes. Quickly. Open it." She motioned with her hand.

He grabbed it, turned it, and pulled. A rush of heavy, wet air swooshed into the door. He found it exhilarating. The best breath of air he'd ever had...in his life. His eyes, wide. Totally in the present.

"Across the street. Into the farmhouse. Run!"

Herb stopped in his tracks.

"I can't!"

CHAPTER 85

"You can't?"

"No. Reese. I've got to grab her."

"Hurry!"

He ran in and opened the bedroom door where Susan had left her. She barked in response to all the noise. "Come on, girl. Come!" He didn't take the time to hook her up to her leash.

Out the door they ran. Herb led the way. Reese followed, barking all the way. Susan in trail. They all leaned into the strong winds.

"Quickly! Get in the house!" She yelled.

They ran toward the front door. Herb and Reese parted, letting her through. She worked her way up to the door and unlocked it.

Upon entering, Herb looked around, wondering what to do next. Knowing Susan had every detail planned out on this expedition, he waited for her next order. Like a marine sergeant, she barked her commands. "Your father, the bedroom on the right. Joe, on the left."

Herb ran up and tried to turn the knob. No luck.

"Move. I've got the key." She entered the key. Turned it. And buried her shoulder against the door.

Upon opening, Herb saw his father sitting on the chair. He looked defeated. Exhausted.

His father looked up.

Herb looked down at this frail frame of a man. The man who shaped his life. Who tarnished his self-worth.

And now he stood over him, here to save *his* life. *Ironic*, he thought. "Come on. We're getting out of here." Herb could see the video camera aimed on his Dad. He grabbed him by the hand, but saw his ankle cuffed to the chair.

His eyes shot to Susan. She got the message.

She fumbled through her keys, eventually finding the right one. Keeping her distance as best she could from anyone's reach, she knelt to one knee and inserted her key and unshackled Herb's Dad. She stood up and backed away.

Herb rushed to his father. "Stand up! This place is going to blow."

He helped him stand. His legs stiff from lack of use, and mixed with old age. His dad asked, "What's this all about?" Scared, the old man stood up. Worry consuming his face.

"I'll explain. Right now. We got to go!"

Susan waved her arm, motioning to the other door. "Joe. Let's get him out of here!"

She rummaged through the keys, finding the right one. Threw it into the lock. Turned, and opened the door.

Joe sat on the ground, leaning against the wall. His ankle also shackled to a large wooden beam, the shackles bolted in with huge bolts.

His face shot up to Herb and Susan, his expression, one of gratitude and confusion. Clueless as to what would occur next.

Susan directed her glance toward him. "I'm letting you go. Do what I say."

Joe nodded. Intense obedience all over his face.

She unlocked the cuffs. Joe took them off. Reese dashed up and licked him all over his face.

Herb rushed to his side and helped him off the floor. Joe's legs weak from the lengthy confinement.

"Okay. Twenty-two minutes. Follow me!" Susan motioned her hand to all of them. She went through the house and out to a garage. She pressed the automatic opener and the garage door opened. Torrential rain blew in. In the garage sat an Explorer. Six passenger. "Get in!"

Herb opened the back door and helped his father get in. He moved slowly.

"Joe and Herb, in the far back." They pushed down the seat and climbed over into the back seat.

Susan opened the front passenger door and commanded, "Reese. Here! With me!" Reese jumped in with joy. "All the time we spent together paid off."

She slammed the door and jumped in behind the steering wheel. Turned the windshield wipers on high.

She popped it in reverse and stepped on the gas. Mindful to not throw Reese off balance.

"Where we going?" asked Herb.

She threw it into *drive* and said, "To get the best seats in the house."

"For what?" asked Herb.

"Watching your house blow up."

Herb ran his fingers through his hair. Looked at Susan in the rearview mirror. "Do you have to?"

She licked her lips. "I've thought a lot about this. No one's going to get hurt. Your house is secluded. No one lives nearby. This will be good for you."

"Good for me? How do you figure?"

She looked back at him in the rearview mirror as she drove away. "Everything in that house is about your accomplishments. Your accolades. Showing off all the stuff you bought on elaborate trips. Your pretentious furniture. Your arrogant jade and pearl carvings from Asia. Your Waterford crystal from Ireland. Your customized Harley."

"You can't knock a guy for liking fine things."

"Yes. But Herb, you valued those *things* more than you valued *people*."

Herb let out a breath in agreement. And nodded.

She could see this in the mirror.

"This will be your chance to purge yourself from those *things*, and move on to caring about *people*."

Herb bobbed his head.

"I have to do this. For both of us."

CHAPTER 86

Susan drove a half mile away from the house. Dirt road all the way. And pulled into a wide open field. She turned her vehicle around so they faced the direction of Herb's house. Debris of all kinds flew past them, some of it brushing against the car.

"Eight minutes," she announced.

In his old raspy voice, Joe asked, "What's going on?"

Susan looked in the rearview mirror at Herb. "You want to tell him or should I?"

His eyes burned back at her. This would not be easy. "I'll tell him." Herb turned around and faced his Dad and Joe.

They studied him with anticipation in their eyes. How could *he* be responsible for *them* getting kidnapped? What could possibly make sense of all of this?

He said, "I said bad things to lots of people over the years. One of them, her mother." He nodded towards her.

"How bad to merit all of this?" Joe asked.

He paused. "Bad. Her mother could've used some encouragement. Could've used some help. All I did was ridicule her and make her feel worse."

Herb's dad looked at Herb, and shook his head. "Am I responsible for the way you are, son."

Herb bit the side of his lip. "You are. But, I need to be responsible for my own actions. Stop blaming you...and do what's right."

Susan watched them both. She could relate. Much of her internal dialogue stemmed from her mother.

She directed her words at Herb's dad. "I heard you were a son-of-a-bitch. Herb saved your life. He's changed. I'm not sure I can. You should be proud of him."

His dad looked at Herb. Dad's eyes moistened by the moment. "I'm sorry for all the harm I caused you."

Herb studied his eyes. Looked into them hard. Then looked away. He couldn't forgive.

Awkward silence filled the car.

Joe sliced into it. "This is because of harsh words someone said to someone? You kidnap and tie people up? And think that's okay?"

Susan shot the old man a look. "Those harsh words did more than hurt my mother. They led to her death."

Joe shook his head. "I don't understand?"

Herb interrupted. "Joe. I won't get in to what I said, but I could've helped someone when they really needed it. Instead, I made her feel worse."

Joe looked puzzled. "Why?"

"Cause I was messed up...to make myself feel better. A sad state of mind. I'm going to seek therapy."

Susan nodded her head up and down. A look of contentment warmed her face. She glanced at her watch.

"Two minutes."

They sat there in anticipation for the inevitable. Susan. Herb. Joe. And Reese.

There was no handbook on what to say when your house is going to blow up right before your eyes in a matter of minutes. And the person responsible is sitting in front of you.

Nor is there a proper etiquette for addressing someone when they decide to let you live and untie you after several days in captivity. Do you thank them shamelessly or scorn them for the experience?

And to make the situation even more confusing, the person responsible has a gun tucked in their pants.

Maybe the best call is to just sit and wait. Like a middle schooler waiting for the principal to whack you with the paddle, knowing its going to burn bad. Real bad. Ready your eyes for what will prove to be an amazing explosion, thrusting someone's personal life hundreds of feet into the air. Watching what were once prized possessions come plummeting down, scattering them in countless directions.

The end result, hopefully allowing that person to start a new life. Erasing away the torment that followed them every day. Dissolving the past.

Maybe, just maybe...blowing up Herb's house was the best thing. For everyone.

CHAPTER 87

Kaboom!

The blast shook the car. The house which stood before them a second ago...gone.

A flash amidst the dark storm.

The landscape changed forever.

The sky rained dark debris. Clothes drifted from the heavens, catching the hurricane winds. Plaster particles plummeted down, pelting their vehicle. Personal articles obliterated into tiny pieces. Rubble strewn for hundreds of yards.

All in the blink of an eye.

The reality of this all unfathomable. They sat there in the vehicle, stunned.

After the debris began to settle down to the ground, the three of them looked at each other. The explosion, the culmination of the entire experience bringing them all together. The final act which would prove to be the catalyst to their new lives. Each in their own new way.

At least that was the plan.

The final choice would lie within each individual as to how they would leverage this experience and set forth with the remainder of their life. Only time would tell.

They examined each other, realizing this experience cemented them together in a way that no other would ever be able to. They'd been kidnapped. Held against their will. Subjected to various types of mental torture and physical abuse. And ultimately, their life was under imminent threat the entire time.

The expression they each exuded was, *what now*?

Knowing Susan paid extreme attention to detail and had thought out every aspect of this ordeal, they knew better than to ask her, *what next*? They decided to wait and see.

She turned around. Gave them all a once over with her eyes. They stared back at her with respect, and with fear. Sometimes fear and respect follow along the same line. "Mr. Keeler Senior, you were kidnapped and taken from your home. I apologize for the inconvenience, but it was imperative that I used you for leverage to harbor Herb's full co-operation in the final stages of this tribulation. And to help gain the impact to hopefully encourage him to change his life around. Let's hope we did."

His father nodded with respect. Too fearful to say anything or show disrespect towards her. After all, she still had the gun.

She continued, "To Joe, you were abducted from Herb's home. You weren't part of the plan. You were unexpected. But, I think your well-being helped influence Herb's decisions throughout this affair as well. For that, I thank you. And I apologize to you for the fear and inconvenience I caused you."

Joe nodded and meekly said, "Thank you." His hands still trembling after the explosion and from the immense duress this nightmare had caused.

And finally, she turned and directed herself towards Herb. They looked at each other like two battled warriors. Two gladiators who had faced off in hand to hand combat, who engaged with each other strategically. Trying to out maneuver, outsmart the other. And now, now it was over. Almost as if they'd miss the cunning, the cleverness the other possessed. The respect of their opponent.

She said, "Herb." And she drew in a large breath. As if what she was about to say was a prepared speech. Only the Gods in heaven knew for sure. "I dreamt about this for most of my adult life. When I decided to do it, I schemed and plotted this for over a year. I invested money, study, time, learned so many aspects of technology, pharmaceuticals, security systems, Smart TV's, Smart thermostats. Interviewed people about so many things I knew nothing about when I began this journey. It's been exhilarating. I've learned a lot. I hope I've grown a lot. And learned more about myself as a person. Because of you." She ran her fingers through her hair. And continued. "I hope *you've* learned a lot about yourself as a person. I hope *you've* grown. I put my life on the line by stepping across legal boundaries in a very big way. I threw it all on the table. Hell, I was prepared to go all the way and kill you. That's how far gone I was. But, something through this journey changed. Maybe I saw *you* change, and it made me think differently about killing you. Giving you a chance to redeem yourself. I hope you take this chance, Herb, and do something wonderful with it. I really do."

Herb looked at her. His throat swelling up with emotion. His chest heaving for breath. His mind struggling to find the right words. His eyes fierce upon her. Full of disdain, respect, awe, and anger. A collection of extreme emotions from both ends all layering upon her.

He swallowed, and began. "I hate you for trapping me in my house. For threatening my dog. And by the way, can you take her explosive collar off? Please."

She reached into her purse and retrieved a small remote. Hit a couple of buttons. Then reached over and removed the collar from Reese's neck, and put it in her purse. "Sorry," she said.

"Thank you." And he continued. "You tortured me in my house. Destroyed my things. You kidnapped my friend. Kidnapped my father. And you threatened to kill us all. For this I hate you." He paused for effect. "But! And I say a big but. I think you freed me from myself. You made me see something inside I didn't see, and made me understand why I am who I am. And I believe I can change. And for that I thank you. And I thank you for sparing our lives and for giving us the chance to live in a new way."

They stared at each other with mutual admiration.

And when she realized there was nothing more to be said, she jammed the vehicle into Drive and pulled away.

She pulled up to the curb at Main St. at the main corner of town in Oyster Bay. Punched her phone for an Uber driver and gave them the coordinates to be picked up. She pulled five twenty-dollar bills out of her wallet and gave them to Herb.

"Gentlemen," she said, "the ride ends here. Get out."

She watched Herb and Joe get out first, the winds still strong. Then helped Herb's dad out of the vehicle. They all stepped around to the curb, where Herb opened the front passenger side door and helped Reese get out of the car. His leash reattached by Susan. She handed Herb the leash. Rain drenching the pooch immediately.

They looked at each other one last time.

Susan looked right into Herb's eyes, took in a small breath of air, and yelled, "Don't make me make that phone call."

CHAPTER 88

In the year that followed, Herb Keeler spoke on all the talk shows, every news station, the USA Today, the New York Times and the Wall Street Journal. Telling people his story. How he was abused as a child. That his insecurities overruled his sense on how to treat people. He admitted he was the biggest son-of-a-bitch. And that no excuse justified the way he made people feel.

He told them he'd gone away for a short trip to do some soul searching. To look inside himself. To find out what was missing. He never mentioned being kidnapped and tortured. Or what he'd been through with Susan. He said after he looked inside himself he learned something new about himself that he found liberating. He became a renewed person.

He apologized to the world in every interview. Live talk. Newspaper. Radio. You name it. He said he regretted every negative thing he ever said to anyone. He wished he could take it all back.

He encouraged writers to send their work to him. To reach out to him for advice. He received so many he had to hire a staff to sift through them all. And he worked close with his staff in responding to every query with encouragement. Even the ones that had no hope of being published. He didn't want to stomp on their dream. He shared a brief bit of advice with every letter. It was imperative.

He eventually created his own Creative Writing School. Fully accredited with college stature. And students came from all over the world to study under his programming. Fiction. Non-fiction. Memoirs. He brought in guest lecturers like John Irving, James Patterson, Sandra Brown, and all the big names he could coddle over to his school. Admission requests overflowed. In five years his school became the most sought after literary college in the country. Once students were enrolled, they couldn't wait to meet him. It was like meeting the rock legend of the century. He kept them in pure awe.

Herb found that *nice* agreed with him.

After having his name and his story being blasted all over the media for weeks, Herb's calls to Katie finally were answered.

They met at their usual place. Central Park. "I've changed," he said.

"I see that. You've been quite the story. I never knew all that stuff."

"Which stuff?"

"Your reputation for blasting people."

"Yes. It's true. I was a son-of-a-bitch."

They walked slowly down the wide path, flowers on one side bursting with color. Katie studied his face closely. Looking for sincerity. He continued. "I had issues. Things that go back to my childhood. The way my dad treated me."

"I'm sorry."

"Thanks. I realize I'm an adult now. I can't take it out on others. It's time to own my life."

"How did you come to that realization?"

He cleared his throat. "After you refused to return my calls, I did some soul searching. Deep soul searching. And I talked to someone who I hurt badly. Very badly. We talked for two days."

"Hmm. What'd you talk about?"

"I learned how my words hurt them. How my words hurt their family. How I ruined their lives." His forehead creased, clear he felt the pain he caused. Regret painting his face.

"It took a lot of courage for you to confront that person."

He looked at her. He couldn't explain he was held captive for two days, threatened, manipulated and toyed with, with his house ultimately blown up. He couldn't say he was forced to discuss his past. That part he omitted.

"It was one of the most difficult things I've ever done. It forced me to be honest with myself. To realize my insecurities. My fear of introducing you to my mother was simple. If I introduced you to her, I was saying you're worthy. Worthy of real love. With me. That I'm worthy of real love."

"But, you are worthy of real love."

"I was too scared to admit that. Too scared to fail. Of being hurt."

She laughed. "Oh Herb, you're messed up." She stepped up and wrapped her arms around him. The embrace raging a force of love between the two of them. At a new level of feeling neither had ever experienced. The hug looking like it would be their eternity. He whispered in her ear, "I missed you so much." Tears of emotion flowed down his cheeks.

"I missed you, too," she said through her raspy voice. Her eyes misting up.

"I can't wait to introduce you to my mother. That's, if you still want to?"

"I do. I do."

"Can you forgive me for being a wuss?"

She let out a chuckle. "Yes. I can forgive you for being a wuss."

He looked into her eyes. "You'll love her. And she'll love you."

Tears rolled down both of their faces bathing their cheeks with love.

CHAPTER 89

A bumble bee buzzed around Herb's tall glass of coke looking for a spot to land. Where could it get the best locale to suck up the sweet liquid?

The sun shone down on the three of them, Herb, Katie, and Herb's mother. Sitting at a linen covered table, red and white checkered. Looked like the quintessential American-Italian restaurant. Except, they weren't at an Italian restaurant. No. They sat on the upper deck of Herb's yacht.

And it wasn't Italian they ate. No. They sank their teeth into American quarter pounders, smothered with cheese, accompanied by French fries. And after the first couple of big bites, washed them all down with gulps of iced cold coke.

"How's your burger, Mrs. Keeler?"

"Katie. Please. How many times do I have to tell you? Call me Lisa."

"I'm sorry. It's just the way I was raised."

"That's good. That means your parents taught you to respect folks."

"They sure did."

Herb's mom responded. "But, if we're going to have a long term relationship, and I hope we are, call me Lisa. Please."

Katie dabbed the burger juice from the corner of her mouth. "Okay. I will, Mrs. Keeler. Oops!"

They all laughed together. "It's a habit." Katie said.

"That's okay. I'll call you on it until you get it right."

Herb finished his gulp of coke and said, "And she will, too."

"Been so long. Herb finally brought someone around. But, I can see why."

Herb and Katie glanced at each other and looked puzzled. "Why Mom?"

"You wanted to make sure it was someone nice." And she smiled.

Katie blushed with appreciation. "Thanks Mrs..." She put her hand over her mouth. "I mean, Lisa." Herb and Mom grinned.

That afternoon they talked about everything. Writing. Pharmaceuticals. Baseball. Single parenting. Even abuse. From laughs to serious stuff. They felt comfortable with each other covering the gamut. All respected each other's opinions.

After lunch, Herb said, "All right, let's take this boat for a spin."

His mom said, "Oh, I really should be going. You kids enjoy the afternoon out on the water. Alone."

"No Lisa. Please come. Besides, Herb said he was going to let me drive the boat. I want a witness to make sure he sticks to his word." She looked over at Herb.

He held his right hand up as if swearing in at court. "I did say that."

"Come on, Lisa. It'll be fun. I might need help at the wheel. Can I count on you?"

Mom looked at them both. "Oh, all right. If you insist. One little boat ride couldn't hurt."

Herb guided it out into the Atlantic and positioned it in a wide open area. Dropped it down into a comfortable speed, stepped back and said, "It's your ship, Captain Katie."

She looked at Herb's Mom, who gave her a reassuring nod, and then at Herb, who nodded as well. She stepped up, grabbed the wheel and away they went for the rest of the day. Sucking in all the fresh air. And even more important, basking in the comfort of each other. Thankful for what each of them brought to the group.

At the end of the day, Herb and Katie dropped Lisa off at the retirement home. Katie said, "Lisa, it was great to meet you. I look forward to seeing you again."

Lisa said, "Katie, it was more than great to meet you. Thanks for the lovely day."

They hugged and said good bye.

Herb hugged his Mom, and with her mouth next to his ear, she whispered to him. "She's a keeper. Don't screw it up."

CHAPTER 90

Susan flew back to her husband and two sons in Michigan and arrived home.

She walked into her house with her small suitcase and yelled out, "Anyone home?"

Her black Lab came running around the corner and slid into her, almost knocking her down in the kitchen. His tail wagged with his entire body. "Oh Herb, I missed you, too."

She got down on her knees and hugged him. He went ballistic. Kissing her face, hopping up on her. True love. All the way. "Oh baby. You missed me?"

A deep voice echoed off the refrigerator. "Somebody missed you."

She looked up.

There stood her husband. Fit and smiling. She stood up. "Yeah. Somebody missed you, too." He opened his arms and gave her a huge hug and a delicious kiss.

"Mmm." He murmured. "How was New York?"

She looked at him right in the eyes. An inch away. "Great. They had twenty hotel companies there. All of them want to work with us on our intern program. This will bid well for our students."

"Excellent."

She flashed her smile at him. "How were you without me?"

"Lost, of course. Missed you."

"Missed you, too."

They kissed again. A long embracing kiss.

Upon coming up for air, he asked, "Want to go out for dinner? Stay out of the kitchen?"

She thought for a moment, crooked up the side of her mouth, tilted her head to the side, let her hair fall down along her shoulder, and said, "You know, I could go for a nice home-cooked meal with my family. That okay by you?"

He paused for a moment. "Sure. I'll hit the grocery store and pick up a few things."

"That's okay. Let me go. I could use a little bit of time browsing through the grocery store. It'll be therapeutic after being cooped up for several days with academic people."

"Could you use a little company?"

"No. But, later on tonight I could use some real company. If you know what I mean." She raised her eyebrows at him.

He smiled back at her. "Sounds good."

"Hurry back. I'm starved. I'll call the boys. They're next door with the Burtons shooting baskets out back."

She grabbed her purse and headed out the door. She jumped in her car, backed out of the drive and headed for the supermarket.

Only problem.

She drove right past the grocery store.

Intentionally.

CHAPTER 91

She pulled into the cemetery and wound her way around the ponds and past the military section and pulled up to the tombstone of her mother's grave. She looked around for visitors. She wasn't in the mood for talking to anyone. Strictly here to see her mother.

After careful reconnaissance, the coast looked clear. She walked past several family tombstones that led to her mother's. By now, they felt like her family.

Hello Mrs. Mooney. Hope they cut your grass Mr. McGillan. Oh, I like your flowers Mrs. Vidmar. I'll come back with a sponge next time and clean your stone up Mr. Jones. Couldn't they put a more interesting family name next to my mother than Jones?

Ah! There it is. Mama's stone.

She walked up to it and looked down at the stone. She knelt down and brushed away the lawnmower clippings resting on the top of it. For a final dusting she put her face up to it and blew the last remnants of grass and dirt away.

She pivoted her head around in all directions and made sure she could enjoy the moment with privacy. She stared at the stone. And gathered her thoughts.

"There you go, Mama. Nice and clean. How've you been?"

She repositioned her legs so she could sit cross-legged facing the stone. It was her usual mode of operandi when visiting Mama.

"I've got good news for you. I did it! Got even for you. Yep. That's right. That plan I've been telling you about for the past year. I did it. I finally did it. I know. Sounds crazy. Doesn't it? But, I did it. I trapped Herb in his house. You should have seen him. He was scared shitless."

She began to laugh.

"You would have loved it. I wish you could have been there. Man, he didn't know what hit him. When he read the letter I wrote him telling him he was trapped, you should have seen him panic. God, I wish you could have seen him, Mama. His body quivering like a little girl. And when I blew his lamp up, oh man, you should have seen him hit the floor. I almost lost my breath I was laughing so hard. You would have loved it."

Her posture sharpened up with her excitement. She ran her fingers through her hair.

"But, the best one, was when I blew the cigar up in his mouth. I swear, if I could have recorded all of this, I could have sold it as a comedy to all the movie companies. I missed the boat on that one. And Mama, you'll love this. I made him apologize to all the writers he scorned in the USA Today. That's right. National newspapers. I humiliated the bastard for you. Plus, I roasted the son-of-a-bitch. How? I turned off his air-conditioning on the hottest day of the year. And then I turned his heated floors on high."

She started laughing. "This was so much fun. And...I had him wire me some money, too. Nothing like a few coins to add to my bank account after all he did to you."

"And to add to the fun, I blew up his prized Harley. I had the best time."

She worked herself up into a bigger laugh.

"There were so many moments that made it worth all the planning and all the trouble to carry this out. But, in the end it was all worth it. I admit, some of the stuff I did was a bit juvenile, but hey, all in the spirit of revenge. He got what he deserved. Ah, the simple things. A couple of things I did I feel bad about."

She hung her head in shame.

"I stuck a device on his dog's collar to make him think it was an explosive in case he didn't co-operate. It worked quite well. Of course it was a fake. You know I have a soft spot for animals. And the other thing I did, I had to kidnap his dad. I knew if I had his dog and his dad under my control, I'd be able to get him to do whatever I wanted."

She stood up and began pacing back and forth in front of the tomb stone. Her breathing quickened. She rubbed her left arm with her right. And as she turned around to start pacing back the other way, she flicked her hair back over her shoulder.

"This next part, Mama, I'm not sure what you're going to think. Remember how you always told me to use men and then move on? Use them before they use me? Well...I teased him. Yes. I teased him. I slapped him, too. And then, I left him unsatisfied. That was for all women, Mama. I thought you would appreciate that. It wasn't just for you and me. It was for all women. I hope that's okay with you."

She stopped pacing. She squared herself up with the tombstone and stared down at it. A serious expression took over her face. An intense seriousness.

"Mama, there's something else I have to tell you. I couldn't do it."

And she began to cry.

"I'm sorry, Mama. I couldn't do it. I couldn't kill him. I'm so sorry, Mama. Please don't be mad at me."

She wiped the tears from her eyes. Tried hard to regain her breath.

"You see, he changed. I changed him, Mama. I made him better. After that, I couldn't kill him. I think he will be a better man because of me. You'll see."

She looked high into the sky, rubbing her hands together. Then, slowly folded them as if she were praying. She pulled her hair away from her face with both hands, so she could face her mother with total clarity.

Then staring down at the tombstone, she said these words, "Mama, I will make this promise to you. The next time I will take all their money. Just for me. All of it. You will be proud of me. You will see. I will only seduce rich men. And when I'm done with them to make me feel good, and when I've taken all their money, I will end their miserable lives. Through this I will balance the scales of justice against all men. It may take a little time to work on each one. But once I do, I'll move on to the next one."

She knelt down and touched her mother's grave. "Just like you told me, Mama. You will see."

More

E.P. McKenna!

Please turn this page for a preview

of

The Grand Secret

Susan's journey continues...

Available on Amazon.com and at Barnes & Noble.

The Grand Secret

Chapter 1

MY NAME IS VINCE WALKER, and not to brag, but I'm one of the nation's leading automotive consultants. I was attending "the black tie affair of all black tie affairs." And right now if I could be face to face with the moron who invented bow ties, I'd punch his lights out. I ran my fingers along my chafed neck, hoping for relief.

It was Monday night, the first of June, and Michigan's business and political power brokers had just concluded their first day of discussions at the Grand Hotel on Mackinac Island in Michigan, and this is where the worst week of my life started.

The Grand Hotel is famous for at least two things, two notorious icons. The first was its 660 feet long, world's longest wooden front-porch. The mere mention of it would drive a nest of termites into a culinary frenzy.

The second notable was an event, the annual Detroit Regional Chamber's Mackinac Policy Conference, where the movers and shakers of the state came to discuss the challenges of the times. I was there to share my eminent wisdom.

I should mention my wife, Susan, and I had just returned to our room after dancing to the sounds of the Grand Hotel Orchestra down in the Terrace Room. The sound of clip-clopping horses drifted in on a waft of warm moist air through our open window while the stars pulsated out over the Mackinac Straits.

As I took off my tuxedo jacket and removed my bow tie, I said to her, "I'm not ready to call it a night yet. Let's go up to the Cupola Bar. It's late. The bar's closed. We can have the whole view all to ourselves."

"No, you go, honey. I'm tired. I'm sure it's beautiful. Tell me all about it in the morning," she yawned, sitting on the bed and kicking off her heels with her danced-out feet.

I might add, she made it tough to want to leave her. She was looking mighty delicious tonight. It was her erotic perkiness and silky black hair that initially attracted me to her. And I could never escape the stare of her glacier-blue eyes. In her late forties, she was still turning heads, especially mine.

The only problem, it had been quite a while since we last rubbed bodies together, naked that is. Maybe the rigors of the job, too much time away, or maybe we just stopped putting in the effort.

I noticed a change in her demeanor upon her return from her New York trip last year. A hospitality conference. I couldn't put a finger on it, but something about her had changed. An invisible wedge seemed to have developed between us. Rigorous questioning by me only seemed to make it worse.

Truth is, we both hoped this trip would reignite the flame between us.

We used to sail here. I'm a sailor. It's my thing. It was *our* thing. Whenever we came here, we stayed at the Grand Hotel. When we checked in to the hotel, we surrendered to its spell. Sparks flew. Sparks hell. More like ten-acre forest fires.

Lately, we were barely a flicker.

I always liked stargazing with somebody, particularly Susan. But, if she wasn't willing to share my lust for the stars tonight, I wasn't willing to miss them myself.

"All right, you're going to miss quite the spectacle," I said, trying to persuade her one more time.

I left my room and swaggered up three flights of carpeted stairs to the Cupola Bar perched high on top of the hotel complex. After being surrounded by hordes of people all day, it was nice to have a moment to myself.

A quaint bar of about 25 feet by 25 feet, its surrounding windows welcomed the gentle moonlight. The room presented dramatic views of the Mackinac Bridge spanning across to the point where Lake Michigan and Lake Huron came together.

I stepped into the dimly lit bar, and found its emptiness contrasted by a flurry of chaos emerging from a dark, damp corner.

I glanced toward the noise, sensing a torrent of motion. The scent of old spilt beer blended with the intuitive sickness that arose from my gut.

If there was ever a sixth sense telling me, *don't look, run like hell*, it was then.

Damnit! My curiosity got the best of me. For some primeval reason, I had to look.

Two sinewy figures pummeled a motionless body lying on the ground. It might as well have been an old rag doll.

Both men wore dark suits. An overhead light placed its subtle presence on their upper torsos. One had jet black hair with a gray spot in it. The other's head was shaven and he sported a goatee. Their sense of purpose was as deliberate as an electronic robot working the automotive assembly line.

I glimpsed at what was supposed to have been a man's face, but instead was an unrecognizable pulpy mass. My blood ran cold. I just stood there frozen, listening. I wanted to yell. *Stop it. Help! Someone!* But, I couldn't.

All I heard was the guttural grunting of the men as they stomped on his abdomen. The boney crunch of the skull followed them imbedding their steel-toed shoes into the back of the head. Physical exhaustion enveloped them quickly.

The injured man's total lack of resistance told me it was probably too late to help. A half a second later my common sense finally kicked in. *Get the hell out of here!*

As I turned to run down the stairs, the wooden floor creaked. I froze for a second. A tension-filled pause followed. Their heads turned. Our eyes met, and the foot race was on.

I leapt down the stairway three steps at a time, my legs trying to keep up with the rest of me. *Lose them! Lose them fast!*

I lost my balance and fell up against the handrail. I steadied my legs and continued downward. I kept zooming down the steps-my legs pumping away like a piston, my blood pumping away through my veins. Only one goal on my adrenaline soaked mind: get back to my room. Fast!

As I descended past the first flight of stairs, I peered over my shoulder to gauge my lead. I was already out of their sight, but not by much. The sound of footsteps and heavy breathing followed close behind.

Hitting the landing below at the third level of stairs, I bolted in the direction of my room, old world carpet flashing beneath my feet. I arrived at my door, half a lung less than what I started with.

My pursuers hadn't landed at the base of the stairs on my spacious floor, yet. The empty hallway was heaven to me, at least for now.

With the key buried deep in my small pocket, my trembling hand couldn't grasp it fast enough. I jammed my hand back in again, as deep as it could go.

My adrenalin raced through me. I withdrew the key and jostled it into the dark tiny keyhole, turning the doorknob. "C'mon door, open! Open, damn it!"

I could hear the hard charging footsteps getting louder by the second. Or maybe that was my heart thumping out of my chest.

Looking at the stairwell, they were yet to be seen. The door opened and in I went. I closed it as quickly and as quietly as possible, not knowing whether or not they saw me entering my room.

Susan stirred and murmured, "What's going on? The view that good?"

I threw myself on top of her and cupped my hand over her mouth. Her eyes bulged with fear.

From the faint moonlight on my face I'm sure she could see the terror in my eyes. It was clear, I'd run into something much more terrifying than frickin stars.

I whispered, "Don't say a word. Please. Someone's after me. I'll explain in a minute."

I struggled to catch my breath, gasping for brief spurts of air. Darkness cloaked our room with equal clouds of fear.

I could see the shadows leaking under the door as the men inched by, listening for any activity from the rooms. After what seemed an eternity, the men moved on.

Trying to keep my labored breath from being heard, I whispered, "I've got to call the police. I saw someone being murdered."

"What are you talking about? What happened? Where?"

"Shh...Listen Susan, I've got to call the police. I saw them. I can identify both of them."

I could tell Susan didn't know what the hell I was talking about. Awoken from a state of tranquility, she'd probably been dreaming of our last vacation in the Bahamas. Oceanic breezes and cold Coronas. Willowing Palm trees. Hawaiian Tropic simmering in the sun. Soft sandy beaches.

Now, she looked afraid for her life. No reason. The wrong place at the wrong time. Just like that. A split second. Serious trouble.

"You have to call the police and tell them what you saw," Susan pleaded. "Call them now Vince, before these guys get away."

"Where's my cell?"

Just then, a small note slid under our old wooden door.

A READER'S GROUP GUIDE FOR DISCUSSING <u>THE QUERY</u>
BY E.P. MCKENNA

1) Do you like Herb? Do you find yourself voting *for* him or *against* him? Do you feel the author wants you to like him? Why or why not?

2) Does the author want you to think of the captor as the bad guy or Herb? Do you distinguish one or the other as a worse person than the other? Why?

3) Do you feel the captor is justified for doing what being done to Herb? Do you think Herb is deserving what is happening to him? Do you feel the captor is the good person? Or the bad person?

4) Herb likes material success. Yet, in some of his assertions on the people he traveled with, they achieved material success as well. He mentions, that is what he liked about those folks. And that's what he hated about them. Discuss his mixed feelings. Discuss your mixed feelings on this matter.

5) Discuss the captor's motivations and the extent of the multitude of details needed in which to carry out this year-long plan directed at Herb. And talk about the obstacles that would have arose in this pursuit.

6) Converse the multitude of emotions Herb experienced during this journey.

7) The media can slant any story and massage a person's image. Converse how the media produced favorable and non-favorable aspects of Herb.

8) Herb has a friend in his dog, Reese. Why do you think the author wrote Reese into the book?

9) You learn early that Herb has an appetite for style and "the finer things." Does this make him a bad person? Why or why not?

10) Under the same circumstances Herb experienced, do you think most people would believe there was indeed a bomb planted in the house and not feel inclined to try and test the door?

11) Do you think people have the capacity to overcome the mental scars of their upbringing and move on to live with inner peace?

12) Do you feel the compensation Herb wired to the Student's family was warranted?

13) Herb displayed negotiation skills. Which tactics did he use to give him the advantage in dealing with his captor?

14) Many of the characters in the travel group were high achievers, acquiring massive wealth and material success. Do you feel this is an obsession of our current society driven by social media? Always trying to brag about our next achievement or event?

15) Herb discovers he is the way he is as a result of his father's treatment of him. Do you think most people would be able to ascertain why they are the way they are, due to significant upbringing events?

16) Does the juvenile method in which Herb's captor tortures him irritate you? Or do you feel he deserves this abuse and mental aggravation?

17) Do you consider Herb's "friend" Joe as a true friend?

18) Both Herb and his captor have control issues. What do you think about the two of them trying to inflict control upon the other?

19) What if Herb would have taken the opportunity to apply revenge towards his father? What direction do you think the author could have taken the story from there?

20) Were there any ways you could think of where Herb might have been able to escape?

21) Do you like the way the book ended? What do you think the years that lie ahead hold for Herb's Captor?

E.P. McKenna lives outside of Detroit, Michigan with his wife and has two grown daughters.